A LARK ASCENDING

John Campbell

Ocean Highway Books
Independent Publishing Consultants

ISBN-13: 978-1502977960
ISBN-10: 1502977966

Cover Design, Richard Sutton

Also by this Author:

Walk to Paradise Garden

I would like to thank the following people in no particular order:
Pamla Campbell, Tanya McCullough, Ann White, Saundra Verstrate, Rachel
Bodner, and Thea Phipps

Professionals: Kyane Howland, Wendy Bertsch and Bob Davidson of Ocean
Highway Books, and Richard Sutton of RS Communications

Chapter One

London's East End 1921

He landed in an alley. A cat shrieked; its complaint shredded adolescent nerves that were already on edge. If the mangy creature hadn't caterwauled, the boy might have escaped detection.

The cat took off, scuttling like a rat in the dark warren of London's East End. It probably felt threatened—Malcolm Roberts certainly did. As he righted himself and slid through a narrow passage, something snatched at his shirt. Fear flashed hot through his body. Then the material ripped, releasing him. He hurried between buildings with a sharp pain awakening at the top of his shoulder. *Must've been a nail; must've sliced my skin.*

The sound of boots scraping against brick and grunting expletives told him the bullies were scaling the wall in pursuit.

Malcolm shot out on White Horse Road and realized he had the choice of returning to his home in Stepney or hightailing it to the Limehouse riverfront. Which should he choose?

His earlier decision had caused this mess. Unable to ignore his curiosity, he'd followed the group of ne'er-do-wells, proud of his ability to shadow suspects almost as well as his penny-dreadful hero, Detective Phoenix. Their operation was almost completed when he sneezed.

Malcolm cursed his sneeze—and his curiosity.

His life depended on making the right choice now. Those thugs would prove as determined as angry bees. Although street noise swallowed up their racing footfalls behind him, Malcolm knew he had to keep going. Should he run to his father or his friend?

If Joe Hasani was docked at his berth, Malcolm could escape across the Thames, putting real distance between himself and the hoodlums.

Malcolm headed for the waterman, running like a thieving urchin.

Along White Horse, he wove and jostled his way against the oncoming throng, aware that the crowd would likely thin out as workers headed for home or pub.

Chapter Two

Lightning flashed behind heavy draperies. The subsequent thunder shook Malcolm's upholstered chair, threatening to snuff out the glimmerings of comfort he felt after his hot bath. Despite sitting near the steady flame, he shivered and pulled the blanket closer around his shoulders.

"Well, that was some adventure for you, son." Captain Roberts settled into the wing chair across from him, holding what Malcolm had counted as his father's third brandy since Joe dropped him home. "You must be proud of yourself."

"But I ran."

"There's nothing wrong with retreat when you're outnumbered. You showed daring and resourcefulness, swimming out to Joe like that. Thirteen years old and you can think like a reconnaissance man behind enemy lines. Intelligent beyond your years. Hear, hear." The captain raised his glass.

"But what if he hadn't been out there?" Malcolm asked, annoyed at the quiver in his voice. "I would've been caught and filleted on the docks."

Malcolm wanted something more from his father. If his near-death experience didn't rattle the captain from his distraction, what could?

Staring at his brandy, the captain said, "I imagine you might have chosen to borrow some dinghy...or dive in the river, as you did, but swim parallel, say, to Duke Shore stairs." The former military man pulled a slow draught of the liquor.

"I reckon you're right, sir."

"You've proven my theory, Malcolm. By allowing you the freedom to explore where you wish, you are, I see, developing manly traits—those necessary for the day you become a soldier."

The 'freedom' was his father's—free of a parent's responsibility.

Having grown up in the aftermath of the Great War, Malcolm had become disenchanted with the thought of such a career. In his mind, 'soldier' meant 'cannon fodder', for he knew of nothing but death, disfigurement or neuroses for all of the war's participants. A victim of the last type of casualty sat before him.

Malcolm fiddled with the edge of the blanket, saddened at another conversation with hope set against vexation. His father's acknowledgement was not empathy; it was not love. Malcolm felt as though he were taken for granted, much like the Turkish rug beneath their feet—the carpet was fine but not necessary; it was something acknowledged but not appreciated.

A vow arose in Malcolm's heart: He would earn his father's love, he would come to matter more than a rug—or would die trying.

His father added, "It was highly fortunate that Joe was there for you, I'll admit. I can't understand why he continues his ferry business. It's not as if we don't have bridges. His Majesty just opened Southwark."

"People still need to go up or down the river, Father. Not just across."

"Well, he can't be making much of a living. At least not from legal custom."

Malcolm frowned at hearing anything against Joe. A spark popped and alighted on the edge of the hearth. Malcolm watched as its pulsating life ebbed away.

Another flash of lightning conjured up an image of himself in the water—this time, as a ripped-open corpse drifting in the Thames.

"Did any of those ruffians get a look at your face?"

"I don't see how they could have. Not really." His mind grappled for details. Had anyone been close enough to have noted his profile?

His father fought down a belch and added, "Before they realized you were there, you surely noticed something about them, something to recognize."

"Well, I saw the solicitor, Mr. Crocker. The rest had their backs to me." Malcolm placed his cold hands in the folds of the blanket and concentrated on what he'd seen. "Wait a tick! One of the lads was taller. His back was huge and hunched. He might have been rusty-haired, but he had his cap on. I think it was rusty-coloured hair sticking out."

"And, what did you actually see them doing beforehand?"

He watched his father take another sip and then replied, "Um, I started trailing them when they turned into the alley from Burgess Street. Something about them didn't look right. Two of them kept looking around in a, uh, a suspicious manner, and . . . well, I began wondering. So, I hung back and then followed. They'd pushed their barrow up behind Crocker's offices. The crates were marked on their sides, with bold letters, five, I think. And when Crocker pried one open, he called them cricket balls—"

The captain jerked, sloshing half the contents of his glass down his shirt.

"Uh," Malcolm continued, "they didn't look like any cricket balls I'd ever seen."

"They were made of metal."

"Right. How did you know?"

"Explosives. Grenades. Must have been stolen government goods."

"That makes sense because of the way they were talking. I couldn't make out most of the words, but—well, it sounded like they were up to no good."

The captain's hands quivered, and with concentrated effort, he set his glass down. It pained Malcolm to see angst settle upon his father's features; it troubled him even more that his father evidently read his thoughts and noticed the pity in his son's eyes. Gathering what dignity he could, the man squared his shoulders and cleared his throat.

"Anything else?"

"Yes. Crocker opened another crate. This time I could clearly see that its sides were marked "Books". But it was full of truncheons. I bet they were stolen from the police." He had hoped for his father's smile, for acknowledgement of his deduction, but the man's gaze was trained on something beyond Malcolm, beyond the room.

The fire hissed. Malcolm picked at a loose thread on the blanket before venturing to look up. His father's face had blanched to the colour of stone. The familiar reaction made Malcolm's insides twist to the point of suffocation. The captain regained his focus and opened his mouth to speak.

"Excuse me, sir," their only remaining servant said, slicing the air between father and son. With her usual wary eyes and shallow breathing in the presence of the captain, Annie stood by the parlour door. "Will you be needin' anethin' else before I go, sir?"

Captain Roberts stood and offered a quick bow. "No, thank you, Miss Annie. Good night." He bowed again. Malcolm had almost grown accustomed to such odd behaviour—bowing to maids as if they were ladies. It wasn't done. But no one visited them anymore. No one knew except Annie and him.

Annie stumbled a half-curtsy, never quite sure what to make of this formal business. "Good night, then." She turned and headed for the back door.

The familiar ache intensified in Malcolm's chest. A household of servants had fled soon after his father returned from the war. When his mum died of influenza, even Cook quit, leaving the two to fend for themselves, which they had done, pitifully, until Annie had mysteriously shown up on their back step.

Music no longer filled the house. His mother had adored symphonic works and her Victrola. Though commanded not to touch it, Malcolm had done so on a few occasions, but then painful memories kept him from it thereafter.

He had been six when his da first crossed over to France and ten years old when the war ended. It had taken hardly any time for him to realize Captain Roberts had returned a different man.

The embers glowed hot. Malcolm wrapped himself up tighter in the blanket. He'd had a hard day. He hoped to heaven he'd get through the night without incident.

Chapter Three

Under a grey Sunday sky, Malcolm skipped his way through the mews and along Bishopsgate, as if yesterday's misadventure had not occurred. A few drops of rain tickled the back of his neck. He capered around the corner to Brushfield Street. The rain eventually gave up and so did his resolve.

Despite the chorus of church bells in the air, mounting unease tarnished his joy in these local amblings. He slowed and found himself checking over his shoulder. A scullery maid bustled past here, an older woman trudged there, each evidently heading for Spitalfields Market. Familiar activity. In the Jewish East End, the market hummed with Eastern European accents today. Most would have already observed their Sabbath the day before.

Malcolm decided to head in that direction himself.

He scanned the throng. None reminded him of Crocker's hoodlums. And, as was sometimes the case on a Sunday, some were recognizably not descendants of Abraham.

"Well hullo, Mr. Phipps. I didn't expect to find you here today."

"Aye, Malcolm, our autumn has been kind to us, and I have so many vegetables to sell—and with the holidays only weeks away—I thought I better make good use of me time." The farmer's stall displayed bushels of beets, parsnips, carrots and such. "Business always picks up end o' November. Me purse loves the happy hols, it does." Malcolm knew Phipps was not a greedy man. But *good use* of the farmer's time did not necessitate attendance at his village church.

Malcolm understood.

His father's regard for the church had waned since the war. The same was evidently true of his aunt. Snide remarks escaped them in his presence. Malcolm had deduced that their grudge was against clergymen rather than scripture. In the context of blessing ammunitions and armies, to what else could they be referring with their mutterings of bloodguilt? Of course, they had never discussed their reasons with him.

The cheery voice of Phipps reined him in. "Thanks for sending your Annie to my stall."

The farmer reached out and caught the wrist of an urchin, stopping the wee lad from stealing. He replaced the larger, choice potato in the child's hand with a smaller one and sent him off. "I'm sure you enjoy a good shepherd's pie now and then, don't yer?"

Malcolm smiled his reply, as much to please the kindly vendor as to confirm his favourite meal.

Phipps nodded to an acquaintance crossing the street, keeping Malcolm in the interchange. If only the captain would include Malcolm so readily.

"She seems a good lass, Annie does."

"Yes. Well, enjoy your ride back to East Horsley." Malcolm turned to leave and stopped. "Oh, where's Mimi?"

"She's being brushed and spoiled by a young Chinese lad back there." He pointed to an alley nearby. "Those two get on keen, they do. That ol' mare'll be good and fresh for our little journey."

"Right." Malcolm offered a farewell nod. "Goodbye, Mr. Phipps."

"Be careful, lad."

Malcolm waved and meandered off.

Why would Mr. Phipps tell him to be careful? He couldn't know of last night's brush with death. Malcolm shrugged off the question. Life in London had enough at hand to warrant daily "be-carefuls".

In fact, he spotted one at the next corner. Constable Hawkins stood watching the crowd with one hand on his hip, the other gripping the handle of his Metropolitan police issue truncheon, as if ready to pull it out at the slightest provocation. What was he doing here? His usual beat was Limehouse.

The policeman's gaze slid right and fixed on Malcolm, causing him immediate breathlessness. If Hawkins had somehow witnessed last night's chase, he would have had to realize that Malcolm was the victim. The bullies had been crying out their intent to slash him. But if Hawkins had been in the shadows, why hadn't he blown his whistle and rushed to help?

No, the man's stare had nothing to do with last night. Malcolm crossed to the far side of the street and rounded the corner.

Last summer, a boy from the Docklands had inadvertently made an enemy of Hawkins. Malcolm didn't know Jiggs well, but he knew enough to understand that the problem lay with the policeman. Malcolm distanced himself as briskly as he could.

He had hardly covered any ground at all when he saw them; two large lads prowled furtively along an intersecting street. Something in the hunched posture of the larger one caused chills along Malcolm's arms and neck. If they had been part of Crocker's gang, they might recognize him today. He was wearing different clothing, of course, and he believed that he possessed no unique mannerisms. Could they have seen his face while in pursuit?

"Don't look their way," he told himself. "Behave naturally; they won't notice." His peripheral vision stayed alert, however.

He couldn't hear their words, but the tone of their conversation carried more urgency than was commonplace. A tingling sensation rose up his spine as he strained to listen.

Just then, two ladies came out of a shop, talking excitedly about a new moving picture show. The cloche-topped females ambled on, talking at the same time and vexing Malcolm as their voices dominated all other sound.

He passed a Chinese laundry with its door propped wide open. Someone inside was being berated, judging by the shrillness of the speech and the sharp delivery of its speaker. He hurried on.

Sudden movement flashed across the street. Feet ran his way. "There he is. Get him!"

Malcolm took off, darting round cumbersome old ladies and a blemish-faced girl who screamed louder than was called for, then past a dark, scampering dog. He nearly knocked over a pram. He kept running. As he turned his head to look back, he collided with something large, stationary and cushioned by tweed, which knocked the wind from him. Before he could push around the person, the black dog ran past, panting.

"Get him, Jack. Here, Pickles, here, boy!" The two lads ran past, intent on their pursuit.

"What is this all about, lad?" the towering man said, now grasping Malcolm's shoulder.

The flood of relief turned to fear. "Oh, um." He tried to catch his breath. "Huh…um, I'm sorry, sir." He breathed in deeply then exhaled. "Huh, I shouldn't've been running. My fault. Did I hurt you?"

The man bent closer and his features warmed. "I got in the way of your chase, as you were trying to catch your friends' dog, apparently."

"Oh, uh, yeah. I mean, yes, it was my fault. Sorry, sir."

The man turned, looking down the street. "I hope they catch him. Now, on with you, but watch where you're going."

"Thank you, sir. I will."

Ignoring a few stares, Malcolm continued on his way to Heneage Street, his neck burning with embarrassment. The fresh upheaval blurred his focus. He tried to clear his head by taking deep breaths. He was passing the Poltava Synagogue when he spotted his mate.

"Sid!"

Sid Shapiro turned from the window of Lever's book shop, waved, and headed his way.

"What's wrong? You look a bit rough this morning." Sid gently slapped him on the back and fell in step, though Malcolm had no particular destination now that he'd found his friend.

"I had a bit more adventure than I care for last night. But all's well today."

"Your da again?"

"No, no." He dug his hands into his pockets. "Say, here. How 'bout if I buy us a coffee? I've got something to tell you." Sitting at Jade's coffeehouse always improved a day. There were no disapproving side glances at their friendship from either Jew or Gentile at that congenial place.

"I'm with you, mate. Thanks."

Coming toward them from the end of the street, Mr. Lever pushed his barrow along.

"Books for sale. Half price."

The man's bandy legs had the shopkeeper's lean frame swaying from side to side, his waddle more pronounced whenever he pushed or carried anything heavy. As a result, the handcart zigzagged, causing some who shared the pavement to veer to the side or stop altogether.

"Fine literature at half the price!"

Mr. Lever was an entrepreneur with gumption. It was his practice to have his plump wife mind their shop as he periodically got out among the people.

"Ah, my two scholars," he said as he neared the boys.

"I happen to have *Cashel Byron's Profession* among my morning's gems. I'm sure you two would enjoy reading about a prize fighter." He lifted the book from his barrow and held it with pride. "Are you old enough to take on some George Bernard Shaw?" The man's gaze endeavoured to bore through Malcolm, as if hypnotizing him to comply. Malcolm could easily ignore the hawker's stare and his *you're-no-longer-little-boys-now, are you?* challenge. Lever seemed a kindly man but his shopkeeper's tone conveyed the belief that a customer would be silly to pass up such a deal.

"I've only got enough for our coffee this morning, Mr. Lever. I'll stop by another time and take a look."

"I always enjoy seeing our youth delight in the treasures of the printed page. Until then, lads." He nodded and careened toward his shop.

"Well, now," Sid said, his eyes bright. "Off to Jade's we go." He danced around a parked lorry at the curb and led the way across Spellman Street and in the direction of Whitechapel's best coffeehouse. Sid was almost the same age as Malcolm but smaller. Their disparate sizes gave the impression of a handful of years between them. Malcolm's shoulders were broad like an athlete's. Sid's sunken chest almost gave him a consumptive appearance but he was lithe and, surprisingly, able to outrun his friend.

They turned down an alley, an oft used shortcut, and Sid began whistling away with attempts at Jolson's tune about a red robin.

The entrance to Jade's hid down an alley off Old Montague Street; one in which the ancient slabs were swept clean. There was no sign announcing the business, nor any lettering on the two windows that looked out over Old Montague. Its heady aroma was enough to signal its existence, providing a temptation Malcolm could never resist when he was in the area. Although the captain did not appear to be wealthy, Malcolm was regularly provided with a shilling or two for things like coffee and books.

He and Sid entered.

The greyish glare coming through the two front windows paradoxically made the long, narrow room darker. Malcolm carefully led the way to the small booth situated in a nook below the staircase. As his eyes adjusted, the familiar smells of musk and mould, which rode faintly below that of roasted coffee beans, assured him that all was dependably the same.

Malcolm told Sid of last night's adventure with hushed intensity. Sid hung on every word. Sid was opening his mouth to reply when a conversation nearby caught their attention.

"I'm tired of Houdini's feats." The voice grabbed Malcolm's attention. The man's head and mane were oversized for his stature. His shirt and bow tie looked fresh while his brown suit sagged from textile exhaustion. The two gents were sitting at a table in the middle of the coffeehouse, close enough for Malcolm to note the seriousness in the eyes of the speaker.

The man's companion shrugged and said, "I'd give my eye teeth to write about all the jolly things to see in the West End. I could watch Lillian Gish all day long."

"You can have her—and Charlie Chaplin and Billy Belcher—"

"It's Bletcher."

"I know. That's me being funny." The bow tie moved up and down as he talked.

"Oh, ha, ha."

"But I mean it. I want to write about life, real life."

Malcolm whispered, "Ever seen those chaps before?"

Sid nodded, a smile of self-satisfaction brightening his features.

Young Billy came to take their orders. Malcolm ordered a piece of sticky toffee pudding for them both to share with their coffees. Watching the boy's back retreat to Jade's counter, he missed what Sid had just whispered. He gestured for a repeat.

"Those men are from *The Daily Telegraph*."

The idea of writing for the public fascinated Malcolm. He thought he heard them discussing a yellow parasol, which seemed unlikely, as their tone was serious.

Large Head continued, "Yes, the Yellow Peril. Now that's real life stuff. 'Community invasion', intolerance, tension. I'm going to ask Mister Peters if I could—"

"Oh, Thaddeus Smith! How nice to run into you again." A woman with a ridiculous bow stuck on her cloche approached the men. She had one of those high-pitched nasal voices that could send a person packing. Her attention was focused on Large Head—Thaddeus Smith.

Billy brought the boys' coffees. Mr. Smith introduced the woman to his companion, after which the journalist manoeuvred an escape as superb as any of those performed by The Great Houdini.

After Jade's, the sky cleared as Malcolm walked Sid home for his dinner.

Mrs. Shapiro whisked open the door and hurried Sid inside with only a mumbled greeting to Malcolm, who turned and headed for the Tube. He would spend the afternoon with his mum.

The shadow of Colonel Basil Green's mausoleum encroached on Malcolm's sunshine. A slight chill settled on his ankles, but late-day light tried to warm the rest of him.

His attention was trained on a large spider off to his right. Its dexterity was as impressive as the tightrope walker he'd seen last summer at the Bristol Fair. The spider was 'knitting' some mittens over the fingers of a familiar stone lady.

The lady was his paternal great grandmother, Hermione Lily Roberts. The sculptor had captured her spirit and legacy, reportedly at the wish of Malcolm's relatives. Malcolm preferred the artist's rendering rather than a fashionable likeness. A simple robe, similar to that of the Roman goddess Libertas, draped the figure to her feet. The hand undergoing the spider's attention stretched low, palm down, as if to rest on the head of a child. Her other hand held a book to her breast. This frozen-in-time gesture represented her life's work, he'd been told.

She had been a proponent of improving the welfare and education of children in London's rookeries. In her day, long before the Great War, she had taken advantage of the only avenue available to a lady in Society, that of capitalizing on social connections. He'd twice overheard his aunt speak of her with admiration. The discussions had never included him. As a boy, he could only listen during the family's Boxing Day dinner conversations. It had been one of the few topics that had captured his imagination. Malcolm would love to have been alive back in the day, to have witnessed Great Grandmama's discreet and sometimes not-so-ethical means of influencing men in government on behalf of London's disadvantaged children.

Now and then, an old question niggled at him: Could you dream yourself back in time? He knew better now and had been younger when the idea had occurred to him—only months after his mother had died. Nonetheless, the question returned like a bad penny. Twilight and dreams sometimes breathed hope into his desire to see her again. And he would let his thoughts dally over the ways in which he might have saved his mum.

A chilly breeze broke the spell, his childish expectations.

He checked again on the spider's work. Taut strands of its web glistened between her fingers in the sunlight. It was as if this creature was getting the lady ready for winter.

Smells of decaying leaves and sun-baked earth wafted his way.

Malcolm's muscles relaxed. The sensation made him aware of his physical well-being and how he had escaped harm in Limehouse. The only damage he had to show for the misadventure was a bruise where his head had hit the pavement and a scabby scratch on his shoulder. Bruises and head wounds were not new to him. He vividly recalled when, years younger, he'd realized, and marvelled at, the body's capacity to heal, and the fact that in time bruises disappeared altogether.

If only painful memories were as easy to efface.

Or worries over fresh dilemmas to allay.

It was unlikely that the Limehouse bullies would be this far north, and they knew neither his home nor his connection with this haven. How could they? Nonetheless, he kept watch on the streets beyond the cemetery's gates. Had any of them seen his features? Not likely, but the anxiety would fester until he knew he was completely safe from them.

What was up with Crocker and those hoodlums? The only other person who might be interested in solving the mystery—the only appropriate person he wouldn't fear to approach—was that news-paperman named Smith. The idea of investigation excited Malcolm despite the risk of failure.

Trusting the police was out of the question. If only the ugly secret had not come to his ears.

He checked the gates again. Nothing but the usual traffic beyond.

Flashing motion high above the gates drew his attention. A seagull glided with ease. Its caw mocked a laugh before it veered back toward the river basin. He thought of Joe manning his boat.

In listening to the waterman's insight, he'd learned that formal education had little to do with wisdom. Wisps of their conversations came back to him, knitting together and forming something whole, like the silky web on his great grandmother's hand. Malcolm always felt better in Joe's company, as he did in Sid's.

The colonel's shadow had stretched to envelope him completely.

Malcolm decided that when he next found Sid free of family and school, he would take him to meet Joe. It was a meeting long overdue.

Chapter Four

"The Russian Steppe begins near the mouth of the Danube River and stretches all the way to here." Mr. Jones pointed to a classroom map, depicting a part of the world Malcolm knew little about; its importance to his life was doubtful. "Almost to Kazan."

If only Old Jones would talk about Genghis Khan or Marco Polo. As dry fact was stacked upon dry fact, Malcolm wrestled with his choice to either allow his heavy lids to close or seek relief beyond the classroom window.

"The climate of the area here..." The man was the sloppiest pointer, Malcolm thought; it looked as if he was indicating the entire continent. "...is semi-arid with nothing to impede the often ferocious winds."

Again, Malcolm considered a means of escape: eyes closed or eyes diverted. A thread of memory brought decision. Having twice been disciplined before the rest of the boys for sleeping in class, he chose the window. He kept his head perfectly still, facing the map, while shifting his gaze to the light and to life along Mile End Road. *Not much of interest there either.* A delivery truck rolled past. Across the road, custom appeared to be dead slow for the apothecary. But shadows were finally tilting to the east a bit, which made him smile. It wouldn't be all that long, really, before school got out.

In the tier of desks below his, Albert passed a folded note to William. Below that, to his right, Jerome's head looked about ready to drop forward. The last time Jerry had fallen asleep, he'd drooled all over his desk. *Got an extra two whacks for that.*

Back to the window. A newspaper truck passed by Malcolm's narrow view, heading east. Why would a solicitor be interested in crates of explosives and truncheons? Would he be shipping them to a relative beleaguered in some hot spot of the Empire? That wasn't how things were done. What were the hot spots now anyway? All he could think of was India. Not very *hot*, metaphorically. The only trouble he'd read about involved occasional skirmishes along the north-western border.

Why would Crocker take delivery from a bunch of hooligans? The captain had taken Malcolm's account in stride. Other than sloshing his blasted brandy, he didn't appear concerned. If Malcolm could do something about it, the hurt from that might disappear. He wrestled once more with the dilemma of whom to trust, but the thought of approaching the police to report Crocker's suspicious activity still tied his stomach in knots. He concentrated beyond the window again.

On the apothecary's awning, a pigeon now perched, basking in the sun. A gentleman came into sight, striding along. His path would soon pass beneath the bird. Would he get bombed? 1-2-3-4. The pedestrian made it through without incident. At that moment Malcolm noticed a newspaper tucked under the fortunate man's arm, and that again brought to mind Thaddeus Smith from the *Telegraph*.

"That'd be best; that, I could manage to do," Malcolm said under his breath.

Smith had said that he wanted to write about real life. Perhaps he could seek out the newspaperman today, after school. First, he'd dash to Stepney Jewish School and collect Sid. His friend would be miffed if Malcolm didn't include him.

". . . mountains of Transylvania."

Silence.

"Master Malcolm."

Malcolm's mouth went dry.

"I consider daydreaming as offensive as sleeping. Come down here."

Old Jones reached for the strap.

Malcolm waited in Stepney Green across from Sid's school, a more attractive building than Merriweather Secondary. Its red bricks and hipped roof looked fresher than Merriweather's soot-encrusted grey.

Crossing the park from Jamaica Street, two bearded men in identical broad-brimmed black hats and black frock coats walked with their heads together, speaking in Yiddish. Malcolm enjoyed the complex consonants and inflections of the language. Two pigeons, moving and murmuring as if in imitation, followed the men.

"Malcolm, my good man," Sid called as he approached.

Malcolm laughed and said, "Don't be cheeky."

He directed them south, suddenly indecisive whether he really wanted to seek out the man at *The Telegraph*. Introducing Sid to Joe would be more fun. He and Sid could seek out the newspaperman tomorrow. Part of him wanted to forget about Crocker's back-alley shenanigans, but he couldn't.

"D'ya want to go down to the docks? We could stop by my waterman friend's mooring."

"Something's on your mind. I can tell."

"Let's have a stroll, at least. I think more clearly when I'm moving about."

"Regent's Canal, then?"

"There you are, *my good man.*"

"Don't be cheeky, Malcolm, *old bean.*"

Sid cuffed him upside his head and took off, sending pigeons into a fluttering mass; the birds, like Sid, looked ready for anything.

The wake of a small barge fluted out along the canal waters, engaging gold and brown leaves in a dance as they bobbed and gathered on the surface. Malcolm caught only a glimpse of the vessel as it quietly disappeared beyond a brick-sided bridge, heading toward Limehouse docks.

In the opposite direction along the canal, just outside the Mile End Jewish Cemetery, stood the spot forever etched into Malcolm's memory. About a year ago, en route to the market, two local bullies advanced on a boy half their size. They jeered at the waif and began shoving him back and forth. It was about to get uglier when Malcolm grabbed up a fallen branch and chased the bullies away. That was the beginning of his friendship with Sid.

Malcolm looked back toward Limehouse and gathered his thoughts.

"You know that fella from *The Telegraph?*"

"You mean the man that lady fussed over? Oh, *Thaddeus Smith!*" Sid's voice in falsetto mocked the woman. "What about 'im?"

"I'd like to talk with him. He wants to write about something more interesting than Belchin' Bletcher, something about *real* life, right? Maybe we could help get him started. And then we might find out what was going on at Crocker's."

Sid threw a stone along the water, ostensibly with no relish, though when it plopped rather than skipped, his shoulders drooped.

He shrugged by way of reply, looked at him and asked, "Why not go to the police?"

Malcolm glared his answer.

Understanding filled Sid's features. "Oh, of course." With flushed cheeks, he busied himself by searching for another stone to throw.

"If anybody could figure out what Mister Crocker is up to, a newspaperman could, I bet."

"What if this Thaddeus Smith doesn't come back to Jade's?"

"We could just figure out how to find him, then, couldn't we?"

They stood outside the newspaper's offices in Fleet Street.

"Um," Sid said, "the nobs'll be looking at us."

Fleet Street was imposing enough, but the new office building loomed in solemn majesty. With the business day still in progress, plenty of respectable activity coursed along. The air here was different. Void of sewer smells and odiferous workers, the breeze carried a measure of hope and Empire, along with a blend of vehicle exhaust and fine cigar smoke.

Malcolm understood his friend's uneasiness and offered an assuring smile. Sid still wore baggy knee trousers. The captain had allowed Malcolm to wear long trousers for over a year. Both wore soft caps. If their hands and faces were not so clean, they'd look like newsboys. "I think we're young enough to be ignored, mate."

"I'll take that up, thanks." Sid joined him at the window.

Inside, an immense amount of mahogany—walls, counters and desks—was dotted with green-shaded lamps. Staid clerks in stiff collars and even stiffer expressions filled the room.

"How are we going to find him in there?" Sid asked.

"Follow me."

Pulling open the ornate wood and glass door was an experience in itself. It was the largest threshold Malcolm had ever crossed. A symphony of sound swept over him as he stepped in: typewriters clacking with a pace that sounded like a pulse pumping below the chordal murmurings of voices, topped and punctuated by countless return-carriage bells. His gaze rose above the mahogany, taking in a wall of proud marble rising up to a palatial ceiling from which three gargantuan light fixtures hung. They weren't like any chandeliers he'd ever seen. Sleek and modern, they glimmered as if Jules Verne had devised them.

"May I help you, lads?" The man's face, bisected by a thin black moustache, peered down at them with hooded eyes. His persona was imperious but resigned to accommodate anything or anyone appropriate to the business of news.

"Um, we'd like to see a Mr. Thaddeus Smith, please."

Without pause or blink, he said in a dry tone, "Sixth floor. Then turn right, down the hall."

"Thank you, sir."

"The stairs that you want are that way." He nodded almost imperceptibly toward the back of the lobby.

Although intimidating, the activity all around them excited Malcolm. Here was where news, of London, Great Britain and the world, was processed and sent out to countless readers.

Walking past a pair of brass-plated elevator doors, Sid said, "Why didn't he say we could take the lift?"

"Probably didn't want to subject the adults to being confined with street urchins."

"We're not urchins," Sid said, indignant before catching on that Malcolm was joking.

They found the stairs and began climbing.

Malcolm added, "Probably because the lift attendants are allergic to boys."

"Enough!" Sid chuckled, his breaths quick and shallow from the climb.

"Let's see," Malcolm said, "the stuffy bloke said turn right and down the hall." The hall, consisting of terrazzo floor, marble wainscoting and countless identical doors, was long enough to accommodate a foot race. Green-gold lettering on the translucent pane of each wooden door identified its occupant. From behind them came more tapping on keys and the odd muffled conversation. They'd reached the end without seeing a Thaddeus Smith.

"Maybe he meant turn left and down the hall," Sid offered. As they headed in the other direction, a click signalled the opening of a door just ahead. An older gentleman came out, dressed similarly to the stuffy bloke downstairs, only this gent sported an old-fashioned beard. He gave them a cursory glance, but was not inclined to offer more. He walked to the elevator doors. Malcolm soon heard the chime, then the operator pushing open the inner caging. In short order, the man and the operator disappeared down the shaft, generating relief for Malcolm rather than regret at missing an opportunity for directions.

No Thaddeus Smith could be found on any of the doors on the floor.

"Maybe we got the wrong floor," Sid said in a whisper.

Reluctant to go downstairs to ask again, Malcolm suggested, "Let's try this."

"What?"

He answered by means of his quickened pace, heading back along the stipulated route, reviewing each door as he went. The lettering on the very last door said, "Staff". The sound of a man mumbling, as if reading to himself, gave Malcolm some hope. He knocked.

A shadow appeared behind the glass. The doorknob turned and clicked, opening to reveal a quizzical gaze from the short man with the large head and mane, Thaddeus Smith. His mouth twitched, poised to smile. "May I help you, gentlemen?"

Propitious beginning, Malcolm thought. "Uh, we'd like to speak with you, sir," Malcolm ventured. "About a disturbing matter."

After introductions, Mr. Smith ushered them into the small room. Malcolm paused and inhaled the sweet smell of pipe tobacco. The pleasant aroma was the room's only redeeming factor. It looked as if it could have previously been a janitor's room. There were no chairs other than the one behind the desk, so they all stood, the boys shifting from side to side as if they were on a rocking boat.

The journalist asked, "What do you have?"

Malcolm explained what he had witnessed behind Crocker's offices. "We couldn't help overhear you at Jade's, saying that you wanted to write about something important. I thought you might wish to investigate the Crocker situation."

"I see."

"We'd even help, if we knew how."

Sid's eyes widened with alarm, surprised at being included in any further involvement. But Malcolm trusted that he could count on Sid, even if his friend was not by nature a risk taker.

"Hm, there are a few possibilities that come to mind." The journalist sat behind his desk, lit his pipe and puffed it to life. He began to mumble to himself while studying the ceiling. Was he praying? Surely not. He pulled open a drawer and rifled through some files.

Looking satisfied, he pulled one out, laid it on his desk and said, "Where can I find you gents if I need you?"

"Uh," Malcolm didn't think he wanted his father to know, no matter how much the captain encouraged manly activities. And he knew Sid's parents would object. "You could catch us when school gets out." He gave the details.

Chapter Five

Malcolm loved Sundays. Sid's family obligations were all dealt with on Saturdays, and the two could while away their free time until sunset. They made their way to the Docks soon after dawn. Malcolm strode with spirit, eager to introduce Sid to Joe.

"The river stinks worse today," Sid complained. They sat side by side on a derelict pier near Joe's berth. "How long does it take for Joe to come back from Southwark?"

"I don't exactly know. A customer could have him going anywhere, out to Gravesend or up to Battersea." Malcolm glanced at the place where Joe moored his water taxi, a short distance from their perch.

Just beyond that, Chinese dock workers trudged from a moored ship to Eggert & Sons' warehouse. He'd never seen a fat Chinaman working the docks. These weary Orientals bore large bags of— Malcolm thought the sacks might contain sugar from the West Indies—on their backs. Each labourer looked as thin as Sid.

Sid interrupted his thoughts. "That sure looks like hard work."

"I imagine it is."

Malcolm looked up and down the Thames. Joe was not in sight. "Those Chinamen shoulder as much as the large Irish lads I've seen."

Sid pointed to the walkway beyond Eggert's. "What's that girl hawking over there? I can't quite make it out, but I can tell it's not flowers or oranges."

"That's Maisie. She sells matchbooks, mostly. Stands round here to be the first to help the sailors part with their money. She's a good lass, though."

"From here, it looks like she is pretty enough to be a lady's maid or a shop girl."

"She was—pretty, I mean. I don't know how it happened, but one of her front teeth got knocked out. Some of the other teeth have turned brown since. She had been planning on more schooling."

"You mean she left school for good? Because of her teeth?"

"Because her father died in Belgium. She and her mum fell on hard times. I guess Maisie is old enough not to be bothered by attendance officers."

From across the expanse, Malcolm noticed the girl's attention trained on them. Or was she watching something farther along the river? He knew their conversation would be eaten up by distance and river noises and shrugged off the concern.

"Joe keeps a watchful eye on her when he's moored here, and so does one of the managers at Eggert's, as I understand it. On the weekend, Joe says she hawks her matches outside some pubs. Not sure which ones."

Sid appeared to consider this and said, "I'm liking your friend Joe more and more. It's good to think he'd look out for a lass' safety in these parts."

Malcolm looked down to the empty boat slip with fondness.

Then the memory of his recent escape from the hoodlums caused his stomach to churn. He scanned the area again, looking beyond the Chinese workers and Maisie, afraid that he might see one of the bullies staked out, watching for his return. They might not have seen his face clearly enough to recognize him, but they could have noted that he called Joe by name, that he knew this area. He would have picked up on that detail were he in pursuit—were he a spy or an enquiry agent. But there were no loiterers in view, apart from themselves and a man smoking a pipe next to a business called Tobin's. The man was a local, not a stranger.

Malcolm resumed his vigil over the Thames.

"Trust me," he replied to Sid's comment on the river. He pointed downward. "It's even worse than it smells. Just pray you never have to jump in." He felt the rise of goose flesh under his jacket as the image of the floater arose to haunt him. The slimy corpse had seemed to cling to him as if by intent. Thankfully, all he could see today bobbing about in the choppy waters were bits of rubbish. Nonetheless, a shiver travelled up his spine.

"I'm not tempted to. Hey! There goes a Jardine Matheson freighter." Sid pointed. The huge ship glided noiselessly down the busy river.

"Just think of the sights that ship gets to see," Malcolm said, grateful for a change of topic.

"You mean: the sights that its crew gets to see." Sid elbowed him.

"Of course that's what I mean. Don't be tedious, old trout." The freighter sailed past the many ships and steamers anchored just off the docks. "I see it has the customary flock of screaming gulls sending it off."

Sid chuckled.

"Anyway," Malcolm continued, "I wonder if it ever docks at Dubrovnik."

"Where?"

"That's where Joe's from…well, where his folks were from. He said that before the war, it was called Ragusa. Now, it's part of the Kingdom of Serbs, Croats and Slovenes. Along the Adriatic. Don't they teach you anything at your school?" Malcolm silently admitted that this tidbit was gleaned during one of those rare times he'd actually paid attention to Old Jones.

He tried out a foreign accent, one which was very roughly East-European, one which he sometimes heard Joe mimic.

Malcolm said, "Allow me to tell you, my friend, about my homeland; my city: Dubrovnik, she makes me happy. Every time I walk her streets, I climb, I descend, I view the sea, the sky and my people. The smell of bread baking wafts from its houses. Our bread is better than anyone's, even the Frenchies'. This aroma never fails to light up my face as I cross its districts. From open windows I hear the voices of women, yelling at their husbands, at their children, at their servants. Our women have spirit like no other.

"Walking next to me, you will always see my Sylvie, my goat. Walking with Sylvie is much more peaceful than walking with my wife. My Sylvie, she thinks she's my daughter, accompanying me on my errands; never a complaint has she. I spoil her so, my Sylvie. But I digress.

"Dubrovnik! My family has walked its ancient lanes for centuries. Marco Polo explored its lengths and was beguiled. She is my home. You will love it here, my friend. You will love my Dubrovnik."

"Sheeeesh! You got all that from geography?"

"That, and from listening to some around here, and from my imagination. There are times when I wish we lived somewhere else."

"I'd like to have a goat," Sid said wistfully.

Malcolm cuffed him and laughed, and concerns over bullies and floaters were comfortably pushed away.

"Are yer waitin' for Joe, lads?"

Malcolm turned toward the gravelly voice and then realized it was the local who'd been smoking next to Tobin's.

"Yes, sir."

The man sank his grimy hands in his pockets while a number of curious expressions crossed his features, none of them optimistic. His pipe shifted to the other side of his mouth.

Speaking around its bit, the man said, "I'm sorry to tell yer 'e won't be back. Got knifed out on the river. The watermen along Gravesend found his boat driftin', his body in it. Whoever done it didn't even take 'is money."

A pang struck Malcolm. Dropping to his knees, he heaved. Tears blurred the dark waters below.

He was to blame. Joe's death must be linked to him. Those thugs had seen his rescuer. They could easily have assumed that Malcolm had explained what he'd witnessed at Crocker's.

Now prostrate, Malcolm rolled on his side and curled up, his chest and throat ached. Sid knelt next to him and held his arm in a gentle grip, offering the only comfort he could think of.

The man's voice came closer. "Yer knew 'im, then. Sorry to 'ave been so blunt, lad." He too knelt nearby.

How could this nightmare get any worse?

Large hands grabbed Malcolm from his warm bed. The pain of the grip and the whoosh past his ears forced his mind to catch up with what was happening. His gut landed on the man's shoulder, forcing all breath from his body.

"Got ya!"

"No!"

His abductor turned and made for the open door; and Malcolm's arms just managed to deflect a blow to his head as the swing brought him in contact with the wardrobe. Each jerky step as they bounded down the staircase punched air from his stomach.

"I got ya!" The laugh that followed filled the hall with its madness. The familiarity of the sound and the jostling robbed Malcolm of his strength. When would his father break free of these episodes? Would they survive this one?

Just then, the captain changed course, and Malcolm's head swung and cracked against the newel post.

"Ah!" Shooting pain and breathlessness had him fearing he would faint and be totally helpless. *Not the cellar. Please not the cellar.* Thoughts of being buried alive had him about to retch, held at bay only by the flurry of sensations. *Please not the cellar.*

The baize door gave way like paper in the wind.

Boots clomped across the kitchen's linoleum and then turned toward the cellar stairs.

"I'll get you to safety, man!"

"No!" Malcolm grabbed for a kitchen chair and missed. He grabbed for another, pulling so hard the top of its back rammed up against his ear. He almost dropped it and again feared he would faint.

The door was swung open.

"No!"

The first plod down again knocked all air from Malcolm, but he was able to hold the chair up and across, catching the door jam with a thud, followed by a jolt.

Malcolm, braced by the door jam, splayed across the threshold; his captor tumbled down the stairs.

The following silence filled Malcolm with dread.

"Are you all right, Father?"

Chapter Six

"How many times has this happened without sufficient injury to have to call me in?" Doctor Adams could not whisper to save his life, which Malcolm counted as a blessing. He could tell that the two men were stationed at the foot of the stairs.

Sitting up in bed, Malcolm leaned in the direction of the closed door but only fragments of reply carried from the remorseful captain.

"I understand combat trauma. But, you have to pull yourself together, man. Your night terrors will soon have the lad's brains beaten into a pudding if you don't work out a solution."

Their retreating steps reduced the interchange to a mere buzz. Malcolm hopped out of bed, tip-toed to the door and carefully opened it. The men reached the vestibule. Other than a snatch of muffled conversation while he was crossing his room, all he heard was a stiff 'goodnight' and the closing of the front door.

The sticking plaster pulled at the split goose egg on the side of his head. A clink of glass came from the liquor cabinet in the parlour. Malcolm crawled back into bed and pulled up the covers, feeling as if he were drifting with the currents under the Thames.

"Chin up. I don't want to see your lip tremble." The captain's own lower lip trembled, however, in between commands to his son.

Malcolm sat in the back of the cab, feeling small and young.

"I'll come round on Sundays." Roberts' face darkened in thought. "Uh, can't next Sunday but the one after."

Malcolm nodded.

Captain Roberts gave the cabbie his fare and a slip of paper with the Newington Green address.

He turned back and placed his hands on Malcolm's shoulders. "It's time to be a man." His breath smelled of coffee. His words sounded hollow. The captain's emotion was again encased like sodden feet in muddy military boots.

Memories of stilted conversations by the fireplace darted through Malcolm's mind. Those times together had been tense, yet he suddenly wanted them all at hand, private and secured behind locked doors.

The captain backed away, stood straight. He shut the door of the cab and stepped up to the curb.

The old cabbie, in respectful silence, shifted the gears.

Panic flashed through Malcolm's body when the vehicle began moving over the cobbles and past neighbouring homes. A sharp need surged, and he jerked his body around to keep sight of his father through the rear window. Their eyes locked. The captain's face went slack. His posture shifted. The vehicle kept on course.

"Wait!" The captain's voice cut through the air. "Wait!"

The cab stopped. Malcolm fumbled with the door. His father strode up and threw it open. His large hands reached in, grabbed hold and pulled him out and into his arms.

Malcolm had never before felt his father's tears.

The embrace, feeling both quick and eternal, ended. The strong arms released him and then hands nudged him away and toward the cab. This time, the parting inflicted pain so sharp as to feel physical, as if some of his skin had stuck to his father and was ripping away.

Malcolm slid again onto the back seat of the cab. The captain shut the door, the sound firm and final; and then the vehicle started forward and gathered speed.

Despite the chill running through him, Malcolm's face, arms and back still sensed his father's warmth. He wondered whether he'd ever feel such an embrace again. Would he forget how it felt?

Chapter Seven

"Your aunt asked me to welcome you in her absence. You may call me Wendell. No need for formality with a rascal like myself."

The handsome man, whom Malcolm understood to be Aunt Jane's neighbour, stood tall with relaxed elegance, wearing a white tunic and loose-fitting pants, the likes of which he had seen on East End merchants from Bombay.

"Uh, yes, sir."

"I don't mean to fuss, but Wendell will do. And I will simply call you Malcolm. Unless you insist on Master Malcolm."

"Oh, no, sir—uh, Wendell."

"Very well."

A young maid with a severe limp hobbled from the back of the main hall. She was new to the household since Malcolm's visit on Boxing Day a year ago. Without a word, she bent down and gathered Malcolm's suitcases.

Before Malcolm could offer to take his own things, Wendell said, "She'll be fine. Come. We're to have tea in my flat upstairs. Your Aunt Jane will meet us there...eventually."

Wendell led the way. A surge of curiosity arose when Malcolm noticed that the man's ankles were bare with his feet tucked into leather slippers of a foreign shape. Not at all like the ones worn by the Bombay fellows. He'd never seen anything like them.

They passed the first landing where Aunt Jane's flat was situated, then another. The carpet on the wide staircase was rich in texture and only slightly worn. Malcolm had been in the house on just three other occasions, twice for Auntie's Boxing Day dinner, which she began hosting after Malcolm's mum had died. He took more notice of details on this ascent. All of it, the stairs, carpets, and light fixtures were in finer shape and of higher quality than those in his home.

Malcolm's chest tightened at the thought. He barely recognized his own voice as it said, "When my father is better, I shall return home."

"Uh, yes." Wendell continued his pace.

"But I'm grateful to Auntie. Where is she?"

Wendell opened his door and entered. Malcolm trailed behind.

"She's attending a lecture. Make yourself at home."

Wendell stood back, and an expanse of deep red and saffron filled Malcolm's eyes, leaving him breathless. Carpets and drapes covered two of the walls, making the large room exotic. A sweet musky aroma reminded Malcolm of pipe tobacco but was from something decidedly different. Piles of cushions and two divans made up the furniture. Wanting to appear as cosmopolitan as Wendell, Malcolm masked his awe, walked to a set of cushions and sank down, righting himself from a clumsy sideways tip at the last second.

"My man will bring in tea shortly." Wendell turned his back, walked to one of the windows with a street view and stiffly glanced below, as if he wished to conjure up Jane Beardsmore to appear and take the waif off his hands. Or was he concerned about something else down there? The man's soldier-like frame stood at ease, but the hands clasped behind his back clenched and opened repeatedly in sync with the ticking of the clock.

The timepiece on the mantel was held fast in the ivory teeth of a copper dragon, which glared across the room with vehemence.

"I like your sitting room, Wendell." Malcolm attempted to sound like his father. "You travel, I see."

The man came away from the window, though he appeared not inclined to sit. "After the war. Mesopotamia, India, Egypt, Spain. I'd spent so much time in cold, stinking French mud, I couldn't bear to come straight back to dreary London. After baking my bones a bit, I brought a touch of the Middle East with me. I'm glad you approve."

Though suspicious of the man's sincerity, Malcolm couldn't help but feel a rush of satisfaction. His opinion had never seemed to matter before.

On the wall, among two metal plates and several framed photographs, hung something that looked like shrivelled flesh.

"Uh, is that from a cannibal village?" Malcolm pointed.

"No, lad. Some of the old Basque shepherds still fancy their wine in Bota Bags—or wineskins. That's made from goat hide."

Footsteps approached from what Malcolm assumed was the kitchen area. Wendell's manservant was a short, hearty looking older boy, fresh-faced, as if straight off the farm. He wore no white gloves as he carried in a laden tray. The lad's brown suit was well cut but informal for one in service.

An ornate trunk positioned between Malcolm and his host became their tea table. The manservant's hands worked with deftness arranging tea things before Malcolm, which was surprising considering how large and strong they were, but Malcolm had seen hearty footmen before. He studied the lad's face and realized he'd underestimated his age.

The young man straightened. "Would that be all, sir?"

Malcolm thought the lilt sounded similar to that of a boy he'd met from Wales.

Wendell said, "Yes, thank you, Bryn."

Without eye contact, Bryn nodded and returned to the kitchen.

Malcolm's fingers were tapping tattoos on his knees. He stopped and waited to be served.

The question of how Malcolm took his tea was indicated by a lift of Wendell's left brow.

"Just a spot of milk, thank you."

"I don't care for milky tea myself, especially in the case of China tea. But you might wish for a bit more than a spot. This tea is strong enough to put hair on your wee chest."

Malcolm accepted his cup and saucer and inhaled the scent. "Hm." He took a careful sip. The flavour was pungent but delicious.

"I like it. I'll check out my chest in the morning."

"Ha! You're not bad, old thing. You might just fit in round here."

A knock at the door was followed by Aunt Jane. In one fluid motion, Wendell was on his feet. Malcolm scrambled to get off the cushions gracefully. He then gaped at his aunt.

She was wearing the plainest black ensemble he'd ever seen. The lady offered a self-mocking smile.

"I know. Not my flamboyant self, Malcolm. Every now and then it's good to blend in."

He took stock of the lack of jewellery, the absence of adornment to her cloche—she wasn't even rouged or mascaraed. A small church in the area came to his mind. Had she forgiven the clergy?

He asked, "You mean, like for church services?"

Aunt Jane sank on a divan.

Bryn strode back with a tray. After arranging her tea things, he went and stood next to the credenza.

She ignored the refreshments and plugged a cigarette into a shiny red holder. A subtle gesture of her brows prompted Bryn to again pad across the rug while simultaneously flicking alive a match. He held the flame to the cigarette's end, and then retreated silently. Aunt Jane inhaled and released a lazy billow of smoke toward the Adams ceiling. Now she appeared more like the woman Malcolm knew. She met his gaze.

"Dear boy, you will find that I'm neither political nor religious, but I have my causes. Without a cause, life would be dashed boring."

Wendell folded his arms at his chest in a movement that was both elegant and uneasy, as if he wished for a different topic. "Pleasure keeps me from boredom."

She lifted her cup. "Oh, pleasure is all well and good." Aunt Jane forced a taut smile. Malcolm leaned forward, expecting her to finish the thought that hung between them, but she instead set down her cup and saucer, stood and walked toward the front windows, her pose unnaturally casual. Standing off to one side, she peered down at the street in the same guarded manner that Wendell had done.

After some moments, she turned back, resumed her seat and said, "It's a sense of purpose that gets me out of bed each morning."

"No wonder I'm content to laze about till noon," Wendell replied with wearied self-disdain.

Aunt Jane's eyes darkened, and Malcolm wondered if Wendell and his Aunt often reached an impasse on such issues. The two adults fell into an uncomfortable silence, and Malcolm asked whether he could go outside.

Quiet hung in the modest expanse that was the landlady's garden. The contrast to the disturbing undercurrents in Wendell's flat, following in the wake of Malcolm's earlier surge of emotions, proved a welcome stretch of still water. Now, he could nurse his feelings away from the pitying gazes of Wendell and Aunt Jane.

He sat in a wood-slat chair that tilted back. A cool breeze brushed his face, breathing hope into his nostrils along with the scent of spent flowers. He wished he knew more about gardens. He reached out and touched the leaf of a shrub. It was aflame with shades of burnt red.

Two of the brick walls were covered with ivy. His gaze travelled along countless leaves, appreciating the depth and texture they offered. Thoughts of his mum, who had loved gardening, arose unbidden. He swept them away, peeved. She had given up *her fight*. His father had been shattered by *his*.

Malcolm sat up to spit, as if to expel his resentment but stopped himself at the last second. This lovely refuge belonged to Mrs. Doran. For all he knew, she could be watching him from behind at one of her windows. If he was to live with Aunt Jane for some time, he couldn't chance losing the right to come into this sanctuary. How can one bury troubling thoughts deep enough? Is there some trick, some psychoanalytic process, to locking them away for good?

A gaze around the garden calmed him once more. His eyes moved along the jasmine, lingered on the alyssum and crept up ivy-clad walls. For all he knew, the greenery could end any day now, could be rendered dormant for months. A quiver of excitement rose in his heart. It was a fine thing to experience natural beauty just before it disappeared, like catching sight of lark before it flew away. He was grateful for this garden.

But it wasn't home.

Guilt at having failed his parents pressed against his chest like a strong hand. His father's hand? His mother's? God's?

Malcolm gulped down a jagged breath and coughed.

Memories of Joe surfaced—an instinctive attempt to allay loneliness. But, in an instant, relief twisted into a sharp pang, and Malcolm dropped his head into his hands. If only the report of Joe's murder had been a dream—if only his friend would be at his river post, waiting for him.

The city's muffled sounds gradually filtered through and filled the air. He wondered at having been deaf to their hum till now.

He wiped away a tear. Just then, fluttery movement in the garden drew his attention. Something had ruffled the little flowers.

With care, Malcolm rose and crept in that direction. Another clump fluttered. His heart leapt. On his knees, he placed his hand among the alyssum, parting its white petals gently. Underneath, on the black earth, sat a toad. Malcolm caught the little thing. Its rapid pulse concerned him. Was it so very frightened? Or was the pulse of such creatures always rapid?

"Hullo, Toad," he whispered.

With his other hand, he lightly stroked its smooth back.

"You seem to be all alone this afternoon." Its gentle pulsations alerted Malcolm's sensitivities. Were toads helpless?

He shared a self-mocking smile with the toad. "You don't know whether you'll be needing me or not. I understand. But if ever I see you in danger, I promise to rush in and help. No need to worry about that. I'll be living here now."

He set it back among the alyssum. Before letting it go, his fingers gave it another soft stroke. Had its pulse slowed? Was he imagining that it had?

Malcolm must have blinked. The toad had vanished. There was the slightest ripple off in the jasmine. Then nothing.

"Well, I see you don't need a protector. You're faster than Sid."

For some time, Malcolm kept vigil in hopes of any other sign of the toad. All remained as still as the painting in Mrs. Doran's parlour.

"You have a nice home here, Toad. I expect we'll meet again." He brushed together the petals as they had been and leaned back on his haunches, preparing to stand.

"I hope so."

Chapter Eight

"Come, come, Malcolm. Wendell's motorcar is waiting out front."

Malcolm raced down the first set of stairs then came to a halt. His aunt stood below on the marble-tiled hall, her persona back in place. Ivory satin flowed to just below Auntie's knees, and she was also wearing a long wrap of poppy red and ivory paisley. As he marched downward, he couldn't help but smile at her final touches: an ivory-hued silk turban, eyelids edged with kohl like Theda Bara, and shocking red shoes.

"Yes, yes. My old self," she said. "Come along. Have you had Chinese cuisine before?"

"No, Auntie. Is it very different from Indian?"

"Heavens, yes."

He held the front door for her and then followed to the shiny motorcar, where Wendell stood at the ready by the vehicle's passenger door.

Dressed in a crimson tunic and fez, the colour on Wendell clashed with Auntie's paisleys. Below the loose-fitting pants, black British boots had been polished.

Malcolm was slightly disappointed not to see the curled-toed leather slippers. He barely managed to refrain from remarking that their attire looked more suitable for a fancy dress ball than a restaurant. Instead, he nodded and said, "Good evening, Wendell."

Wendell bowed and replied, "And now I escort my fair neighbour and her dashing nephew to the palace of Genghis Khan for a meal befitting a prince."

Malcolm smiled but instead of playing along, said, "Swell motorcar."

Wendell slipped on leather driving gloves and replied, "A Dalage D1. Glad you approve."

There it was again. Did this man, this eccentric but virile man, give a sow's ear what Malcolm thought?

For now, he suppressed the questions and enjoyed the anticipation of their destination. He turned to watch the passing bustle of life once they rounded the corner onto Regent Street.

Either from intuitive awareness or from boredom with Malcolm's company, Auntie and Wendell clammed up. Perhaps they had their own worries—the earlier image of each of them in turn looking down from the flat at the street below concerned him. He was somewhat familiar with neuroses. Surely these two were closer to normal. He snuck a glance, taking in their choice of dress, and shook his head. Was he going to end up crazy? Was it infectious? No, he knew it wasn't. He was fond of his aunt. Her self-mockery indicated awareness and intelligence. His jaw clenched. Enough *brooding!* There was dinner to look forward to.

Recognizing Shadwell's streets, he asked, "Where are we going?"

"Donny Foon's, just outside Limehouse. I know your father never took you there, but surely you've passed by the place in your explorations."

"Not that I know of, but maybe, when I see it . . . ."

Nearing Limehouse, Wendell pulled over to the curb and turned off the engine. Malcolm looked up and down the dark street. There were respectable people walking along, but none of the buildings indicated a restaurant.

In short order, he and his older companions were walking down the street, attracting restrained attention. Malcolm cast off a wave of embarrassment and followed the two with his head held as upright as theirs. He wondered at their relationship. Auntie was probably fifteen years Wendell's senior.

A Chinaman in Western dress, sporting a bright tie, came out and held open a wood and glass door as they approached. He bowed to each of them.

Before entering, Malcolm noted the small unlit lettering *Donny Foon* above the doorway while even fainter Chinese lettering ran down a plaque next to the entry. The Chinaman cleared his throat, and Malcolm slipped inside, crossing a small foyer to stand behind the adults.

A blend of aromas, some pleasant, some dubious—but none familiar—met him. How had he overlooked this place before? Malcolm thought he might bring Sid here someday.

The tables, chairs and linen were all Western, but a string of glowing paper lanterns hung across a mahogany bar. Against the opposite wall were two lacquered panels, a vibrant dragon painted on each.

The Chinaman, whom Wendell addressed as Lee, led them to one of the last available tables. Again, Malcolm chose to ignore the heads that turned and the voices that murmured. He heard a snatch of one comment, however, which indicated a measure of awe for Aunt Jane. He would have held out his aunt's chair but Wendell and Lee fussed over the privilege.

Seated, menu in hand, Malcolm whispered, "I don't think the Chinese workers I've seen at the docks come to this place."

"They wouldn't," Auntie agreed, distracted as she rummaged in her handbag and retrieved her cigarette holder. She inserted a cigarette and held it for Wendell to light. After inhaling slowly, she blew a smoke ring above the table, sat back and studied the entrée list. "They could hardly do so."

Wendell said to Malcolm, "Someday, I'll take you to a place that the coolies do frequent. You'd think you were in the most common part of Shanghai. Terribly scruffy, but an adventure you'd long remember."

"Uh, thank you, Wendell. Perhaps."

After their orders were taken, Wendell began discussing the various offerings of London's theatres and his voice became serious as his attention was fixed on Aunt Jane's reactions.

"The Royal Opera Company is a poor echo of what it was before the war...." He began tossing out names like Wilde, Strauss and someone named Salome.

Malcolm didn't understand the need for Wendell's intensity on the topic. His gaze wandered to an archway where strands of beads curtained off an alcove, in which three musicians strummed Oriental stringed instruments. The space beyond the curtain was dimly lit, but the countless, many-coloured glass beads glowed.

He sat back and enjoyed the sensations washing over him: delicate, Oriental music, the occasional clink of glassware or china, an intriguing array of bouquets—he was becoming even more hungry.

Dinner was served. A crispy duck, shiny with sauce, was set before Aunt Jane and another before Wendell. The waiter placed a silver tureen of chop suey before Malcolm's plate, along with one of rice. Malcolm took a careful sip of his tea; it had a softer flavour than that in Wendell's flat.

Wendell said, "Do you know, Malcolm, what chop suey means?"

"No." He was happy to be included again.

"Garbage bits."

"Wendell," Aunt Jane scolded.

"Or tiny bits. Not to worry, old man, Donny Foon uses the finest ingredients. No dog or rat meat, I assure you."

Aunt Jane cleared her throat in another protest.

Malcolm grimaced his reply.

The flavours and textures were delicious. Malcolm patted his lips with his napkin, sipped his tea—and met the gaze of a form behind the beaded curtain. A shiver went down his spine as the figure held its stance for several long moments then receded from view.

The motorcar's backseat felt cold and stiff when Malcolm slid in next to Auntie for their return home. As Wendell crouched to manoeuver himself into the driver's seat a boy ran up to him. Instead of holding his hand out in hope of money, the smudged-faced ragamuffin held out a folded piece of paper. Wendell took it without surprise.

"Here you go, lad." Wendell dropped a few coins in the lad's hand. The boy ran back toward the restaurant.

"What is it?" Aunt Jane's voice was tight.

"I'm to meet a chap in the alley, an associate of ours." He bent forward as though removing something from under his seat.

"I'm going with you."

Malcolm expected a chivalrous refusal. Wendell turned and met her gaze. "Are you prepared?" Aunt Jane's hand touched the side of her purse.

"Yes."

Wendell then reached over to grab a coat that Malcolm hadn't previously noticed. The motion was swift, casual, but close enough for him to catch sight of an item partly concealed beneath the topcoat that was now draped over Wendell's arm. The weapon looked similar, he was sure, to those seen in crates at Crocker's back door: a truncheon.

Aunt Jane composed herself on the pavement. Before taking Wendell's arm, she slid a pistol from her purse, endeavouring to block Malcolm's view by adjusting her wrap.

The proud crimson tunic and the paisley silk ensemble strolled away as naturally as a couple coming from a ball. After several yards of amazing nonchalance, the two disappeared into a dark alley.

"Wanna know what they're doin', mate?" The boy appeared next to Malcolm's car door as if he'd been there all the while.

Malcolm lowered his window.

"Oi could do a bit o' eavesdroppin' for a price. Foon's cookies, if ya took some along, or a few pennies?" The youngster's eyes were Asian yet he seemed like any other English lad soiled with poverty.

"Ha'pennies?"

"Three, at least." The boy sniffed.

"What if my people come back before you can report to me?"

"That's a risk. They might not come back at all. Did ya think o' that?"

Masking his panic, Malcolm reached into his pocket. "Here's one half-penny. If you get back with word, I'll give you two more."

The coin was snatched before Malcolm felt it, and the boy ran off.

"Great. Now what?" Malcolm said to the air in the motorcar.

The yearning to sit before his own hearth with his father crested with even greater intensity than before. For the moment, he could do without adventure.

The street scene grew darker. Hooves clomped on the lane from behind, moving at a lazy pace until they came alongside then headed north. The driver sat as if in a stupor; the wagon, from what Malcolm could see, looked empty, large enough to move a piano . . . or a couple of corpses. He sat up and considered its course. The wagon passed by the alley Wendell and Aunt Jane had ducked into and rumbled on down the street. Malcolm relaxed and released a sigh.

A ghostly face rose at his window, startling him.

The boy's eyes darted toward the dark alley and back. "They're talkin' to a man about cricket balls. And somethin' about Limehouse. They don't seem to be in danger. Can't say the same fer Limehouse." He held out his hand.

Malcolm handed over the two half-pennies.

"Got any cookies?" the boy ventured.

"Ugh, yes." Malcolm's stomach was in knots. "Here, take them."

"Thanks, mate. If you're needin' me services again, me name's Jun and you can sometimes find me behind the restaurant. I mean, I'm there washin' grubby dishes, just two steps in from the back door. The boy indicated Foon's and then disappeared like steam.

Cricket balls and truncheons. Malcolm's hands quivered in his lap. Were his new housemates in league with Crocker? What about Limehouse? Did their plans involve the Chinese part of Limehouse? How could that be if they patronized Danny Foon's? Maybe their meeting was on behalf of Limehouse. But it smacked of trouble. Weapons, messages, alleys. He dared not ask them outright. He wished he could meet Sid now to discuss this, or to stow away on a steamer together and escape all the drama and uncertainty.

Chapter Nine

The landlady's face, etched with lines, reminded Malcolm of Wendell's shrivelled Basque wineskin. Poor little goat. Poor old Mrs. Doran. She handed him a plate of cake to go with his tea.

"I'm so glad you admire my little garden. For a boy who revels in running freely in the East End, I find it intriguing to hear that." Her little eyes glowed with the kind of insight that is both comforting and disturbing to its target, as if she understood his need for solace—as if she knew his family secrets. Yet, his paranoia soon abated, aided by the woman's air of kindness and the texture of her delicious cake as he munched away.

Freddie, Mrs. Doran's calico cat, stirred and stretched in a pale sunbeam, seconds before the mantel clock struck four, as if reminding the clock of its duty. After the fourth chime, the creature curled back into a ball and in short order resumed her somnolent breathing.

On the wall above Freddie, a painting took on more brilliance in the sun. It might be of the garden here. He wondered whether the artist was the serene older woman serving his tea. He tried to check the room discreetly for evidence of a painter's tools but saw none.

The lull in conversation proved neither awkward nor companionable. The landlady probably understood Aunt Jane's need for respite. Taking in a nephew was no little task. And Wendell had no reason to shoulder more of Malcolm's care than was necessary for a friend and neighbour.

For the first time, Malcolm wondered if Annie would have remained as his father's maid-of-all work. It would be seven long days before Malcolm could enjoy his first visit. Had the captain scared off the young girl by now? What his father needed was a battle-axe-of-a woman to come in and take charge of daily chores. Malcolm made a mental note to discuss this with Aunt Jane later that evening.

Mrs. Doran cleared her throat. "Did you read of the big ceremony yesterday, Malcolm?"

"Uh, no, ma'am." He waited expectantly.

"His Majesty unveiled the new Cenotaph in Whitehall."

Malcolm recalled that the wood and plaster memorial was to be replaced by one of stone. Old Jones had taught the class that the term meant an empty tomb and that this Cenotaph had been erected on behalf of all the soldiers who had not come home.

Her voice swelled. "It sounds as if it were quite the ceremony, and such a lovely way to observe the anniversary of the war's end.

". . . and those broken by the war." Had he said that aloud? Had she realized that he was talking of the men, like his father, whose lives were forever haunted?

Malcolm's throat tightened.

He regained his composure, wiped away a tear, and took another sip. The landlady's eyes kept a respectful, understanding distance. The clock ticked away, measuring moments of relative comfort. He breathed in the delicate fragrance rising from his cup.

"You do a lovely tea, Mrs. Doran."

In the diminishing hues of daylight, Malcolm meandered through the garden. It was silly to think that he'd see the little toad this time, but an ache compelled him onward. After a slow circuitous check, he sank into a garden chair and listened for any sound no matter how faint.

Darkness was quickly taking over and a dog barked in the distance. A motorcar casually rumbled over the cobbled street out front. Malcolm's senses detected a slight motion among the alyssum off to his left. He leaned forward and peered. The flowers fluttered again, and Malcolm was on his knees. Gently, he parted the scented growth here and there, but unless the little creature actually leapt into his hands, he wouldn't find it now. Darkness completely enveloped the garden.

Malcolm whispered, "Goodnight, little fellow. Another time, perhaps."

Chapter Ten

Malcolm's measured efforts at stealth were thwarted when the door to Merriweather Secondary's rooftop scraped open with a shriek. If he were caught, he imagined he would be facing more than just a whipping. A driving need outweighed the risk. He strained to listen for some reaction down the stairwell.

Nothing.

School was out; students and teachers alike had only one thing on their minds—having their tea.

He stepped out onto the flat roof, anticipating relief. Carefully, he closed the door. It was an odd sense of freedom, one of limited space with an endless vista. Up here, he could enjoy the lack of people, of their gazes, whether curious or not. He walked in a small circuitous pattern, taking deep breaths before leaning against the door.

Stepney spread out, its details made sharper in the late-day sunlight. The top of the Poltava Synagogue in Spital Square caught his eye. Quick, flashing images, memories of times with Sid, at Jade's coffeehouse or Lever's bookshop, lightened his mood.

Something pulled his gaze southward, to the low-lying river basin in shadow. The Thames wended through London like a snake. From the rooftop, he could see snatches of it between buildings. One could sense its presence even when all sight of it was blocked.

A bird rose from the Docklands, catching the last of the golden rays. It soared above the area and brought strains of a Vaughn Williams piece to mind, bonding Malcolm to his surroundings in that odd way that music could. His mum had loved the composer's work.

For long moments, he stared at the basin. His mind drifted to a place so dark that his vision faded. He should be down there, the Thames as his grave. If it weren't for him, Joe would still be alive, alive and winking at Bess in Town of Ramsgate Pub or sipping brandy at home or rowing a customer somewhere.

He ached for Joe's company, sitting at the docks and listening to stories of river life. The man had offered him more advice than his father ever had.

A cold breeze slapped Malcolm back to the present, to Merriweather's rooftop. Poltava and Spitalfields now hid in darkness, as did his father's house. A revelation stirred up more regret—he himself had been too self-absorbed. He was guilty of the same fault for which he'd blamed his father. Though he'd never voiced his resentment, the captain might well have read his dissatisfaction.

Malcolm was up and at the door. He turned the knob and its rusty hinges shrieked. He bounded down the stairs.

Mr. Crebs, the janitor, paid him no heed as he dashed through the small concourse. Malcolm slid on the wet floor but righted himself and kept going. Pushing through the double doors, he was out onto Mile End Road.

I've got to see Father! I've got to, got to, got to. His unspoken words drummed in his mind like a mantra, its rhythm in sync with his gait. The street noise pressed around him as if he were running through a tunnel of water. A large horse, pulling a delivery wagon, plodded toward him. A motorcar purred from behind. The sounds of pedestrians, peddlers and buskers fused into one cacophonous hum.

He turned sharply into the alley leading to the back of his house and then tripped through the tangle of weeds in the garden.

The door was locked.

We never lock the door before bedtime. He stepped aside and bent to the loose brick, slid it out and grabbed the key.

He entered the kitchen and called out; the sound of his voice fell flat. The kitchen was tidy but the air was stale; its silence gave him a chill. He called out again, hearing the suppressed panic in his voice. After pushing through the baize door he went into the parlour and up to the hearth. The fireplace was swept clean and the brandy bottles and snifters were nowhere in sight.

At the bottom of the staircase, Malcolm steeled himself for what he might find. His feet failed to cooperate and in the silence, he realized the clock had wound down. The first step creaked. Every one of them creaked or moaned in turn. He swallowed down nausea.

He walked past his own bedroom, not even bothering to look in. The door to his father's was shut. He turned the knob and pushed. The bed before him was made. He stepped in and looked around.

Chapter Eleven

Nothing.

Then Malcolm recalled the basement. *Lord in heaven, help me.* At the main staircase, his steps descended heavily. He ran along the central hall, across the kitchen. His shallow breaths came faster. He turned the knob of the basement door.

A sound drew his attention to the back porch. He could see the shadow of a figure beyond the window curtain. The door opened.

"Aunt Jane!"

"Malcolm, dear." She walked up to him, concern creasing her features. "Forgive me, dear. I was going to tell you." She placed her gloved hands on his shoulders.

"Tell me what?" His voice quivered.

"He's in a hospital. In Surrey. He is getting some help."

Malcom slumped with relief. "Can we go there? Tonight?"

"No. Sunday, though. Possibly."

Malcolm fell into her arms. She held him tight.

"I know, I know, dear. This has all been too dreadful for you."

Sobs erupted, wracking his body. When the waves of emotion eased, she sat him at the kitchen table. And true to an auntie's calling, no matter how unique, she turned and prepared his tea.

The milky tea soothed Malcolm's throat and calmed his jitters. In the parlour, flickering candlelight enlivened Auntie's jewellery as she sat across from him in his father's wing chair. Down on the hearth, in lieu of a fire, she had placed the dining room candle sticks. He struggled to find a way to express his gratitude—her talent for creating atmosphere proved to have healing power—but any arrangement of words fumbling around in his mind fell short.

Meeting her gaze, he nodded, and felt relieved when she appeared to understand all that he would say if he could. He also saw in her eyes an underlying concern. Rightly, she would be perplexed at having to care for the needs of an adolescent boy. Images returned, however; he remembered her checking her pistol outside Donny Foon's. Maybe he had read everything wrong. What did he know about people? This aunt whom he'd only met on holidays was a mystery.

She said over the rim of her cup, "I was using Wendell's car to meet someone when, lo and behold, I saw you racing down Bishopsgate."

To meet someone?

Malcolm wanted to ask, *who, for crying out loud? What are you up to, Auntie?* Instead, his throat gurgled. He took a mouthful of tea and glanced at the little flames.

"I try not to worry about you." She reconsidered her phrasing. "I try to allow you freedom, as your father has done. I envision you and that friend of yours—what's his name?—to be a couple of mudlarks, hunting along the Thames."

Malcolm opened his mouth to object to the term 'mudlark' but instead said, "I made you miss your meeting."

"Don't concern yourself with my doings." A softening smile came a moment too late.

She lightly brushed away invisible lint from her sleek jacket. This evening, she looked the part of a cabinet minister's wife, sitting there in a well-tailored ensemble: pleated skirt, a silk blouse under her jacket, the impression made all the more respectable by a string of pearls. Not flamboyant. Not austere. For what occasion was she dressed this time?

She diverted his attention with a comedic flicker of her brows then looked down her nose at the plate of biscuits between them. "My kingdom for a piece of Mrs. Doran's lemon cake."

"Hear, hear!" Malcolm offered, trying to please her while wanting to dismiss his suspicions.

"Alas."

Aunt Jane lifted her handbag and retrieved an onyx and gold cigarette case and then an ebony holder. After fitting a cigarette in the holder, she leaned toward a candle and lit up. In short order, one, then two, smoke rings were released from her rouged lips.

She leaned back and said, "He can't help himself, your father."

"Tell me more."

"What? Tell you more? Yes, yes, I should." She took a slow drag and released a hazy spiral overhead. "We, none of us, can control nightmares."

The cigarette holder trembled until she stationed her elbow on the arm of the chair. "He'd hoped, like many do, that they'd fade away in time. I gather that his symptoms are not uncommon. These dreams are so real and . . . and enveloping . . . that he enacts them. You know he truly believed, in the moment, that he was rescuing you from harm."

"I know." He couldn't tell her how he had feared his father would hide him from harm by burying him in the basement. Rational or not, that concern would surge at such times.

"So," his aunt continued, "we decided that he needed to get help from those doctors who are frantically trying to learn how to treat the malady. Your father is at such a, uh, hospital in Surrey, as I said."

"An asylum?"

"Um, a kind of asylum, yes. One for soldiers. I understand that they try to talk things out, to get at the fears deep inside." Ash grew long on her cigarette, threatening to collapse on the carpet. He met her gaze and saw her lips draw tight. She was holding something back.

A flame sputtered on one of the candles.

"They tie my father down at night, don't they?"

She looked at the growing column of ash and tapped the ebony holder against the nearby hearth fender. She settled back, took a slow drag and spoke through the smoke.

"They might do. I won't lie to you, Malcolm."

The room swam around him but he focused his attention. "Why—why couldn't he stay here? If I'm gone, if no one is in the house, he can't hurt or scare anybody."

"He could hurt himself, Malcolm. And, um, he ventured out of the house during the last episode." She checked his gaze and decided to continue.

"He grabbed a woman off the streets in the middle of the night. I'm sure she thought it was *Whitechapel* all over again. Fortunately, a bobby came upon them. Once he got matters under control, the policeman realized what was going on."

Another puff, producing a failed smoke ring. "I had to step in, Malcolm. I had to help save him."

"How did you learn of the episode?"

"Tedious detail. Doesn't matter."

"So, we can go see him on Sunday?"

"Possibly. I need to ring ahead."

"I have to see him, Auntie."

"I know, dear."

Her mouth twitched while she considered something. "Malcolm, I am not sure how to say this." Shadows came and went across her features.

"You inherited your father's broad shoulders. Your father and I have discussed this. Though not especially tall for your age, you have a mature look, as if a few years older. You think clearly. And, well, we both of us seem to forget how young you actually are."

Internal butterflies fluttered with need, hurt, and pleasure. His brows rose.

She noticed. "Well, what I mean to say is, oh—you have to be patient with me, Malcolm." She inhaled and puffed. "I'm trying to say that you don't have to take so much onto your young shoulders. There's no need to explore or scrutinize every enigma out there. Books are much safer."

She was masking something significant with her artifice; he was sure of it.

"After Boxing Day, I will be leaving you to fend for yourself for a few days. I trust you will keep to my flat and stay out of trouble."

He would commit to no such promise. "A holiday trip?"

"No. Business, of sorts, in Leeds. Pity me. The place is too dull for the Happy Hols, I'm afraid, but there's no helping it."

She tapped a cylinder of ash onto the hearth and her smile turned cool. "Now, finish your tea. I'll drop you at the flat and see if I can make amends over my earlier engagement."

Chapter Twelve

"I can't be long at Jade's, mate." The two boys turned from Stepney Jewish School and headed for Whitechapel. "My mum will give me what for. I have to get through the rest of my homework. It's due tomorrow."

In many ways, Malcolm envied the Shapiro household.

Sid added, "I bet you are getting up pretty early these days to take the tube to Stepney for school. How's Old Jones?"

"Today we moved on to Mongolia and China. I'd give anything to see the Great Wall."

Malcolm described his new household and the dinner at Donny Foon's. Then the words spilled out about his aunt, how she and Wendell had taken along weapons to meet someone in the alley, and that somehow Limehouse might see trouble.

"Wow," Sid enthused. "You're talking about explosives and truncheons in the same breath as Limehouse. I wonder what it's all about." He slapped Malcolm on the back. "I'd never had such fun before meeting you."

Malcolm shrugged. "And I will be trapped in Wendell's motorcar with them all the way to East Horsley soon, to visit my father."

Sid and Malcolm entered their hangout and settled into their usual booth. On their second serving of coffee, Sid said, "Do you think their secret meeting might have something to do with the Chinese?"

"Sort of. But...I'm not sure...why do you say that?"

"Mr. Smith mentioned the 'yellow peril' before that lady interrupted them. You've not heard that phrase before?"

Malcolm recalled his ambles along the docks. "I've heard it." Joe had put one worker in his place for using the term. "Only once."

"Anyway, Smith said that he wanted to write about that kind of thing. You heard 'im. Some folks don't like the Chinese—just as some folks hate my people. Has Old Jones or any of your teachers covered the pogroms in Europe? They did in my school. Gives me the willies, it does."

"Dreadful stuff, sounds like," Malcolm said with sympathy. "If that's what could be in store for Limehouse and the Chinese, it seems strange that my aunt and Wendell dined at Donny Foon's. I mean, isn't it a bit of a coincidence that they chose Foon's and then had that meeting about Limehouse in the alley?"

"Your mug looks like you don't care for coincidences."

"Yep. I don't. And you look like we're talking about something that smells fishy, right?

"Yep," Sid mimicked.

A smattering of regulars sat talking in low tones or staring down into their cups, oblivious to the sensational possibilities being discussed between the boys.

Malcolm took a deep breath, hating the slight quiver in it. "There's more, I think. Auntie and Wendell are both nervous over something. I've noticed each of them checking outside to see if the flat was being watched." He leaned forward and added softly, "We know Wendell has a truncheon. It could be one of those I saw getting delivered to Crocker. And Aunt Jane told me herself, in her cryptic way, that she has *her causes*. And it looks like she's been pressuring Wendell to join her."

Sid fidgeted.

"For nights on end, Sid, I've suffered the sleep of the damned."

Sid's eyes widened at the curse, but he said nothing.

Moments passed. Malcolm watched Billy bustling behind the counter, wiping up spills and wrestling with bags of beans. Then Malcolm added, "I'm exhausted. In class today, I barely stopped myself from nodding off. I don't fancy another whipping from Old Jones."

Cool air rushed in from the entry.

Sid recognized Thaddeus Smith first and gave a tentative wave, a mere twiddle of his fingers.

The newspaperman walked up to their table. "I was hoping I'd find you gents here." He took his welcome for granted and pulled up a chair, ordered a coffee from Young Billy, and then plopped his elbows on the dark table. "I have to thank you two for bringing this business of Crocker's to my attention. I haven't had this much excitement since I met, uh . . ." His eyes looked from one to the other as if assessing their life experience, and then his face flushed. "Well, never mind that."

"What's going on?" Malcolm asked. "Does it involve the Chinese? Are they planning some kind of mayhem while Crocker's men prepare for vigilante action? Or is it the other way around?"

Smith replied, "Oh, it's the other way 'round, that's for sure. You see, I was able to get into one of Crocker's secret meetings."

Malcolm considered the man's clothes, narrowed his eyes and waited for more details.

"Oh, I didn't dress like this." His hand absently ran up and down his top coat. "I picked up some old labourer's clothes at the mission store on Three Colt Street. Then I rehearsed a story just in case I was found out. The worst of it was preparing my mind to violate The King's English and the grammatical rules I hold so dear." He snorted a self-mocking laugh. "But no one asked me anything. Impressions and illusions go a long way."

"What was it like?" Malcolm asked.

"Oh, it was a colourful discussion. Lots of anger. Some complained about being out of work because of the 'stinkin' coolies working 'ere for less.'"

"How did you find out about the meeting?"

"A little investigative work."

"So, are you going to write about it in the paper?" Sid spoke up. "And expose their plan?"

"Are you kidding? That would sign my death warrant. Crocker's followers would only regroup after I'm cold in the grave." He kept their curiosity at bay while he took another taste of Jade's java. "No, no. The danger isn't immediate. They plan on blowing Limehouse to smithereens during the New Year's celebrations."

"All of it?" Sid asked, horrified.

"No, lad. I exaggerated. But it's a messy business nonetheless and I've seen enough to know how things can get out of hand."

"New Years? That's just four weeks away!" Malcolm said.

"More like ten weeks. No, eleven. Chinese New Year is early February—the eighth, actually."

Dread washed through Malcolm. No one deserved to be bullied let alone have their head bashed in or get blown up. He envisioned the Chinese people he'd seen: dockworkers, Jun and the man called Lee at Donny Foon's, those peacefully minding their own business while moving about in the Chinese part of Limehouse.

Sid asked, "So, how is this going to help you with the *Telegraph?*

"I plan to be on hand when it happens. That's the ticket for a newspaperman."

"And do nothing to stop it?" Malcolm, incensed and incredulous, glared at the man.

"Of course I'm going to do something. Crocker and his men need to be caught in the act to be properly tried and sentenced. I will be alerting the police. I'm hoping to report, afterward, how London's civil protectors thwarted utter destruction. And I intend to be right in the middle of the action."

Something about Smith's reply sounded off key. Malcolm wondered whether the man would really contact the police. Without them, Smith's story could be more newsworthy. But the man otherwise came across as upright. It was too soon to judge, but Malcolm intended to keep the thought in mind.

"Me too," Sid cried, despite himself. "In the middle of the action!"

Another rush of cool air announced a newcomer. Standing in the open entry—left hand on hip, the other gripping a wooden spoon—stood Mrs. Shapiro.

Chapter Thirteen

Malcolm almost flew into the front seat of Wendell's automobile.

"Sorry about that, Jane, Malcolm," Wendell said. "Stupid dog. Can't it see a motorcar coming along?"

"I'm glad you didn't hit it," Aunt Jane said, craning her neck to follow the pooch's excursion.

A three-storey stone building with red-brick trim stood at the corner of a village street. It was a butcher's shop.

"Where are we?" He rubbed his eyes. Despite his interest in leaving London and the longing to see his father, Malcolm had dozed off a number of times en route to the asylum.

"East Horsley, old man. Got a ways to go yet, but the worst is behind us."

"Biscuit?" Aunt Jane lifted the small basket she'd brought along.

"No, thank you."

A grey sky filled the landscape with drabness.

"Now," Wendell said to himself, "a mile down Crocknorth Road, I should turn left onto Gravesditch Road. Ah, there it is."

Wendell slowed for the turn, but Malcolm's pulse accelerated. The dirt road followed a gulley then ascended a wooded hill dense with undergrowth on either side. At a bend, numerous chimney tops spied on them from above the foliage. Upon cresting another rise, the old manor loomed tall.

"We've come to Guildford Park House, which has served in its present capacity since the Boer War." Aunt Jane patted Malcolm's hand.

There were no gardens that Malcolm could see. Tall grass and weeds predominated. Its front rose up like a sheer cliff of yellow stone tinged with grey. Malcolm peered at each window, intent on discovering some clue to life within. A round, moon-like face stared blankly out of an upper window, into the distance.

Malcolm's attention was then drawn to six stone vessels crowning the top story. These ornamental appointments should have relieved the structure's monotony, but their similarity to cremation urns made matters worse, he felt.

"Lovely," Aunt Jane said, her tone dry, as if reading his thoughts.

The air blew cold as their feet crunched on the fine gravel up to the main entrance.

A bald man in a dark suit answered the door.

"May I help you?"

"Yes," Aunt Jane spoke up, "we called yesterday. We're here to see Captain Roberts. We've brought his son."

"Yes, we have been expecting you. I am Samuel Boggs, the admissions steward." He spoke in a low tone; whether it was out of discretion or weariness, Malcolm couldn't say. "We've arranged for your visit with Captain Roberts to take place in the library. I will take you there now." He indicated that they should follow him down the main hall. After a few steps he turned and said, "Should you have any need to speak with The Deputy Medical Superintendent, Mr. Smithers, just step into my office over there and I'll arrange it."

"Thank you," Aunt Jane replied.

The smell of old wood, freshly polished, dominated the main hall. Their footsteps echoed in the silence. The door to each room facing the hall was closed. Malcolm's lungs ached, as if they were shackled.

Samuel Boggs took out a key and unlocked one of the doors. They stepped in. Malcolm heard the click of the lock behind him but his gaze darted ahead to the lone figure at the end of the room.

Captain Roberts choked on his welcome and, with restrained motion, waved them over to the fireplace. He was dressed neatly. Malcolm noted that his father's face was freshly shaven though his eyes emitted an uncustomary dullness.

The captain shook Wendell's hand and nodded to his sister and Malcolm. He met Malcolm's gaze directly and offered him the familiar 'chin up' expression.

"Sit, sit," he directed, gesturing to the nearby chair and settee. Wendell and Aunt Jane allowed Malcolm the chair closest to the captain. The captain's face revealed little.

Coal hissed in the grate. Most of the wood furnishings, as well as the mantelpiece, was either ebony or painted black and the carpet was patterned in black and ivory and grey.

Malcolm wanted to blurt out an apology to his father. He was sorry for possibly adding to his burden—if it were true that the captain had seen pent-up resentment and hurt in him. But, of course, a private chat would be needed.

Ridiculously mundane conversation passed between the adults while Malcolm looked for any physical evidence that his father had been cruelly restrained at night. How would they do that? Sedate him and bind his arms along his sides while strapping him down on the bed? He could envision his father's face filled with horror as he screamed helplessly during an episode.

A noise by the door drew Malcolm's attention to Mr. Boggs who escorted a portly man, carrying a laden tray.

"Ah, our steward, Mr. Albright," said the captain.

Mr. Albright set down a tray bearing what looked like curried egg sandwiches among the tea things. The steward fussed with the various items till all was arranged before them. Both men turned to leave as Auntie began to pour.

Wendell said, "Ah, I'm famished, that—"

Just then, the captain shot to his feet and barked, "Mr. Albright, Boggs." The two men turned at the door. The captain gave a sharp salute.

After a long pause, each returned the unwarranted formality with limp-wristed salutes. They left, closing the door.

Malcolm heard the lock click. He restrained an urge to sigh and tried to mask his disappointment. He'd hoped that by now the doctors here would have helped his father overcome his odd compulsions, to regain his sense of proportion. *If they haven't succeeded with that, how will they ever quell the night terrors?*

Wendell and Auntie took their tea casually, their performance studiously calm, as if nothing out of the ordinary had happened.

Malcolm yearned to contribute to the visit and wrestled with which interesting bit of news or adventure he might share. After sensing the undercurrents between them, he held back.

The captain settled in his chair. He looked at each of them and said, "Have a sandwich. We have a marvellous cook here."

Malcolm took two for his plate. He prepared to take a bite, then— in the lull—felt that now would be a good time to speak.

"Father, I learned the most astonishing thing."

From the floor above, what sounded like baritonal humming increased in volume. It grew to a low howl and then exploded into a shriek.

The captain attempted to detract their attention from the patient above. He said to his sister, "I am glad that the weather cooperated well for your trip here."

She sat still, her brows arched, her kohled eyes looked upward.

Malcolm bit into a sandwich, despite his loss of appetite.

Wendell brushed some lint from his lapel.

Silence.

Then the cry started again.

The captain scratched the side of his ear, and then cleared his throat.

Aunt Jane whipped open her handbag and fiddled with her cigarette case.

Wendell and the captain began discussing economic troubles, as if Malcolm had said nothing. After a few puffs, Auntie joined their conversation.

The floor above creaked in pace with each footstep crossing the room. The howling stopped.

Wendell visibly relaxed and asked the captain, "Tell me, what's the latest on the Shackleton-Rowett Expedition in Antarctica? Have you read much on it lately?"

As interesting as the topic was, Malcolm's face burned with vexation. He blinked back tears.

"No, I'm afraid I haven't," his father replied to Wendell, "have you?"

Before Malcolm knew it, the admissions steward was at the door again, indicating the end of the visit.

The captain steeled himself for a stiff farewell. They stood, lingering; Aunt Jane began chattering. Malcolm yearned to run to his father's arms.

Then he heard: "Yes . . . Yes, son. Come here. Quick, now." His father knelt down and embraced him, his arms strong and warm, his damp cheek pressed against Malcolm's. A soft, quick cry escaped the captain's lips. He took a moment to regain his composure, then leaned back and looked at his son, as if he just realized a need to talk to him alone. He cleared his throat and said, forcing lightness into his voice, "Oh, I should tell you, Malcolm, that you had a visitor. Uh, the day before I left Stepney. A young lady."

Malcolm couldn't think of any young lady who would come to see him.

"Olive-coloured skin, dark hair, a pretty thing. She wanted to talk with you about your friend Joe."

How would a girl know him or Joe?

"Now, where did she say you could find her?" As the captain strained to recall the detail, his confidence faltered; and Malcolm dreaded his father's embarrassment.

"At a café in Whitechapel," the captain said with triumph. "She waits tables there. I've never been to an eating establishment in Whitechapel. Let's see. She said it's on Wentworth Street, and the place is called, um, The Black Pot—no, The Black Kettle Café."

Heat rose up Malcolm's neck and his peripheral vision dimmed. He didn't want to take in any details now; he didn't know any olive-skinned girl—he wanted to stay with his father.

"Now, son." The captain stood then bent toward him and said in a low tone, "I trust you will use caution. She could be a decoy sent by that fox Crocker, for all you know."

Aunt Jane released a quick plume of cigarette smoke.

"But I thought I should inform you." He took hold of Malcolm's shoulders. "You have shown me that you are capable of anything that a man, a soldier, an intelligence officer might be called upon to do. I want you to know that I have confidence in you, son."

His father leaned down and kissed his forehead. Malcolm had never been kissed by anyone since before his mother had died. The hazy comfort felt at once suspended in time and brief.

The captain then stood at attention.

"Carry on."

The visit was over.

Malcolm sank into a welcome sleep on the way back until he became aware of low-toned talk.

". . . such people deserve neither respect nor freedom," Aunt Jane said.

With his eyes still closed, he kept from fidgeting and breathed with a deep rhythm. He must appear to be dozing. Did she sense his awareness? His mind went over what he had just heard. Wendell had said something about coolies in Limehouse Causeway and Pennyfields Street.

Malcolm's stomach knotted and his hands went cold.

Wendell resumed conversation—it turned to troublesome details of the past summer's drought and unemployment. Malcolm couldn't tell whether the man's conversation was contrived to cover the possible gaffe or not.

Aunt Jane let silence take over, as if she couldn't be bothered with a ruse of chit chat. Malcolm could hear her digging in her handbag.

With a sigh of relief, she produced her onyx cigarette case.

Beyond the car, he could hear the sounds of city traffic. He wanted to look out the window but didn't. How much longer, how many days, weeks or more, would he have to agonize over his problems?

Of all the aunties in this world, his was the most disturbing mystery.

Chapter Fourteen

"This must be Pennyfields," Malcolm said. The Chinese part of Limehouse buzzed with activity.

Sid looked around, as if needing to see the street name.

Malcolm led the way down the narrow lane.

"It stinks here," Sid complained.

"Not so badly. You're just not used to Chinese cooking."

"No, there's something else, something sweet and musky." Sid breathed in and gestured for Malcolm to follow. The two had explored many a derelict stretch of East End blight, but Pennyfields was new territory for Malcolm. Would he discover what all the fuss was about? Why did Crocker and Aunt Jane and all who attended Crocker's meetings care about this district?

Sid pressed on toward his particular destination.

"Cooking supplies?" Malcolm asked, coming to a standstill. The shop at the end of the alley displayed woks and baskets in its window, along with the establishment's name, which was painted on the glass in Chinese letters. He preferred Russian Cyrillic to these stick formations, not that he would ever read either; but as a matter of art, the Russian lettering held a measure of beauty. Anything foreign interested him, but the exception to that might be whatever it was that now mesmerized his friend. A familiar tautness of muscles and sinews signalled alarm. He knew he should acknowledge this innate warning. But *what* was that unusual odour? He paused, unable to leave.

Sid sidestepped him and the shop entrance and bent to peer into a place on the basement level.

Coming from a dark, open doorway, down a number of steps, a sweet, cloying odour arose. Sid uncharacteristically ventured down, albeit with tentative steps. Malcolm grabbed Sid by his suspenders and pulled him back.

"Wait a tick, mate. Why do you want to go down there? You said it stinks, and it does."

"I want to know what it's about. The door is open. Come on." Sid descended like a reconnoitring soldier, wary but confident. Malcolm had never seen him as brave as this before.

The smoky odour floating up from the place made him cough. Refuse littered the way down the steps. The unmistakable smell of urine became evident.

"This must be an opium den," Malcolm said in a forced whisper. A penny dreadful story had situated a murder in such a place. He wanted to grab his friend and haul him out, but he couldn't let Sid get the better of him.

Malcolm followed his friend through the threshold into the dark. Two steps inside, he bumped into Sid's back. His eyes took time to adjust. A table and chair sat unoccupied to their right. Two long rows of berths lined the room and there were prostrate bodies in most of them. At the end of the room, a door opened.

A short figure came through but it was impossible to tell gender, age or disposition. The advancing figure lugged in two large buckets. It was a boy—it was Jun, the youngster from Foon's alleyway.

"Are you gents investigatin' something or 'ere for pleasure?"

Jun set down his uneven burden. One bucket was full of soapy water, the other was empty. He sallied up to the table, as if he were assuming the role of proprietor.

"If yer want a pipey, they'll let yer share one, unless you can afford one each. Only three pence more to share, on top of the farthing for the first 'un."

"You run this place?" Malcolm asked. "I thought you said you could be found behind Foon's."

A sheepish smile lit up Jun's smudged face. "They let me have a few hours o' work on Saturdays and Tuesdays." He nodded toward the buckets. "Mostly cleanin' up what should'a been done in the slops room. But I can get you set up.

Sid turned to Malcolm. "Do you have a farthing and three pence?"

"Uh, I think we should go."

"Aw, come on."

Curiosity overcame Malcolm. He ventured a few steps into the room, his gaze lingering on Jun's, checking to see if he had the freedom to look around first. Jun shrugged, his expression turning conspiratorial. Sid, more true to his nature, now held back and stayed by the table.

The smell intensified with each step; and in the dim light, Malcolm looked from berth to berth with morbid fascination. Chinese men, English gents and an old woman ignored him as they lay inanimate with the exotic-looking pipes. He wondered what the effects of the drug would be like while a simultaneous dread arose, goading him to leave. He expected serene, dreamy expressions but as he peered through the haze, most of the facial features hung slack, trapped in stupor. Two gents looked as if they were downright dead.

"Mad—mad, I tell you." The hoarse voice came from a bunk to his left. Malcolm turned, his gaze locking with bleary eyes, small like a pig's, and deep-set in a pudgy pale face.

"I feel sorry for you, lad—for all lads now coming up in this world." The man's brow arched. "It was a good life, before the war, but mankind went completely mad. I can't tell you how it happened, how it all went wrong, but it did…terribly wrong."

There was nothing to say. Malcolm thought of returning to the front exit but his knees locked and his feet took on unbelievable weight.

"We're doomed, sonny. Doomed."

How long had he been standing, transfixed? Twirling bits of light invaded his vision. Sid coughed while remaining by Jun. The smelly smoke and effluvia surrounding Malcolm began to close in, as intently as flies on raw meat. Two steps later, his head felt as if his skull would squeeze his brains to mush.

He turned back, surprised that he could move. "We'll go now, Jun. Thank you."

"I'd hoped you'd stay, mates," Jun said, his voice low with defeat. Malcolm wondered how lonely and difficult the boy's life was.

"Where can we get a cup of tea 'round here, Jun?" Malcolm asked, wanting to do something for him.

"Just round the bend in the lane. Hong's." He seemed to shrink into himself.

"Can we buy you a cup? Can you take a break?"

Something drew Jun's gaze to the rear of the room. He paled.

Malcolm spun around. The door beyond the berths was filled with a large figure; and Malcolm saw, for the first time in his life, a Chinaman who was fat, like Buddha. Though his feet were planted, an aggressive energy emanated across the room; and he looked as angry as a fire-breathing dragon.

Malcolm nodded acknowledgement to the man and took a step backward toward the door. He said to Jun under his breath. "When do you get off?"

"Not till late."

"Do you work tomorrow?"

"No."

"Do you know where Jade's Coffeehouse is?"

"Yeah."

"Meet us there tomorrow, mid-day."

"Thanks, mate."

Malcolm stumbled up the steps with Sid in tow. He gasped, needing fresh air. It wasn't until they had walked on a bit that his lungs cleared.

The cloying smell, however, clung to his clothes. Aunt Jane probably wouldn't notice, but he worried what Mrs. Shapiro would do when Sid got home. Perhaps he should throw his friend into the Thames. That would produce an entirely different odour.

"Can you swim, Sid?"

Chapter Fifteen

A familiar-looking figure walked briskly toward the opium den. The man recognized them with a lurch, stopped, and then turned a few degrees.

"Oh, hello, gentlemen." Thaddeus Smith waved, recovering his composure with difficulty. His feet, which had abruptly shifted direction on the pavement, now faced—Malcolm peered at the dreary building off to his right—a corset factory.

Smith fussed with his bow tie. "I, uh, was just looking for an establishment to, uh, better understand the area, the Chinese, that is." He sniffed the air. "What were *you two* doing over there?" he asked.

"We have a friend that works there, Mr. Smith," Malcolm said, his tone full of innocence.

"Hmm. I could use some tea right now." Smith adjusted his bowler hat.

Malcolm pointed beyond the corset factory, as though he were an expert. "Then Hong's would be the place to go." He hoped he had understood Jun's directions correctly but led the way, his head high.

A mix of Westernized Chinese and those dressed in Oriental garb converged on Pennyfields. No salutations or even acknowledgements sallied back and forth. Conversations between those at hand were carried on quietly. Most of the men in Western dress had a newspaper tucked under an arm or protruding from a neat satchel. The headlines that caught Malcolm's eye were in English.

The "coolies", as Wendell had called the Chinese working class, gathered at the occasional news post to read what was tacked up in their languages. Malcolm knew of Cantonese and Mandarin and wondered if there were more.

After half the distance to the bend, Malcolm suddenly became aware of the absence of Chinese women. A British-looking woman hugged the far side of the lane as she trudged along with a young son in hand. Even at that distance, Malcolm noticed the mixed heritage of the boy.

Thinking of Jun and his lot in life, Malcolm almost walked right past Hong's. The name in English stood in squat letters above the door while the gold-painted stick figures were splayed across the street-side window. "Here we are."

"Ah, just the kind of place I was looking for," Smith claimed.

Before entering, Malcolm noticed that the lane didn't actually bend here. The buildings were disjointed, giving the impression of a bend. Most would not have noticed. He made a mental note of the fact that Jun had an eye for detail.

Crossing the plank floor to a vacant table, Malcolm wondered at the lack of curious glances. Oriental inflections carried on, hardly missing a beat. Punctuating the mass of foreign words were the rhythmic slurpings of soup or tea, reminiscent of crickets in a garden.

The room was devoid of decoration; its occupants created the ambience. Sid and Thaddeus Smith gawked like two owls. The locals were careful to appear disinterested in the three visitors.

"You come here!" a male voice commanded, each word staccato.

Behind the counter, a middle-aged Oriental gestured to a large chalkboard that stretched wide, busy with stick-like markings.

The three approached the counter.

"Order here. Take to table yourself."

"This will be on me, gentlemen," Smith said. "Uh, just tea, that is."

After deliberations, the menu being impossible to understand, each of them returned to the table with a cup of grey-green tea that smelled not unlike the Thames.

They settled at a table in the middle of the room.

"They say—I mean—the Chinamen say—that if you slurp, the taste improves." Smith gave it a try to support his point.

Malcolm yearned for black tea laden with milk and sugar but he slurped away. "Not as bad as I'd expected."

Sid slurped, unimpressed.

"Have you learned anything new, Mr. Smith?" Malcolm asked.

Smith replied, keeping his voice down. "I've been thinking a lot about this. Yes, I have. Last night I began wondering what could be lurking behind the facts."

He waited until their expressions suggested that their attention was appropriately engaged, then continued, "I've heard the usual complaints: *They steal our jobs and our women.* I won't include the expletives that often accompany these sentiments." He smiled. "Ethnic intolerance has been behind many an act of violence."

"They've covered plenty of cases of that in school, Mr. Smith," Sid offered.

Malcolm had learned that most of the cases discussed there would naturally have focused on of the pogroms wrought on the unfortunates by anti-Semitism in Russia and Poland.

"However," Smith continued, looking pleased, "I have been moving about various circles and learned of a Chinese student, living in Montargis, France, just south of Paris. Apparently, there are a number of Chinese students—a small number but an intense group, I understand—who have connections with the Comintern."

"The what?" Sid asked.

"A communist group. In addition to boycotting Japanese goods— I'll spare you the issues surrounding that rigmarole—they apparently would like to help Marxism get a stronger foothold in China."

Malcolm's efforts to make the connection were interrupted by a commotion out in the lane. A procession beyond the café window had materialized. A handful of instruments, thin in timbre, played a melody with an Oriental tonality like that heard at Donny Foon's. Cymbals and drums set the pace for the marchers. All conversation in the room ceased. Out in the street, the number of drably dressed folks was occasionally augmented by those wearing bright Chinese costumes. Malcolm caught a glimpse of the actual participants; all facial expressions were solemn.

Finally, a casket, carried on poles shouldered by young men, came into view. When it had passed, conversations resumed.

"Notable among these students," Smith continued, "is a Zhou Enlai. Young men like this chap appear to be as ruthless as the anarchists were before the war." Smith stopped and read their expressions. Despite himself, Malcolm realized he must be looking dreadfully dim."

With near desperation, Malcolm stared hard at the perpetual motion of the newsman's chin as words kept coming, phrase after phrase. Malcolm was out of his depth but he'd hate to lose the thread. He believed this monologue contained something relevant.

"You see, China is a mess, politically, as is Russia and a number of other places. A Dr. Sun Yat-sen is trying to unify China as a republic. He'd studied in London, as a matter of fact. But the man is back home now. Having been against China's Imperial government during the war, he seems to be trying to garner support for the Republican ideal amidst some dreadful warlords. I'm not exactly confident of his position and true ideals, however. At least, not yet."

Sid scratched his nose and sniffed.

Malcolm sipped his tea without slurping and kept his eyes trained on the newspaperman.

"British relations with his government, which may prove short-lived, has not been especially chummy. Now, if those of communist leanings, like this Zhou Enlai, could destroy the tenuous relationship altogether, then the Republic would likely not get support from the West when the Communists plan their next coup in China."

Sid's eyelids began to droop.

Malcolm said, "Ah, you mean, if someone like Mr. Enlai could create a disturbance here, making it look like the English hate the Chinese, uh, then this could sever those weak ties."

"Brilliant, lad. Yes. He would have to be an expert manipulator, fuelling hatreds that already exist, getting them to actually ignite."

A low buzz of a snore escaped Sid's mouth, bringing him back to life; his now wide eyes darted from Thaddeus to Malcolm.

Malcolm cuffed him, just enough to get his attention.

Sid said, "Excuse me, sir."

Smith waved away the apology. "But, well, that's the theory I came up with last night. It's amazing what a good bottle of brandy can do for the grey cells."

Malcolm considered the details. Open space often stimulated his comprehension as he sorted through problems. Casually, he looked out the window and his concentration fell apart.

Standing in the middle of the lane, talking with their heads together, were a boy his age and another, larger lad, whom he recognized. His shoulders were hunched and he had rusty red hair sticking out from around his cap.

Chapter Sixteen

"Now, take for example the earthquake in Ningxia last year," Smith said, his voice more earnest. "His Majesty's government as good as ignored the plight of the Chinese. Why, there was at least one entire village near Gansu that disappeared altogether."

Malcolm couldn't take his eyes off the two youths outside. He was sure the larger one had been at Crocker's and had chased him to the docks—and might possibly be Joe's murderer. Had those two recognized him after all? Were they feigning ignorance of his presence here? Or were they scouting out the area, planning their incendiary attack? The pair headed in the opposite direction to that of the funeral procession.

"Ah, excuse me, Mr. Smith," Malcolm said, "but Sid and I have to leave, now. Duty calls. I'll explain later. Thanks for the tea." He offered a quick smile in parting and added with a grin, "Such as it was."

Smith chuckled with understanding and waved a hand.

They exited onto Pennyfields.

"What's up?" Sid asked, his tone urgent.

"We're following a member of that gang I told you about."

"Uh, do we have to?"

"Yes, come on."

Sid fell in step at his side; puffs of vapour hung before their faces in the cool November air.

Before Malcolm, normal pedestrian traffic began closing in. Fortunately, the hunchback was visible, lumbering on, his rusty hair bobbing above the Asian population. Sid began to lag.

"Come on, I don't want to lose them."

"Uh, okay." Then with more bravado, Sid added, "I'm with you."

The street suddenly seethed with activity, possibly with those who came out to observe the procession; their murmur grew to an aggressive roar.

Just ahead, a parting expanse told him that they were approaching a major intersection that must be West India Dock Road. Utter cacophony rose to almost deafening levels. At the crossing, lorries and wagons snarled the road that ran north from the river. There were no bobbies in sight to enforce any semblance of order on the traffic. The scene seethed. For a moment, Malcolm could find neither Sid nor the villainous louts.

"I'm coming," Sid's high pitched voice called from behind.

A flash of rusty hair across the road compelled Malcolm to weave his way through the treacherous current of vehicles and jaywalkers. The bumper of an insistent lorry nudged his side, threatening to topple him over, but he jogged across, surprised to see Sid there waiting for him.

They turned down Limehouse Causeway, which swallowed up sound in its narrow passageway.

"I'm pretty sure they went this way."

A now familiar whiff indicated the presence of another opium den somewhere among the laundries, factories and tenements.

"But I don't see them ahead, Sid." All of the pedestrians were Orientals.

"I don't mind if we call it a day, mate. Sun's going down."

This simple fact surprised Malcolm and he checked the evening's gunmetal sky.

"Wouldn't mind going home for a proper tea," Sid prompted.

"We stink like opium, Sid. We'll have to do something about your clothes before you see your mum."

"She wouldn't know the smell."

"Are you willing to risk that?"

Sid said nothing.

A muffled commotion came from an alley. Malcolm pulled Sid along, off to the side. He peered down the dim passageway. It was the rusty-haired youth gripping a small Asian man and pinning his arms. The other bully landed a punch to the helpless man's gut. A Chinese woman and child cowered just beyond.

"Hey!" Malcolm cried. "Stop." He hurtled down the alley, his attention on the one delivering the blows. The thug's shock was enough for Malcolm to ram both hands square in his chest, sending him flying back into a pile of broken barrels. The Asian man was tossed aside and the hunchback's large hands reached out and grabbed Malcolm's head as if he were about to snap it from his body. Malcolm felt the grip suddenly go limp, following the sound of a whack. Sid had walloped the brute over the head with a thick piece of wood.

The Chinese family ran to the street and merged with the throng of their countrymen. Hunchback was bent over, shaking his head, while his mate tried to decide whom to attack.

"Come on, Sid." Malcolm grabbed his friend's arm and took off toward Stepney, rather than back into the obstructing crowd.

Bags of rice and rubbish made negotiating the alley a challenge. Once they emerged, they darted left, then right onto what Malcolm recognized as Emmett Street.

Curses and footfalls burst from behind, goading Malcolm and Sid on. Fortunately, Emmett Street allowed for a full sprint. Complete nightfall would soon be upon them. A blessing and a curse. Malcolm headed for Stepney where familiarity might present options for ditching the thugs.

Finally, they raced past the terraced homes on Salmon Lane.

"My side aches," Sid gasped.

"Here." Malcolm ducked into an alley. It was pitch black but he and Sid both knew its many connections with other back ways. He estimated they had only a handful of moments to find a hiding place. He grabbed Sid's hand again and pulled him to the south route, running behind Wysocki's cobbler shop. Half a block later, he led him behind Markov's, a Russian eatery that smelled as unappetizing as Hong's. He knew Sid needed to rest, and his own lungs were burning. He happened upon a generous mound of rotting cabbage and other refuse outside the kitchen.

"Crawl under and breathe as softly as you can."

"Ugh." Sid obeyed. Malcolm worked his way next to him, clawing at whatever he could to cover them: chicken bones, general muck.

He heard footsteps and whisperings from around the bend near Wysocki's. Malcolm's heart hammered. He muffled a gasp and tried to regulate his breathing. Sid must be in worse straits but he was doing a great job of blending in with the slop. Malcolm prayed no one from Markov's would open the door and flood the alley with light as their pursuers passed by.

Bits of debris crunched underfoot along the alley. Malcolm had no doubt they now shared this stretch with the bullies.

"Eeeuwwh. Worse than the stinkin' drains," the younger of the hoodlums whispered.

"Quiet. Listen," said the deep-voiced one.

Malcolm held his breath and prayed that neither he nor Sid would sneeze.

Footsteps approached. A hot flash of panic surged through Malcolm when the feet became silent nearby. Measured breaths, as if the bullies were listening carefully, sounded within arm's length. Sid's pulse throbbed against Malcolm's chest. Or was it his own?

"Come on, Jack," a thin voice urged. "It stinks to heaven here."

"I want to get my hands on that one's head again, the older one, the bugger. I ache to hear that neck pop."

Jack added, "Let's go that way."

Scuffing sounds faded around a bend as the two took a passageway heading out of the warren. A ripple of elation brought a smile to Malcolm's face as he lay buried in refuse. Hunchback's name was Jack. And Jack referred to him as *the older one*. It wasn't proof that Jack didn't connect him to Joe, but at least he couldn't go inquiring about him by name.

It felt like a full hour that they hid there, waiting, aware that the bullies could double back or catch them when they made their way out. There were five options for exit. Malcolm decided the least likely chance of being caught would be to go back on Salmon.

At Malcolm's signal, Sid stood and began brushing himself off. "If I weren't so miserable, I'd—"

"Save it, Sid. We need to keep quiet," he whispered.

Once on Salmon, they headed toward Sid's home near Spitalfields. A number of people were still moving along the walkways, despite the approaching supper hour. Malcolm strode with relative ease, though his eyes were wary. They just needed to avoid the pools of light beneath the street lamps.

In the gloom, Malcolm saw an on-coming gentleman look their way with distaste, pulling out a handkerchief and covering his nose.

Sid resumed his complaint. "Why did you have to get us involved?"

"You could have held back," Malcolm said, quelling a flash of annoyance. "You could've pretended not to know me back in Pennyfields." He brushed off debris stuck to his jacket and then looked down the street. "Um, I'm sorry. You are a really good sport for all you've done—for all I've put you through." As they walked on, he began to notice the dampness in the air, as if the river had changed its course inland. He took a deep breath and added, "You saved my life when you walloped the one called Jack. Thank you."

"Well, I'm well and truly miserable now." Sid's complaint sounded hollow, as though he didn't know how to accept the credit.

Malcolm grinned at a bright thought. "There's one good thing, Sid. Now your mum won't smell the opium on you."

They parted at Charles Street. Malcolm was about to turn toward Stepney Station to catch the tube back when he caught sight of an elegant lady draped in white fur and leaving The George. He stopped to stare. It was Aunt Jane. He was about to call out when he saw the gentleman with her. It wasn't Wendell, though the man was familiar to Malcolm—it was Julius Crocker.

Chapter Seventeen

After a vigorous bath—then cleaning the dreadful ring left around the tub and refilling it—Malcolm leaned back in the hot, sudsy water to ease his nerves. His breath quivered, as if he had just wept, but he hadn't. The water soothed his body but failed to reach that inner something. For too many months, his spirit had been dark. Had his father's been *dark* every day since the war? Probably.

Three soft raps on the door accompanied a male voice. "Master Malcolm? It's Bryn. Mr. Harries suggested that I bring you some things. May I enter?"

Malcolm sat up, glad for the layer of bubbles. "Uh, sure." How had Wendell known of his plight?

Bryn entered and closed the door. The hallway bathroom on the second floor was shared by Wendell's flat, the attic flat and Malcolm. The top-floored tenant was reportedly on the Continent for the time being. Malcolm had yet to meet him. Aunt Jane and Mrs. Doran each had their own bath.

"Mr. Harries heard you come in and, uh, thought you might be needin' these." He set some folded night clothes on the chair next to the sink. "I expect they might be a tad large for you but shouldn't be too bad." Bryn also held a set of towels.

Malcolm hadn't dared to enter Aunt Jane's flat directly when he came in and hadn't thought how he would deal with such practical matters following his bath. Wendell must have seen him enter the house, either from his front window or by cracking open his door as Malcolm entered the bathroom. Malcolm's smell alone could have signalled distress as he passed down the hallway.

As if sent to serve as Malcolm's valet, Bryn hung one towel on a large hook and unfolded the other. "Would you like me to tend to your sullied clothes, Master Malcolm?"

A glow of relief and gratitude shimmered inside Malcolm. He had vaguely thought he'd clean his own clothes in the tub afterward. He couldn't allow Auntie's crippled young maid to deal with such a reeking mess.

"Um, if they look hopeless, we might have to burn the lot."

"Mr. Harries said that you are welcome to have a cup of tea in his flat, if you wish but not to feel obliged." Malcolm fancied that Bryn's smile revealed understanding and a kind of respect, as if he approved of manly adventures.

"I think I'll just take myself to my bed."

Bryn spread the open towel over the heaped pile and gathered it all up. Before leaving, he asked, "Do you have anythin' in the pockets, Master Malcolm?"

"Ah, no. My coin purse is there on the shelf."

Bryn nodded and turned to leave.

"And, uh, thank you, Bryn. Thank you very much."

Malcolm turned out the lamp. It should have been heaven to slip between fresh sheets after a hot bath. But every nerve in his body perked with attention, as if still reacting to the threats of the bullies. Would they discover where he lived? Where he went to school? He pulled the covers up under his chin, eyes wide open.

Down the hall, he heard the door to Aunt Jane's flat closing, alarming him all the more. What had she been up to? Adelaide's uneven gait lumbered from her quarters in the back and she softly spoke a welcome to her mistress. She must be taking that white fur from her now. He couldn't hear the few words Auntie said. The closet door closed and Adelaide hobbled back to her bed. Straining his ears, Malcolm could hear little from his aunt's room.

He chided himself for his over-active imagination, realizing how tired he was. Nonetheless, the silence weighed on him.

What was to become of the Chinese district? His father? His own life? He turned on his side while his knees came up nearly to his chest and his face slid under the covers. Malcolm tried to silently recite some Wordsworth to calm his thoughts.

At evening, when the earliest stars began to move along the edges of the hills, rising or setting, would he stand alone?

After "The Boy of Winander", he came to realize that for the past three weeks, unnoticed by anyone, he had been fourteen years old.

Chapter Eighteen

Malcolm took a noisy slurp of Jade's hot coffee and realized too late that he was not in Chinatown.

Sid stifled a chuckle. His hair stood out in all directions, having been scrubbed with some kind of carbolic soap. Evidence of his mum's displeasure over last night's messy adventure could be seen in the fact that Sid half-knelt on the bench with his elbows propped on the table. His hind end had yet to touch the wooden seat and likely would not do so this time.

Malcolm said, "I sure hope you'll be able to sit tomorrow for school."

The thought robbed Sid of his smile.

After several moments of companionable silence, Sid said, "You look kind of rough this morning."

"I've got a lot on my mind, old thing." The playful tone fell flat. "Couldn't sleep."

Sid nodded, evidently recognizing Malcolm's pain as worse than a sore bum.

"Hey, there's Jun," Malcolm said. "He's standing outside. I'll go get him."

Malcolm opened Jade's door and looked out. The boy appeared to be peering in the front window while keeping his distance. A thick fog was slowly invading the area, bringing darkness to mid-day, and shrouding the boy's form.

"Come on, Jun. It's me. Malcolm. D'ya like coffee?" He waved him in.

Jun approached with measured steps, looking smaller and younger here.

"It'll be on me, mate," Malcolm assured him. "When did the fog roll in?"

"It started soon after I left Limehouse and sorta followed me 'ere."

Malcolm chuckled.

Sid fidgeted nearby, his attention on the darkness outside. "I can't be staying much longer."

Malcolm nodded with understanding. Sid's mum probably didn't approve of Sid being out in the fog. "I'll see you home after a visit with our friend here."

The three settled in. Malcolm ordered him coffee and a piece of cake and talked of their experience taking tea at Hong's. Jun's gaze surreptitiously checked on Billy who was slicing cake behind the counter.

"I enjoyed the funeral march," Sid offered, his tone bright. Then a shadow crossed his face as if he questioned the appropriateness of his comment.

Billy came up and placed the order in front of Jun and then returned to his station. Jun's eyes lit at seeing the cake. He then sniffed his coffee warily.

"Have you never had coffee before?" Malcolm asked.

"No. It smells toasted but wet." He tried a taste.

"Well?" Sid asked.

"Let me have some of this cake."

Jun used a fork with a measure of gentility. He wasn't the typical East End guttersnipe.

"A lovely cake, is this." He savoured another bite. After a second sip of the coffee, he said, "Takes some getting used to." He sniffed the brew, took another sip and said, "I hear you two ran into some excitement after leaving Hong's."

"How do you know?"

"Word gets out. Heard you are somethin' of a hero." He left Malcolm wondering while he raised his cup and tried another taste. "And that Jack Carrothers wants you both dead."

Distress struck Malcolm. "Is he the Jack with the hunched shoulders?"

"That's him. A bad 'un."

"What do you know about him?"

The door to Jade's clicked open. The newcomer glided in as silently as fog personified and, after closing the door, she stayed near the wall and settled at a table in the corner farthest from Malcolm's group. She did not remove her damp wine-coloured cape and her posture was neither elegant nor uncouth. Rich contralto tones wavered across the plank floor—she was humming a tune. Only Malcolm and Sid appeared to be curious about the woman who proved to be lost in her own world and whose face was covered with about as much paint—

rouge and eye makeup—as a Dutch Masters' painting. Jun sipped his coffee with slower, fuller draughts and a glow of satisfaction on his face.

"That's Madame Thibodeau," Jun said, his tone matter of fact. "She's a bit Bedlam but nice enough. Used to sing in the opera."

Malcolm pulled his gaze from the newcomer. "What can you tell me about Jack Carrothers?"

Jun munched away.

Billy served the aged diva a cup of coffee and a glass of some dark liquid. She nodded, though her head quivered as she appeared to be considering which to imbibe first. Or was she hearing some inner accompaniment? After a taste of the liquor, she warbled a fresh array of soft tones.

Speaking around another bite of cake, Jun said, "I know where 'e lives," he wiped a crumb from his lower lip, "and, I know where 'e goes to school."

"He's still in school?" Malcolm asked, his tone incredulous. "I can hardly believe it."

"Aye, he is. A fancy one at that."

Sid cleared his throat. "Um, it's late. I'd better be getting home."

By the time the three left Jade's, the fog was smothering Old Montague Street, distorting sound, obscuring distance.

"I had to get an old fop into a taxi yesterday after my shift at Dingxiang's, you know, where you saw me working. He was such a noodle, the driver had to get out and help me."

Filled with cake and goodwill, Jun talked all the way to Brady Street.

When Malcolm led the way north, Jun said, "If you don't have anythin' else planned, mates, I'm heading the wrong way for home."

Jun turned to go.

"Wait!" Malcolm cried. "Uh, do you know where Merriweather Secondary is?"

Jun's eyes narrowed to slits at the mention of it.

"I mean, in case you want to find me," Malcolm clarified. "I know I can find you at either Foon's or Dingxang's. And I can't say when we might pop in to Jade's next, but the school schedule is regular."

"Oh. Good idea. I'm sure I can figure out how to find it. Uh, thanks."

Sid said, "And I go to Stepney Jewish School."

Jun nodded.

Malcolm added, "I hope you'll look us up sometime, Jun."

The fog obscured Jun's face, but Malcolm thought the boy looked pleased.

"Swell, gents. Someday. Someday."

Jun took off toward Limehouse.

Malcolm watched him get swallowed up by the fog and wondered how Jun managed to avoid school and whether he evaded attendance officers altogether. Maybe the truancy people didn't bother with Limehouse.

"It seems late," Sid said, clearly not wanting to upset his mother again.

"I'm sure it's only maybe half-past four."

"That sounds confident."

Somewhere in the distance, or maybe it was closer than it sounded, the clatter of a horse's hoofs and the rumble of a wagon moved along. The comforting noise soon diminished to nothing.

Walking by the Jewish cemetery, Malcolm trailed his hand along the brick wall, a pattern of smooth and rough surfaces brushing against his fingers.

They had just passed a familiar pub on Three Colts Lane when he heard the footsteps.

Sid heard them too. Malcolm could sense his wariness. Sid closed in, walking about an inch from his side.

It was silly to be afraid just because fog concealed the presence of other folks until they were upon you. The others might just be neighbours. The two had passed a pub. Of course there could be someone else along the lane, heading home after a pint or going to the pub to enjoy one. But neither boy said a word, hoping their presence would not be noticed.

The rhythmic cadence of a train diminished to a distant drone in the direction of The City.

Footsteps approached.

No one, not even the menacing Jack, would be able to see well enough to recognize them. But fog sometimes waxes and wanes with air currents.

The heels and soles that clapped the pavement from behind sounded like those of a man.

There were some who would have noticed that Malcolm had the means to buy books and coffee and would kill for mere pennies. And there were men who preyed on the defenceless, like PC Hawkins has done, with a thirst for violence and power.

Fog would make the perfect circumstance for assaults. Good thing he and Sid were together. Malcolm believed that, between them, they could fight off one man.

An alley appeared to the side. Malcolm grabbed Sid's arm and pulled him left. Sid knew to keep quiet. The two stood pressed against the near wall.

The steps advanced.

A figure came up and stopped. He turned into the alley.

"Oh, it's you boys."

"Mr. Lever," Malcolm cried, relieved.

"Funny how fog can make a person nervous. I was as worried about your presence on the lane as you obviously were about mine."

"I can't deny that, sir," Malcolm said. Sid said nothing and leaned hard against the wall and Malcolm's side.

"My wife went to her sister's this afternoon and I'm on my way there to help her get home. I do hope you pop round the shop soon. I just got a few bound collections of Sir Conan Doyle's stories. Perfect evening to be reading them, isn't it?"

"Yes, sir. We'll pop in one of these days. G'night, sir."

"I'll be on my way. Take care as you go. Though you're not far from home now." He walked on and was soon swallowed by mist and darkness.

"Ready, mate?"

"Yes." Sid fell in step next to Malcolm.

"I see word hasn't spread that I'm staying up in Hackney. That's good, I think."

"Yes, old thing."

Malcolm said goodnight to his friend at his doorstep and turned toward Stepney Station and the long ride to Aunt Jane's.

Chapter Nineteen

Whenever Malcolm dropped by Lever's Bookshop, he couldn't help but think of the childish rhyme: *Jack Sprat could eat no fat; his wife could eat no lean.*

Mrs. Lever was not at her table. The woman, who had been fairly cross since her daughter had flown the coop, always waddled and shifted as if her feet were tired of holding up her girth. Of late, an aura of discontent left her with even less verve, as if she were a potato long kept in the bin.

The shop's cash register sat on a smart-looking counter, a counter so ample that it invited patrons to buy books by the case. On the other side, beyond a wide aisle, stood the wooden table and chairs where she would often station herself.

Until recently, Esther, their daughter, had been kept busy cleaning house behind the back curtain or upstairs. She only came out, as far as Malcolm knew, to wait on her mother. But Esther was gone, and today, as far as Malcolm could tell, so was Mrs. Lever.

"Is Mrs. Lever all right, sir?"

Mr. Lever was leaning forward, elbows on his counter, reading a daily. He said, "Right as rain, Malcolm. She's out spending my money. Thank you for asking."

Malcolm held up a well-bound copy of *Captain Brinkley's China; its history, arts and literature* which he had selected from one of the shelves. "Do you have anything more on China, Mr. Lever?"

"On Chi—?" The shopkeeper's face fell with something like consternation pulling together his gaunt features. "Oh, I forgot we even had that in stock." He shook his head. "I'm afraid not, lad."

Something behind Malcolm's shoulder drew Lever's attention. The shopkeeper added, "The gentleman behind you is a regular encyclopaedia on that country, aren't you Professor Worsley?"

Malcolm turned at the sound of a gravelly hem-hawing. The scholar looked down on him and asked, "What do you wish to learn about, lad?"

"Um, well, I suppose I want to understand China's relationship with Britain."

"Most interesting," the man said.

Lever hovered closely, his interest piqued. "Well, well, why don't you two gentlemen sit at my wife's table and have a chat, if you wish."

The professor's beaming expression indicated that he'd enjoy nothing more, and he nodded twice as if acknowledging the offer with a stiff imitation of an Oriental bow.

In good humour, Malcolm also did a quick bow before Lever and then followed the professor to the old wooden table.

Lever added, "Allow me to bring you two a pot of tea."

"Oh, that would be most appreciated, Mr. Lever," the man said, his eyes bright under bushy brows.

Lever's hospitality struck Malcolm as strange, but he welcomed it.

After courteous chitchat followed by Lever's fussing with tea things and a plate of biscuits, Worsley stirred some sugar into his steaming cup and asked, "Where shall we begin?"

Malcolm took a careful sip. "If the common workers of China and Russia wish to govern themselves, if I've got that right, why would that matter to the average Englishman?"

Lever pulled a duster from under the counter and began wiping at his cash register, trying to mind his own business or perhaps wishing to give that impression.

Professor Worsley smiled, possibly at both Lever and Malcolm. He then sat back and shifted his gaze to an old globe, which stood waist high near the front window. A large manila price tag hung from it, indicating that it was for sale. Despite that, the older man looked as if he wished it were close enough for his fingers to spin and point.

"Would you like me to get the globe, sir?"

Lever bristled. Malcolm gave the shopkeeper an apologetic look in case he had transgressed with his suggestion. He didn't mean to take liberties with the shop's wares. Lever put away the dust cloth and returned to perusing his daily. Perhaps Malcolm had misread him.

"No, lad, thank you."

Worsley cleared his throat and continued, "The British Empire, as you know, connects a fair portion of the planet. If we were living in the days before Napoleon, such a thing as communism in the Orient or elsewhere, were it present then, would not have made as much of an impact here. However, now trade and resources matter very much, indeed, to the British economy. And, I suppose, just as important today is the issue of trust with our neighbours, even those across seas and steppes."

"What exactly is communism?" Malcolm asked.

"Yes, well, where to begin." Mr. Worsley took his time.

Malcolm glanced out of the window as he waited, his attention drawn by snowflakes drifting and then melting on the street, making the cobbles glisten.

Lever continued reading with his bony elbows on the counter.

"Communism, or Marxist thought," Worsely said, "appeals to the common man because it looks as if it could offer equality. Various things can look good at face value, like a young tart."

Malcolm waited for him to moderate his statement somehow, as adults often had done when they reconsidered their spicy remarks in the face of his youth. The professor, however, kept the point out there.

"Communism aims at an economic and social system in which all property and resources are collectively owned by a classless society. However, if you give credit to the Scriptures, as one point of reference, they assure us that until Judgment Day, mankind will 'always have the poor' among themselves and that 'man ruleth over another to his own hurt.' My point is that communism can only present a different set of circumstances wherein mankind faces the same types of problems: corruption, violence, the odd plague now and again and, as I said, the ever-present downtrodden."

Malcolm knew precious little about the Scriptures. But it was clear enough that Mr. Worsley's perspective sounded reasonable.

"Right," Malcolm said, "but a friend of mine, a journalist, in fact, feels that supporters of change tend to take drastic measures. My question is mostly *why*; why would some Englishmen wish for China to become communist?"

A brisk jingle of the bell signalled a new customer entering the shop.

"Welcome, Miss," Lever said, beaming beatifically.

The young lady, a pretty thing about Malcolm's age, nodded in acknowledgement and headed toward an aisle featuring fiction.

Worsley kept his focus and said, "Ah, well, we can debate the term 'Englishman' all afternoon. Place of birth doesn't necessarily indicate values or ambitions."

Malcolm considered this as he took a bite of shortbread. Its fresh crunch melted into the familiar flavour that for millions of His Majesty's subjects represented order and goodness.

The professor said, "China is experiencing a surge of Intellectual Radicalism in the face of, what many observers see as, humiliation, which was heaped upon it by Western powers and the treaty of Versailles.

Intrigued, Malcolm pushed away the rest of his shortbread.

"Germany's rights in Shandong and Qingdao, areas with considerable assets, were transferred to Japan by the treaty."

"How was that fair?"

"Life and political hooliganism are seldom fair, lad. It appears to me that the Western powers were aiming to satisfy Japan, because Japan has the wherewithal and the strongest motivations to become an ally, one willing to prevent communism from gaining hold in Asia."

"I'm afraid I'm a bit thick, Mr. Worsley. Why would anyone with British sympathies wish to see communism take hold over there?"

He raised a digit for his first point. "Today, it helps to step back."

Sleet began pecking at the window as the wind picked up. Malcolm looked around. A frenzy of snowflakes mixed with pelting sleet attacked Whitechapel.

The young lady walked up to the counter and paid for her purchase. She then turned and looked at the snow squall outside. Malcolm wished she would notice him. He had his smile ready. Without a word, she tucked her package inside her coat and left. A whoosh of chilled air swept through the place.

The professor continued, "One needs to step back and weigh the balance of things. There is the matter of dependency—"

"Gentlemen, I am sorry," Lever said, "but I must call a halt to this hearty conversation. My wife will return soon and will undoubtedly need to rest at her table. Thank you for stopping by today. I hope to see you both soon."

With that dismissal, Malcolm and the professor left the shop and parted ways, each holding down his hat and hunching into his jacket.

Malcolm's mind should have been swimming with politics but it, instead, quickly filled with thoughts of a young lady. Not the one who left the bookshop, though she was an attractive girl, but the one at a certain café mentioned by the captain.

Chapter Twenty

"Does she work here? In Petticoat Lane? That's funny." Sid was full of himself today.

"It's actually Wentworth Street," Malcolm said, not in the mood for silliness.

"Oh." Sid scanned the busy intersection more seriously. "I thought they called it Petticoat."

Since they had never actually investigated Wentworth and Middlesex Streets as a duo, Malcolm explained, "Before my grandfather died, he said this street had something to do with hogs, then petticoats. This is Wentworth Street today, but the market—with all those garment hawkers—is called by its old name. Anyway, I think I see our destination down there. Come on."

"Do you think she'll know what you look like?"

"I can't even imagine how she knows I exist."

Petticoat Lane Market on Wentworth Street clamoured with activity, giving Malcolm adequate cover for his reconnaissance.

"Everyone's shopping for the hols," Sid said, stating the obvious after forging through a crowd surrounding a popular merchant's stall selling pies.

"Yes they are, old thing."

Tables with a variety of goods held the attention of countless shoppers. While Malcolm and Sid were inching their way along, two women began fighting over a fancy piece of underclothing. Their histrionic behaviour confirmed their lower station, perhaps dance hall women, if not prostitutes. The merchant reached under his display table and brandished a large pair of scissors. "Shall I snip that item in half for yers? You can pay full price each for yer half." The older of the two dropped her hands in disgust and turned away.

As Malcolm, with Sid in tow, walked on, the reference to wise King Solomon evoked bittersweet memories of extended family members. Recollections of his grandparents reading stories to him only reminded him of the loss. He usually managed to keep them under wraps. Influenza had decimated the family, leaving only his da, Aunt Jane, and him.

Despite Sid's company and the crowd, loneliness overtook him.

"Are you feeling sick, Malcolm?"

He tried to shake off the hazy visions and realized that he had stopped walking. Stepping over to the brick front of a building, he leaned against it.

In front of them, along the curb, more merchants enjoyed a brisk business. On Malcolm's left, a man with greasy hair was selling used boots. On his right, a woman sold jellied eels. Across the street, blazoned just above the crowds, large painted letters identified The Black Kettle Café.

In its window stood a dark haired girl whose large eyes were trained on him. She was wearing an apron over a skirt and blouse. Her look of confidence met Malcolm square in the face.

"So much for checking things out while going unnoticed, Sid."

"What?"

"That must be her, there, in the window."

Sid released a soft whistle between his teeth. "Lovely, that. She's looking right at you."

The girl turned away. Most of the tables that Malcolm could see were occupied.

"What are we going to do now?"

He set out across the street. "We're going in to eat and have a look around."

"Uh, do you have enough money for me?"

"Of course, old bean. Let's go."

Malcolm pulled open the restaurant door. The girl was not in sight, but delicious aromas greeted him, along with the gentle sounds of conversations and the clink of cutlery. Eastern European utterances reminded him of Joe's imitations of his hometown accent.

A woman came out from the back and approached. Her eyes were bright, her nose distinctive.

"Would you like the table by the window or along that wall?" She gestured to each option. Despite matronly girth, her face would wrest attention away from most other women. But there were none competing today. The girl was not in sight, and the clientele for lunch consisted of businessmen.

The table by the wall was closer to the kitchen entry, through which the pretty girl must have disappeared. A small stage occupied the area to the left of that door, an ornate bar to the right.

"Uh, along the wall will be fine, ma'am. Thank you."

"This way, gentlemen." Her broad, shapely hips swished in a girlish sway. And Malcolm's neck and face flushed with prickly heat.

After being seated, Malcolm tried to relax while remaining alert. The familiar hum of table talk played against the bustling sounds from the kitchen. A busboy laid out their cutlery and left.

Sid's eyes settled on Malcolm, as if waiting for direction, but something behind Malcolm caught his attention. The diners fell silent like birds before a storm. Malcolm turned.

It was the mature woman with the flashing eyes. However, her costume now presented a significant gap, leaving her stomach exposed. At the back of the stage, two dark-skinned men sat, waiting. One held a stringed instrument and the other, an odd pair of drums. The music started and the woman began a sinuous dance unlike anything he'd ever seen before. He checked on Sid who was beaming a moon-faced smile.

The diners began clapping in rhythm. Malcolm and Sid joined in.

Her moving midriff reminded of him of a large ball of dough that was being kneaded. Fascination lifted his spirits amid nagging wisps of guilt.

He was so engrossed in the performance that the girl's presence at their table caught him unawares.

"Have you never been to a Serbian restaurant before?" The girl stood, hands on hips, with an air of superiority—or perhaps it was just self-possession. Her colouring and beautiful eyes told him that the dancer and the girl must be related.

"You like the dancing, I see. My gran taught us, my mum and me. Our family history is complicated." She gestured to the stage. "That was not a Serbian dance. What do you think of our place, eh?"

Malcolm collected himself with effort.

"Uh, right. Th-the food smells wonderful." He did his best to sound nonchalant. "What do you recommend?"

"Most first-timers like our burek—that's layers of phyllo dough, spinach and cheese baked to perfection."

"I'll order that." He knew he hadn't ever seen this girl before. He would remember. Yet, she behaved with disconcerting familiarity.

She looked from Malcolm to Sid. "Our burek is quite large, if you two wish to share." She shrugged lovely shoulders. "Or would you like to see our menu, sir."

Sid sat straighter at being called *sir*. He replied, "If it's okay with you, Malcolm, we can share."

Malcolm nodded his agreement.

The girl left. Just then, the music resumed with a quickening beat, filling the place with energy. This time the woman's fingers began clinking tiny cymbal-like instruments while her hips rolled rhythmically.

Sid's fingers tapped in time on the table top. Malcolm smiled at him, then realized his were doing the same.

The girl returned with a hint of ceremony and the flaky brown burek. Before Malcolm could fully appreciate its appeal, the afternoon show came to a sudden end. A number of men tossed coins on the stage at the feet of the woman. Emboldened by a new type of enthusiasm, Malcolm stood and tossed a few as well, shocking himself. Sid stared at him open-mouthed. The girl appeared unimpressed. Hoping to appear as if he were an old hand at this sort of thing, Malcolm sat casually. He then turned his attention to lunch.

In the moment his back had been turned, the girl had served Sid his half of the entrée.

A hearty voice cried from across the room, "Miss, I need a bit more of the plum. Would yer kindly?" She complied, heading for the bar, her demeanour business-like.

Malcolm's first bite of the burek released a fountain of delight across his palate. The texture of warm flaky pastry, with its essence of some marvellous oil, mingling with the creamy cheese and spinach, made him savour each mouthful for as long as he could.

With unmasked suspicion, Sid examined his but was soon trying to chew his first bite while his lips stretched, smiling.

The girl returned. "I see that you two are worldly wise chaps. Since this is your first time here, you each get a shot of slivovitz, our plum brandy, on the house." She set down two squat glasses and turned to deliver *a bit of the plum* to the man across the room.

Sid sniffed. "Whew! Smells like medicine to me. You can have mine."

Malcolm raised his glass and admired the liquid's clear golden hue. "This looks like it's more than a shot to me." When he inhaled above the glass' rim, his nostrils flared, enticed by its gilded promise. He took a sip. The feel of it on his tongue was both cool and hot; smooth and yet he had to quell an urge to cough. "Whoa." He closed his eyes in concentration and took another sip, then another.

"Go easy on it, lad. First time? That stuff will end up tasting you more than you will taste it." It was Joe. Malcolm opened his eyes. It was not Joe, but a man at the next table. Malcolm nodded to him and said, "I believe you, sir."

Nonetheless, he sipped on. The plum brandy began to go down with more and more smoothness.

Sid talked between bites about his cousin's bar-mitzvah. Malcolm nodded amicably, set down his glass and polished off the last of his lunch. After some time, Malcolm realized that the girl hadn't come back to their table, nor had she been in the dining room. A taller busboy with dark bushy brows and rather distinct body odour cleared away their dishes, after which the woman presented their check. Malcolm paid and left a generous tip.

He got up to leave, but his knees buckled. With concentration, he willed his feet forward.

The man who had warned him clucked his tongue but said nothing. Malcolm felt as conspicuous as an elephant.

A swimming sensation blurred his vision and he tripped on a chair leg, righting himself just in time. A few men chuckled. What if he had fallen flat on his face in front of *her*? Malcolm flushed hot with embarrassment. Before he got to the door, which Sid had been holding open, the girl approached.

"Are you Malcolm?"

"No."

He stepped outside. Under his breath, he muttered, "Not now, I'm not." He took a deep breath. "Come on, Sid." He needed to distance himself from the place. The gauzy sky filled the street with glare. Malcolm flung his arm around Sid's shoulders and said, "Get me out of here, mate."

Sid helped him along.

The bustling market clamoured against Malcolm's ears. In the throes of a mounting headache, he vaguely noticed a short figure blending with the shadows of an alley, leaning against a building as if watching him. He didn't want to be seen by anyone.

Stumbling on, Malcolm then noticed a lone person that did not fit into the scene. She ploughed through the throng despite her tottering gait, as if intent on approaching him. When she veered and passed him by, he heard a familiar warble. He turned. Not only was she entering the Serbian restaurant, the old woman stood at its threshold and bellowed a Wagnerian war cry to all inside.

He'd had enough of mystery and oddity. Malcolm wanted to be with his father.

And he needed more details about this girl. Surely the captain could recall more particulars of the encounter when not rushed and observed.

How to get to Guildmore Hall without Aunt Jane, without Wendell?

He knew he couldn't walk so far, even on a good day. And he had read too many stories of danger to go it alone. Those old tales of such highwaymen as Dick Turpin and Claude Duval were etched in his memory. Images of possible assaults floated in and out of his mind, elusive yet haunting. Malcolm tripped over his own foot, righting himself with help from Sid's steadying arm.

He gave up on planning anything for the present.

"Sid, I need to get to my bed. Thanks for the shoulder."

"Any time, Malcolm."

Chapter Twenty-One

Morning frost dusted the low-lying jasmine that blanketed much of Mrs. Doran's garden. With a start, Malcolm realized how late it was in the season; and that he hadn't come up with a solution to any of his concerns.

How could so many events slip past at such speed? Why couldn't time fleet by as quickly in geography class?

He leaned back on the cold bench. His little toad must surely be in hibernation. He wished he could hold it, speak with it.

Some shrubbery off to the left attracted his gaze. Each sculpted bush stood proud as a Grecian urn, rich with blood-red berries, the tops of which glistened with caps of hoarfrost. The captain had neglected their own for years. Those images of tufted weeds saddened Malcolm.

The sun cast a muted glow along the wall to his right. Now naked vines clung to it, entwining in fascinating patterns, as if drawn by pencil. And each offshoot and juncture mirrored his broken and blending thoughts; the Serbian girl, Jun's revelation about Jack and his fancy school—the very idea of a street bully living in a Regents Park townhouse.

Why should that surprise him? No one had claimed that the poor held title to criminal activities. He tried to reconcile newsy tidbits about corruption that he'd read or heard about.

His father had complained of none other than Lloyd George himself. That was months ago—last spring, on a cool night before their hearth—one of many instances when Malcolm had felt his father was only marginally aware of his presence. On that particular occasion, Malcolm had wondered whether his father was speaking to him or to the glass of brandy held at the ready. But his father's grumbles revealed an insight into a misuse of power that Malcolm had never thought possible. The prime minister had offered the captain an Honorable status...for a hefty price, under the table. Quite illegal, Malcolm had gathered.

Jack had never looked like a nob out on the streets. With a dawning smile, Malcolm realized he hadn't either. The captain's approval of adventure had resulted in a wardrobe that included clothes appropriate for East End exploration, in addition to his staid and proper things.

What could possibly make a young man, like Jack, whose father was apparently wealthier than Malcolm's, turn to heinous crimes on the street?

A stentorian voice broke the silence. "I say, there."

Malcolm shook off the feeling that Heaven was calling him. He turned and looked up at the dormer windows. A large, silver cropped head with a moustachioed face peered down.

"Are you Master Malcolm?"

"Um, yes, sir."

The man must be the tenant who had been touring the Continent.

"Do you have a moment to meet properly? Either up here or I'll come down. I've been wanting to meet you, lad. I reside here. As you can see, top floor, I am."

The joviality in the man's inflection matched the good report Malcolm's aunt had given of the neighbour.

"I'll be right up, sir. Uh, thank you."

The top-floor neighbour stood waiting by his flat door. A baritonal chuckle came from somewhere deep inside his stocky body.

"I wish I could run up those steps like that," the man boomed.

Malcolm took the last flight two at a time.

Mr. Gold held out his hand and shook Malcolm's firmly. "Ah, to be young. Never take it for granted, young man. It's all gone before you know it." Another jovial chuckle.

"Now, Mr. Herman Gold is my name, to be sure, not a lie nor a stage name, the genuine article, I am, and it is." More chuckles. "I know your name, as you know, seeing as I called you up here. I also— and I hope you don't find this rude—but I have learned a bit about you already, all of it good, from the fine folks of this residence. Not to worry. Come in, come in."

Malcolm followed him across the threshold in a state of wonder.

Mr. Gold let the flat's door remain open, then retreated into a closet-sized kitchen and said over his shoulder, "Would you like milk to go with assorted chocolates."

"Chocolates? Um, why, yes. Thank you, Mr. Gold."

Herman Gold clinked and clanked his preparations, then bellowed, "On the table there. I opened the box in your honour as you were coming up. They're from Ghent, or Lille. I can't recall exactly where I picked those up, but they are fresh, to be sure. Be they French, Belgian or Dutch, all of those folks know their chocolate—unlike the Ruskies, let me tell you."

"You've been to Russia?"

Mr. Gold entered the parlour with two glasses of milk. "Oh, brushed past it a couple of times. Close enough to smell the fumes of its vodka." His features went sad, and Malcolm studied the man to see whether it was genuine or well-practiced stagecraft.

"I wish I'd been able to visit its cities, particularly Saint Petersburg, when I was young, when the country—Imperialist, then—was open, but I wasn't traveling the Continent in those days." Gold puffed out his chest. "Now, the Big Bear is shut up as tight as a, uh…as tight as an Aberdeen landowner's grasp on his bottle of single malt whisky." He nodded for emphasis.

Malcolm could only smile a response to that.

Gold handed Malcolm a glass of cool milk. "Now, there you are. Let's sit at table round these yummies, shall we?"

Malcolm's first bite contained a nugget of rich caramel, which was encased in chocolate that was so fine, it began melting in his mouth straight off. Fresh *yummies*, indeed. The caramel was such that for long moments he could only chew, delightfully captive to its control. Gold handed over a napkin.

Malcolm wiped his lips and ventured a bold but good-natured inquiry, "I understand that you're an actor, sir."

Gold's jowls lifted. He shot back, "And I understand that you fancy adventures…sir." He popped a small candy in his mouth and talked around it with care. "Who would think, to look at us," he made a self-mocking gesture at his size, "and say that we share such similar traits."

"Traits, sir?"

"For one, being extroverts, surely."

"Extroverts? How?"

"Never mind. It's dreadfully tedious to go into." He caught himself and added, "Not that I'm dismissing you, but I loathe talking about myself, you see."

"Oh, blast," Malcolm ventured, tongue in cheek. With sincerity he added, "I'm interested in learning about your travels, sir, as an actor."

"Oh, all right." Without batting an eye, Gold discarded his excess modesty. "So, what would you like to know."

"You travel throughout Europe, except Russia. Do you perform in all those languages?"

"Brilliant question, lad." He beamed, paused for effect, and then, with a lift of his brows, replied, "No." Reclining back, he added, "If I tried out my French in Belgium, they'd run me out of Flanders. If I tried to speak it in Paris, they'd burn me alive…or, more likely, cut off my head."

Malcolm laughed with ease.

"As to German, I only ventured into the Teutonic territories on a handful of occasions. On one of them, I went to see Vienna, to visit with some old friends. It was at that time that I ventured east, a small detour, you see, where I quite inadvertently had gotten close enough to, as I'd said, smell the boozy breath of the Bear.

"Love can make a fool out of a man," Gold said openly. "I met this actress, you see, a pretty thing who hailed from Warsaw. We met while working in Paris. It was she who took me to Vienna where we encountered some thespians of my old acquaintance. After that lovely bit of frivolity, she was determined to have me meet her family in Poland. This was during the last days of that crazy rigmarole between Poland and Russia, about eighteen months ago, lad."

"Ah." Malcolm hadn't read about it, but his ears pricked up all the more.

"I was fortunate—I'm both glad and embarrassed to admit—to escape the Land of the Slavs with just the shirt on my back, so to speak."

Herman Gold looked off through the nearby window.

Malcolm allowed the actor some time with his reverie and selected another piece of chocolate.

Gold said, "I perform mostly in Paris and Amsterdam, to expats, at the English theatres and clubs. Thus, our plays and variety shows are in English." He grinned with a nod at finally answering the question.

"Fascinating, sir."

"I'm glad you think so, sir. The modest income, with the occasional residence offered to us players, allows me to see the world before I'm too old to do so."

"That would be a great way for His Majesty to manoeuver a spy," Malcolm said, surprised again at his own gall. He checked his host's features for any sign of annoyance.

Mr. Gold's eyes remained bright. "It would, indeed. They told me you were a bright lad. And, as you know, a spy would never admit his true position, except, I suppose, under the most grievous of tortures." Gold shuddered, possibly out of fear—more likely, a comedic gesture to lighten the idea or to give it more colour, Malcolm supposed.

Gold added, "But, I confess to no higher calling than that of merely entertaining myself abroad."

"And I must confess, sir, I wish you could teach at Merriweather."

"Is that your school? Well, I'm sure they'd listen for one moment and wish to toss me out on my ear the next."

The man's gaze shifted to the clock on a bureau. "I have yet to get to know you better, young man. And it would be my pleasure to do so. However, I see that I have prattled away our visit. If you'll excuse me, I need to run to the greengrocer's as I wish to present your Auntie's kitchen helpers with a little something for our family dinner tonight."

Malcolm descended the stairs feeling better than he had for days. His spirits lifted even higher when he realized how Mr. Gold's mention of the greengrocer held the key to Malcolm's quandary; he now saw how he could arrange to visit his father. The timing was perfect, for Auntie would be leaving him alone while away for a weekend in Leeds after Boxing Day.

But first, he needed a disguise. Not a full-blown disguise like those Sherlock Holmes had mastered. Just a little something to throw off the two men who had seen him at Guildford Park House. What was the admissions steward's name? Boggs? Malcolm could not dredge up the name of the other one, the man who had served their tea.

He entered Aunt Jane's flat and listened. Silence hung in the entry hall. He stepped to the parlour. Nothing. The door to his aunt's room was closed, as usual.

Just then, a squabble of something boiling over on the stove erupted. Adelaide must be in the kitchen.

"Oh no, not again!" she cried.

Malcolm pushed through the door. Adelaide looked up from the steaming mess. She was holding the pot's handle with a towel. Green muck dripped over the pot's sides. Her spectacles were trained on him.

With their foggy dullness behind the rising steam, it took her a moment to recognize him.

"Thank goodness it's you." She clucked and said, "It was going to be such a lovely pea soup. Now it looks like sea poop." She burst out laughing, a self-mocking hysteria that lightened the moment.

Malcolm laughed too, surprised to hear her speak like a schoolboy. It kindled a rare camaraderie.

"Can I help, Adelaide?"

"Oh, no, Master Malcolm, bless you." She dropped the pot in the sink and took off her specs. "Good thing the lady is out this afternoon."

She began wiping the lenses with her apron when Malcolm realized his opportunity. He had to refrain from clapping his hands together.

Instead, he smiled at her. "Maybe we should have tea. Why don't you sit, Adelaide. Allow me to serve you this time."

She donned her cleaned specs and stared at him; her magnified eyes gleamed twice their size through the lenses. He read in her features some shock, likely due to his friendliness. Was he over-playing his role? He wanted those spectacles, or some other pair, for his clandestine visit. How blind was Adelaide without her glasses?

He took a moment, then said, "Yes, you deserve a break, if my opinion counts. Sit. You'll feel right as rain afterward." He looked at the disaster in the sink. "Do you think it's salvageable?"

"I'll check it in a tic…and I'll take you up on that tea. Thanks."

Malcolm fussed over the teapot, milk jug and sugar bowl while the kettle on the stove began to patter and build up steam.

Just before sitting down across from her at the table, he reached for the cookie tin. Its weight confirmed the available offerings. He opened its lid and set a plate before her.

"I'll be mother," Adelaide insisted. She lifted the teapot and began to pour.

Malcolm took a hot sip.

"Have a biscuit?" She touched the side of the tin. "Made them myself, I did."

"Uh, no, thanks. Just tea for me. I, uh, had some delightful chocolates with Mr. Gold a minute ago."

"Yes, he's back. Friendly fellow. Always pleased to hear him on the stair, knowing he's home."

"Mr. Gold returns and Auntie leaves—that is, she leaves after Boxing Day. Do they get on all right?" he asked.

"Absolutely. He'll be one of our dinner guests for the holiday. It's just a coincidence that she'll be away just as he has returned, and it's only for a few days. Madam said I should take the opportunity to visit my family while she's away, which I shall, to my sister's."

Malcolm grinned at the advantage this gave him. Now he wouldn't have to concoct a story for Adelaide. His visit to the asylum would be a success. Only he and his father would know. He couldn't wait to see his father's look of surprise—and to hear his praise for pulling off the venture. *My clever son.*

Adelaide began elaborating about her sister, her only living sibling, who can *walk and talk like a lady.* How *she went and married her such a nice man. Alistair Warwick. He owns a successful haberdashery in Kent.*

She said, "I imagine you will be getting a lot of studying done while you have the flat to yourself."

He nodded, noncommittally.

The young woman prattled on about her doings, and Malcolm soon got the impression that Mrs. Warwick might not return her sister's admiration. Was Adelaide aware of that? He would be more mindful of Adelaide's feelings, he decided, but first...

He said, "I've been having trouble with my studies."

She again gaped at him. It was the first time he had brought up anything of a personal nature since his aunt took him in.

Squinting his eyes, he added, "The print in my geography book is quite small."

She leaned forward. "Does readin' give you headaches, then?"

"Yes, yes it does. Fierce headaches."

"You probably need spectacles." She nodded for emphasis.

His heart leapt.

She said, "I'm sure Madam or your father will provide them for you, if you ask."

He frowned. He needed to maintain control of the situation.

He said, "Well, uh, I don't get my next allowance for some weeks yet."

"Oh, well, in that case, I have a spare set of spectacles you could use in the meantime. They're scratched up a bit. Enlarge the letters just the same, they do. They're simple reading specs, mind you. I don't need to see one of those opt—, um, those doctors for your eyes."

He couldn't believe his luck. "That would be much appreciated, Adelaide."

He hadn't thought of specs before this encounter. Granted, he could use some of his remaining allowance to purchase a pair, but these were at hand. And the scratched lenses might even enhance the touch of disguise.

"I promise to treat them carefully and return them later."

"Oh, I don't know why I even keep them. Just in case I break these, I suppose. I'll go an' fetch them."

"Let's enjoy our tea first." He leaned back and smiled.

The first to arrive for Aunt Jane's Boxing Day dinner party was Sylla Le Feuvre.

Wendell's man, Bryn, took charge of her fur coat. A subtle something passed between the two. Either Bryn suddenly developed an eye tic or the valet just winked at this guest. No one else appeared to have seen it. Bryn had been instructed to cater to her ego, Malcolm had heard. But a wink seemed beyond the call of duty.

Malcolm sat back and considered the adults; it was going to be an interesting evening.

Auntie approached Sylla and the two made a pretence of kissing each other's cheeks.

"You look smashing, my dear." Wendell bowed to kiss Sylla's proffered hand.

Sylla's style, like Auntie's, aimed for drama. Her black gown, tubular in form, draped long with green-gold trim and jet bead appliqué. The neckline ran straight across her décolletage at a daring level.

Bryn served her a glass of Champagne and returned to his station near the drinks cabinet.

Sounds of rustling and clinking from the kitchen, along with appetizing aromas, added festivity to the flat.

Malcolm remained on the sofa. On the small table by his right elbow, a glass of ginger ale effervesced, as if it were having a conversation with itself.

"Wish me luck," Sylla said to Auntie, her tone breathless. Malcolm looked up, wondering what she wanted luck for. Had he imagined her moment of vulnerability?

Following a friendly tapping at the door, Herman Gold entered. After thanking Aunt Jane for the invitation, he dispensed with the obligatory chatter with those standing around and sought out Malcolm. The actor made a production of saluting him.

"How's our young scholar this evening?"

Malcolm searched for an appropriate reply. "Feeling very ordinary, Mr. Gold." He smiled to assure a good spirit. "Thank you, sir, and you?"

"Well, yes, well indeed."

Gold then entered into a conversation with Wendell.

Malcolm sipped his ginger ale.

The adults conversed with banter and throaty laughter.

Malcolm sat alone and sipped his drink.

Another knock preceded the appearance of Julius Crocker. His fair hair stretched from just above one ear across to the other and was lacquered taut. A handsome brow and strong chin were his better features; the nose was thin with a bump on the bridge.

Crocker made too much of the business of kissing Sylla's hand, after which, he sported a smile that masked any evil agendas.

For the moment, Malcolm was glad to be invisible. The cast of characters were worrisome.

He would need to keep his wits about him and appear to be minding his business. Things would not end well were he to slip-up while in the company of at least one covert criminal.

Aunt Jane's dining room had been fashioned to charm guests with its hints of warmth, decorated with crimson walls, brass sconces with black shades, a bevelled mirror, and a painting by Frederic Church. Tonight, candlelight glinted off jewels and crystal glassware. It was as good a place as any for cloak-and-dagger undercurrents.

They'd had their soup course—Bryn proved to be a capable server—and all were enjoying a delicious pheasant when Wendell changed the subject from the mundane.

"Mademoiselle Le Feuvre, I understand you have a broad understanding of the political shenanigans in China."

Sylla Le Feuvre breathed in slowly. "I can't take credit for that, Wendell. It's my friend Elspeth. She's reading history at University of Cambridge and has gotten interested in world affairs, just for the hell of it." She leaned forward. "You know how it is, now that women can earn academic degrees and all that. We lunch. She talks. I'm merely a good listener." She shrugged.

Crocker laid down his fork and knife. "What is your understanding, Miss Le Feuvre, of Dr. Sun Yat-sen?"

Her lips pursed seductively while she gave the impression of processing Crocker's question. "He seems like a charming man, from what I've heard." She took a sip from her wine glass, as if she expected no more on the topic.

"His activities? I mean, I understand he's gaining some power there."

Aunt Jane and Wendell became as still as statues while Mrs. Doran and Mr. Gold carried on, conversing in low tones.

"I couldn't really say, at least not anything truly enlightening," Sylla replied. "I don't believe the man has garnered much support if any from Western powers. I'm sure he must be quite disappointed." Her fingers twitched, as if they wished to hold a cigarette.

Malcolm guessed she had more to say but had decided against it.

Silence filled the room.

Gold cleared his throat.

Sylla then said, "But I don't think Britain is especially interested in seeing a united China."

Crocker grinned. "I see you actually know much of this topic."

"As I said, I'm a good listener…and, I read the papers. Who doesn't?"

Aunt Jane rescued Mrs. Doran who appeared bored with politics by initiating a whispered conversation about fairy cakes. Something in Auntie's demeanour, however, told Malcolm that she was keeping up with the main interchange at hand.

Mr. Gold rested his hands over his ample belly and said, "I don't really trouble myself with Asian matters, but from what I have read, many of the warlords have made a hash of things over there."

For quite a few beats, no one said anything.

"I am aware of three governments vying for control," Sylla offered, "and, God only knows, that's enough mayhem for one country, I'm sure.

Malcolm wondered at the game she was playing. He tried not to look at her with awe.

Sylla's elegant fingers began to run along her beads, daring the men to notice her neckline. "I can't recall whether it was in the *New York*

Times or, perhaps, *The Illustrated*, but somewhere I saw the man's picture with the briefest article on reunification. He is quite attractive and, reportedly, charismatic. I'd root for him. I guess, in a way, I am." She lifted her Cotes du Rhone. "Three cheers for Dr. Sun Yat-sen."

Julius was the only one to take her seriously. He raised his glass, reached across Malcolm and clinked it against hers.

Wendell's tone was casual as he said, "It appears to me, as well, that Western powers do not share Yat-sen's interest in seeing China united. I imagine it has to do with maintaining a measure of control over trading activities at its ports. If China were to remain as a house divided…" he gestured as if the phrase were enough for his point, but then added, "The Chinese are practically allowing themselves, or at least allowing parts of the country, to remain as Britain's minion in Eastern trade."

Jane turned toward Julius. "Do you think, Julius, that Lenin's government will have much impact on China?"

Another several beats of pulsing cogitations.

"I cannot say, dear lady." Julius shrugged. The casual observer might take his gesture as: *enough of this silly prattle*, but Malcolm noted a pent up energy about Crocker's features. He was sure that whatever Crocker thought of Aunt Jane's question, it was anything but prattle to him.

The candles bled wax over the silver holders. The table had long been cleared of dinner and dessert. In time, Crocker and Sylla took their leave and ostensibly went their separate ways.

Auntie had allowed Wendell to introduce Malcolm to the pleasures of port after dinner. His head swam a bit as he slouched down on the sofa in a golden haze. Only two dim lamps glowed in the parlour. Mrs. Doran and Mr. Gold remained at the table and were now singing bawdy songs with occasional spells of giggling. Wendell and Jane talked softly in the study.

"Shhh," Auntie then hissed. They lowered their voices further.

What were they up to? Was she for or against Crocker? Had Auntie been going to communist meetings? His head throbbed.

Tonight was the first 'family' gathering Malcolm had experienced for several months. Part of him resented the intrusion of intrigue. Part of him found it exciting. He would prefer normalcy.

The port had at first warmed his insides, but as Malcolm reviewed the piquing urgency surrounding Crocker's agenda a chill ran through him. Would the solicitor's machinations really lead to tragedy in Limehouse? Would it have far-reaching results? He worried over his aunt's safety. Would the small semblance of home life Malcolm had with her and this household shatter to smithereens?

He needed to see his father.

Chapter Twenty-Two

When they crested a hill, Malcolm could finally see beyond the hedgerows; undulating fields marked by patches of grey-green and brown resembled a lumpy quilt stretching out in all directions. Drifting cloud shadows bestowed mesmerizing depth onto the landscape. He was unused to wide open vistas, the Thames and the city view from the rooftop of Merriweather having been his only experience with anything vast.

Malcolm had known when to catch Mr. Phipps, the time of day when he would be packing up to leave the market in Spitalfields for the journey back to his farm. The kindly man was happy to oblige.

En route, Phipps and Malcolm fell into frequent spells of silence, grappling awkwardly for the odd topic both could enjoy. The wagon coursed over and down the hill. At times, the lack of conversation came from a kind of reverence for the beauty around them. Although the view was familiar to the farmer, Malcolm sensed a mutual appreciation for it.

"Quite a change from the mayhem in London," the man finally said. "Yer can't get this kind of peace there."

"You are right, Mr. Phipps." Thoughts of the Chinese bustling around Limehouse flooded his mind and heightened the contrast. Once at the bottom of the hill, the hedgerows again loomed high, walling them in like a corridor and submerging them in dark shadow.

The reminder of Limehouse quickened Malcolm's pulse. His confrontation with Jack Carrothers rose to haunt him: the bully's attack on the Oriental family in the alley, Malcolm's flight through the warrens and the fear of being discovered under the heap of rubbish.

"Are yer all right, man?" the farmer asked.

Malcolm was pulled from his disturbing memories. "I was just...thinking."

"Thoughts can be troubling sometimes, even for the young."

Although annoyed at his own transparency, being understood by the farmer strengthened Malcolm's spirit. He nodded his acknowledgement and turned his attention again to the passing scene of earth's bounties.

Ahead on his right, fluttering light enlivened an old maple's stubborn leaves. They rustled proudly in the breeze.

Mr. Phipss pulled on the reins.

"This is where yer go your own way, lad." The horse came to a stop, and Malcolm fished a half crown from his pocket and gave it to the farmer.

"Thanks again, Mr. Phipps."

"Gen'rous, of yer. Thanks. Now, if yer'll be wanting a lift back to London, yer need to catch me before dawn on a Thursday or a Monday. My farm is down that lane and then left on Stuckney Road."

"Yes, sir. Thank you."

"I hope your visit goes well." With that the older man flicked the reins and cooed some nonsensical words that Mimi the horse responded to. Malcolm stood in the middle of the crossroads and watched the duo head for home.

Malcolm walked on and wondered whether the landscape of China was very different. Now and then Old Jones brought lessons to life. Earlier in the week, the teacher had him imagining Hong Kong and its dense population: rickshaws and bicycles caught in tight traffic while masses of commoners on foot swarmed through the streets and alleys.

He relished the ensuing visions of the Chinese countryside, especially those opening west: goat herders staring off over the peaceful plains, and then across the steppes with Cossacks yelping on horseback, their pursuit roaring like thunder.

The gentle sound of a lark brought him back to England. It was a treat to feel himself to be part of the land here, away from the soot and grime of the city. Would he want to live here? He couldn't answer that, not with certainty. The countless untapped discoveries within the metropolis still held his interest. He liked its hubbub and the energy. He hoped to attend concerts someday, like Wendell did. And the Docklands would forever draw him back with its influx of ships, goods and people from around the world.

Limehouse fascinated him. Hong's and that opium den had introduced him to the exoticism of the Far East. He saw no reason why the varied ethnic groups couldn't carry on peacefully. He then recalled the tensions between the English and the Irish, the Catholics and Protestants; he shook his head.

What on earth did his aunt want to see happen? Why would she care? He'd like to think that her resolute feelings targeted those who threatened peace. Could that be it? *...such people deserve neither respect nor freedom.* He grappled to remember the context. But he was pretty sure her words were said in response to Wendell's mention of the Chinese.

Rhythmic snapping sounds echoed in the air. Malcolm turned to see a crow flapping past a copse; he'd been standing still for some time. The shadows now stretched longer, and to his left lay the narrow road that wound its way to Guildford Park House.

Walking on, he tried not to fret over his aunt's intentions.

The air smelled clean. If he weren't so stiff from the ride, he'd feel compelled to skip about and revel in the open freedom. But the sun hung low on the horizon. He picked up his pace, for he didn't know yet how or where he would spend the night.

Passing himself off as a would-be worker to get entry to the asylum would take some finagling. Nightfall would not be ideal for that.

Movement off in a field to his right caught his eye. A farmer rode across his property in a wagon of some sort, pulled by a large horse. They were heading for the farm buildings, both of them to their suppers. Malcolm wished he had brought something more comforting than bread and cheese.

The old manor home, the asylum, came into view; it loomed atop the next hill. A fork in the drive offered a choice to the right, where the stables sat among tangles of weeds and briers.

He approached the outbuilding and entered, leaving the door open for light. He wasn't raised around horses but it was evident that there hadn't been any kept here for quite some time, probably since the war. Sadness panged through him at the thought of horses being sent to the Front, at the images of their terror and violent deaths. He hated the thought of war. If there was anything he could do to thwart the plans of Crocker's group, he would.

In the surrounding silence, he wished the animals were here for company and warmth. But it was ideal that the place appeared neglected. He might be able to sleep here and be safe from whatever prowled the woods at night.

He made a circuitous inspection before closing the door. Pitch forks hung along one stretch of wall. An array of shovels and other implements hung at hand as well, looking rusty and draped with cob webs.

A scrabbling sound drew his attention to one of the stalls; he was relieved to see that it was a mouse and not a rat foraging. For the most part, the stables looked as if they'd been well cared for before the years of disuse.

He tried to imagine the place before the war, perhaps even before the century. How many horses? Grooms? Stable boys? Even at this time of evening he thought the place would have been full of life. Perhaps the hostlers would be playing cards and exchanging stories while horses nickered contently in their boxes.

Where to bed down? He thought he would choose another stall since he knew this one had at least one active rodent. In the next, he welcomed the sight of hay on the ground. He checked the next stall and then the next and on down the row. The rest of the stalls were completely empty with hard dirt floors.

Before settling in the hay, Malcolm walked to the door and looked up the hill at the large house. A few windows shone with interior light, casting amber splotches down on matted grass. All was quiet. He closed the door and found himself in utter darkness. He opened it again. The western horizon was a thin line of dusty pink, darkening upwards into brown-grey then to black. Malcolm turned back inside and groped his way along the row of stalls, deciding to settle for the third one down, farther from the mouse. Kneeling, he was undecided whether to use his coat as a bed or a blanket. He decided on the latter but for the time being, sat with his back against the wall. He would have his dinner.

He removed the bit of bread from the folded napkin and began munching away. Spending a night in an abandoned stable was an experience he wouldn't forget. *Sid's going to love hearing about this.*

Something pulled him from sleep. It was not the sound of a rodent but of a human; and it bore the intensity of stealth. Amber light shone above the stall from the direction of the door. Metal scraped earth, taking up a rhythmic and determined pace. He could hear the person breathing hard as the thrusts were made, quick scrapes followed by cascading plops of loose earth. He assumed it was a man; the efforts and exhalations sounded masculine.

Every fiber of Malcolm's body came alive. He wanted to move, to twist round and peek over the stall. Prudence told him that his movement would be awkward and give away his presence.

Was this man digging a grave? Hot blood coursed up Malcolm's neck and around his ears. Was this a patient, escaped from the house? Was it his father?

Malcolm willed his body to move without sound. First, he lifted his wool coat up and slowly laid it next to him. He would have to be upright if he were to defend himself. Amazed at the strength of fear, he rolled, twisted and was up. Soundlessly, he straightened and his head rose above the stall.

The figure bent to his task. It was not the captain. The man was small and wiry. Just then, he stopped shovelling.

Malcolm held his breath and stood motionless in shadow, watching the figure stoop to lift something from the hole. The man exhaled in satisfaction when fingers brushed at an object with a hollow sound. Two clasps clicked and hands fumbled, as if arranging treasures in a suitcase. Or placing them inside. Air passed through teeth, almost whistling in delight. After a few moments, the clasps clicked again. In short order, the digging resumed. This time it was returning the earth upon the treasure.

The figure stopped and stretched—it was Guildford's admissions steward. Malcolm couldn't recall his name.

Malcolm sank down with the same measured efforts. He would have to sit and wait. And worry.

Chapter Twenty-Three

He kept to the woods in the early light and made his way to the rear of the manor home. In the crisp December air, the rustling of grass and cracking of twigs underfoot all but shouted out his presence. The grounds remained empty and not one of the many windows of Guildford Park House revealed an interest in him.

A slight breeze carried the smell of wood smoke; and as he faced the rear, of what would be the kitchen, he smiled at the sight of its windows, opaque from steam.

Malcolm pulled Adelaide's spectacles from his pocket. After they were in place, he marched up to the door and knocked. Something inside clattered, then a flushed-face dumpling of a woman opened the door. Her stern look melted as she gazed at him. After sleeping rough, he must look pathetic.

"Good morning, ma'am. Sorry to disturb you. I am in the need of some work and am willing to do anything."

"We aren't taking on any more staff at this time, young man. Sorry."

Though the response was expected, his heart fluttered in panic.

He added, "I don't mean for a wage, ma'am. I'm willing to work for meals and sleep in the cellar, if there's no other place." He filled his features with as much charm and pathetic need as he could muster.

The woman cocked her head as if she recognized him.

"What's your name, lad?"

"Jack."

He hated using the bully's name, but it was one that would arrest his attention, one he would not ignore, raising suspicion.

"Where are you from?"

"Um, I'm from London. I was on my way to visit a relative but could only ride along with a farmer as far as East Horsley."

"You slept in the rough last night, did yer?"

"Yes, ma'am. It wasn't so bad." A breath of caution caught in his throat. For all he knew, even this friendly cook could be in on whatever was taking place in the stable. She might know full well about the items hid in the stalls.

"Won't they, this relative, be wondering where you are? There's a telephone in the administrator's office. I could ask him—"

"No, that's, uh, kind of you. They don't have a phone. And they aren't expecting me to arrive just yet. I was hoping to set out tomorrow morning, if I could just earn a meal and a place to sleep for the night."

"Where is it you're headed?"

He was grateful for having looked over a map yesterday. "Not too far from here. Near Wormley. Tomorrow, if I don't catch a lift along the way, I'm sure I can make it on foot before nightfall." He half marvelled at his ability to improvise.

"Well," she conceded, "my knees are feeling a bit arthritic, with the change of seasons and all. I could use some help taking things upstairs to those unable to use the dining hall. Come in." She stepped aside.

He entered and a warm glow filled him, more from success than the heady aromas in the kitchen.

"First thing," she announced, "go to the sink and wash your face and hands. I'll get you a towel."

He happily complied.

"When was the last time you had something to eat?"

"I can't say, ma'am." That avoided a lie.

"Well, you don't look too skinny, but I reckon I should feed you something first. By the way, my name is Mrs. Hopkins."

"Thank you, Mrs. Hopkins."

She set a bowl of porridge, a cup of tea and a small jug of milk before him on the table.

As he ate, he looked more closely at the activity in the large room. Two large pots simmered on the stove. There were two ovens. At least one of them was evidently baking bread. The walls were painted a sickly pale green while the floor was covered with brown linoleum. But everything looked tidy.

Standing nearby, she followed his gaze. "I used to have a young girl in here to help with this and that. Hester was her name; but havin' a girl wasn't a good idea, I suppose, not with the patients we have. One of them frightened her silly and that was the end of that." She looked at him. "I reckon you'll be fine, though. You look like you can take care of yourself."

Her reddened hands went up and patted back some loose hairs around her head, with little effect.

"Me?" she carried on, as if he had thought to worry about her welfare, "as long as my pots and skillets are within reach—" She slapped the edge of the table. "Ha. That's just me being silly. I never had no trouble here." She went to the sink and began scrubbing potatoes. "If you perform well today and need a job—after your visit with your relatives, that is—I could ask the administrator about it."

So they needed help after all. The idea gave him pause. He could see his da everyday—and be done with all the mystery at Aunties. He mumbled his thanks.

"Mrs. Harries comes in to help me or spell me a few times each week. I don't expect her till Friday. She'll cover for me on Sundays. She's nice enough, but I make better pies. All the officers in here will tell you that, those who talk, that is. Some, poor souls, are mute and so very miserable. Breaks my heart, it does."

She dried her hands, came over, sat across from him and poured herself a cup of tea. "If nothing else, I dare say you could use some wages to buy a new pair of spectacles."

"I should take them off when playing with my mates."

"Hmph. Well, about this place. You realize its patients are officers whose minds' are a bit off after livin' through the horrors in France and Belgium. Some men rock and sway, some twitch, mostly 'round their eyes or with their hands. A few gentlemen get better and get back to regular life. One poor chap here, however, likes to run 'round without his clothes when he can get away with it. We're used to it."

She leaned forward and added in a hushed tone, "I live in the village, but I've heard that at night, when the patients sink into their dreams," she looked around the room, as if checking to see whether the doors were still closed, "quite a few scream their heads off." She shook her head. "I also heard that the patients at an asylum in Sussex are getting out sooner. Either they've been getting more mild cases or the doctors there are better."

Malcolm looked down at the remaining porridge; he was no longer hungry. What awful surroundings for his father to be incarcerated, unable to break out. Just then, a shiver ran through him. How did they keep men like his father from escaping?

Just then the door to what must be the dining hall opened with a thud. Both he and Mrs. Hopkins flinched with alarm. A man wearing a tunic walked in.

"Henry," Mrs. Hopkins said in acknowledgement.

"Good morning to you," Henry said, ignoring Malcolm. The man was probably in his thirties, stocky. Perhaps his strength was needed when patients got out of hand. He began the noisy process of dropping flatware on a large tray.

"Be sure to polish the silver well, Henry. His Majesty will be attending luncheon today." She winked at Malcolm.

"Right you are, Mrs. Hopkins." Henry said, carrying on with the charade. "Nothing but the best today." He picked up the tray and went into the dining hall.

"Guildford House has only male stewards," she explained. "No matron, no sisters. The Deputy Medical Superintendent, the one who runs this place, Mr. Smithers, he's a tough one, he is. They say he thinks women would be too soft on the poor officers, that the patients need to be made into men again, like real soldiers."

She added, her tone conspiratorial, "If you ask me? I'd say that they need just the opposite, some softness, some compassion. But I'm not the ruddy Deputy Medical Super, and that Mr. Smithers doesn't want to hear from me."

Over the rim of her cup, she added, "It didn't help one bit when young Hester carried on like some hysterical fool the time Old Piggy— that's what he calls himself; I wouldn't be so cruel—grabbed onto her in the dining hall. I'm sure he didn't mean anything by it, not really. But Hester ran out never to come back, and after Piggy got out of solitary confinement—that'd be a room in the cellar—some of his fellow patients blackened his eyes for him."

She then breezily explained how the house was laid out, the upper west wing's occupants being comprised of those who could enjoy relative freedom to move about, the ones who ate in the dining hall, the ones trusted not to use forks as weapons.

"Those chaps are the ones who have the eye tics or who are learning to control their hands and legs. A few of them mumble to themselves but are gentle, like children."

The east wing patients were impaired enough, for one reason or another, so that their meals were brought up.

"Since I've been here," Mrs. Hopkins said, "none so far has needed to be fed as a babe would, though a few need to be watched by the stewards. Some of those patients are prone to having seizures of one kind or another. Still, most behave like the refined gentlemen that they are."

She explained further how in either wing, those officers of greater financial means had their own rooms. The top floor housed, in what had been the ballroom, those who bordered on complete madness. Only their military status and funds kept them from the horrors of an actual lunatic asylum.

"Not that it really matters," Mrs. Hopkins said. "I don't see how it could be worse there, not when such sternness is being meted out here. Old Smithers, that super I'd mentioned, behaves as if he's ashamed of these poor men. The stewards are mostly a nice lot; and it is them wot take trays of food to the top floor. Good thing. I can't stand seeing some of them chained up. War is such an awful thing. God help us all."

His blood ran cold.

She stood. "You and me, Jack, we got the dining hall and maybe the first floor, up where they needs it brought; that is, if Henry gets tied up on the top floor and can't get to it on time. And, Lord knows, they'd love to do just that to him up there. I'd like to see it myself. But never mind my silliness. Are yer ready for an education you'll never find in books?"

"Yes, ma'am."

Chapter Twenty-Four

There were only four men sitting at the long table when Malcolm entered the dining room. His father was not there. It was early; he judged that from Mrs. Hopkins' unhurried pace since he hadn't seen a clock yet. Perhaps these officers had never left after breakfast. For those who couldn't concentrate to read or enjoy a regular conversation, he supposed that there wasn't much else for them to do.

After setting the tureen of onion gravy on the table—they were serving bangers and mash—he looked around surreptitiously while adjusting place settings. Evidently more patients were expected for the mid-day meal. Two men occupied the closest chairs, their backs to the kitchen door. They were older, looking to be about his father's age.

Malcolm looked away and considered the room. Once elegant, its walls bore a number of battle scars, as if chairs had been thrown about, perhaps, on more than one occasion. Other than the grand size, the tall cove ceiling and millwork, the room offered little personality, having no carpet or paintings.

Before returning to the kitchen, he shot a glance toward the younger officers sitting at the far end. One sat stone-cold still; if his fingers hadn't been twitching, he could have been mistaken for dead. The other man met Malcolm's gaze with intensity, sending an icy shiver down his spine. The patient's eyes betrayed a busy mind, a mind that must have a measure of sanity since the man was in the dining room. Malcolm tried to tell himself that the malevolent expression had nothing to do with him. He left to get the platters of sausages.

After taking care of the dining room, Malcolm stood in the middle of the kitchen while Mrs. Hopkins introduced him to Henry and another steward named Johnny. The men were arranging trays to take upstairs.

"I'll be glad to help serve upstairs, as well," Malcolm offered, looking from Mrs. Hopkins to Henry. "If not now, for tonight."

"We're on it, young man." Henry gathered up his loaded tray. Someone pushed through the door.

Johnny said, "Ah, 'morning to you, Mr. Boggs, sir."

Boggs! The admissions steward. Malcolm's breath caught in his throat.

Samuel Boggs adjusted his tie, shot his sleeves and brushed his lapels. Malcolm couldn't imagine why the man's appearance would matter in this mundane setting. He hadn't noticed Boggs' vanity or self-consciousness while here visiting his father with Aunt Jane and Wendell. But this was the same man that had been digging in the stables.

Malcolm shoved his borrowed spectacles up tight against his brows, hoping he'd not be recognized, hoping the scratched lenses blurred his features enough. He next looked around for something to do and grabbed a towel to begin drying dishes. The position allowed him surreptitious glances toward the room's occupants.

Johnny lifted up his tray and followed Henry out. The sound of the door swinging closed garbled a comment. Their footsteps receded.

"Now, you don't have to do that, Jack," Mrs. Hopkins cried. "Come over here and meet Mr. Boggs, our admissions steward."

That was exactly what Malcolm had hoped to avoid. If anyone was going to recognize him, it would be Boggs.

There was nothing for Malcolm to do but set down the towel and cross the linoleum floor.

"This boy, Mr. Boggs, is a wonderful worker. I took him in today so he could earn a meal or two."

Boggs only glanced at him, as if he couldn't be bothered. Relief flushed through Malcolm. It was the first time he'd welcomed indifference.

She added, "We never did replace Hester," her meaning clear.

"I will consider it, Mrs. Hopkins, and I will speak to the superintendent." Boggs looked to Malcolm and clarified, "that is a Mr. Smithers, lad." He nodded to the cook. "We shall see."

He touched her elbow and guided her away from Malcolm. "Now, we're having a little trouble with . . ." His whispering became a mere buzz.

Malcolm resumed drying the dishes. With that worry set aside, he could now consider how to get upstairs. His father must be staying in the east wing. Surely he wouldn't be on the top floor where those fit for Bedlam were kept. He had assumed Mrs. Hopkins was teasing when she mentioned tying up Henry. How dangerous was this place, really?

His stomach knotted.

Father, where are you?

"Well, there you go. You'll be comfy enough here for the night, I should think." Mrs. Hopkins stood straight after making up the cot Henry had brought down. It looked inviting with its clean linens and pillow.

"Thank you."

"I'll be on my way home now."

"Would you be wanting someone to walk you there, ma'am?"

"You are a sweet one. No. It's not far. Now, will you be heading out tomorrow or working another day?"

He didn't know. It depended on his mission tonight. "Uh, I just might stay another day, ma'am."

"Then I'll see you before breakfast, bright an early. Goodnight." She left the large pantry, her steps sounding quick on the floor until the back door opened and shut, followed by the click of a key lock.

He looked around the pantry, seeing it differently from the few trips he'd made here during the day. The room was wide enough for two of him, lying head to toe, and at least three times as long. He stayed in his clothes, set Adelaide's specs on a table and then stretched out on the cot. He would just rest his eyes before embarking on his search upstairs.

Chapter Twenty-Five

He awoke with a start. Had he heard something? At the moment, it was so silent he pinched himself to make sure he wasn't dreaming. Nights in the city always carried a constant hum in the air. It was different here.

The wind picked up. Leafless shrubbery tapped against the window and the woods around the property murmured complaints. But their sounds wouldn't be sharp enough to pull him from sleep.

Then, from upstairs, came that same low-toned wail that he'd heard while visiting before. He envisioned his Auntie's reaction, fumbling for her cigarettes; and despite her mysterious dark side, Malcolm missed her and wished he weren't alone.

Sid would have made a better companion, though. Together, they could have explored the wings above. He hoped he wouldn't have to look for his father on the top floor. The voice rose again, and a chill ran through Malcolm; but the wail was cut off, as if Henry or some other steward had wakened the patient...or smothered him.

Malcolm sat up, ready to soldier on. After taking a few steps into the kitchen, he stopped to listen for any indications that the stewards were about. He thought he heard something then realized it was the branches tapping at the pantry window again.

His muscles tightened as he pushed through the dining room door. When he was on the other side, he guided the door to a soundless stop and took a deep breath.

A flutter in his chest arose when he realized that dim lamps had been left on. He wouldn't have the cloak of darkness. He exhaled and analysed the situation. No one was on to his plan. The stewards would naturally need to see where they were going, should trouble occur in the night. At least with some light he was less likely to stumble and attract attention.

The stairway off the dining room was not the main staircase he'd earlier seen from the front entry. Yet its proportions were far grander than a servants' passageway. A threadbare carpet muffled his steps as he ascended. He had prepared a reply in case he was caught. *I heard someone cry out.* Beyond that, he could improvise or just accept the consequences.

At the top of the stairs, he took a moment to orient himself, recalling the morning sun in relation to the structure. The east wing would be to his right. Footsteps creaked above, and Malcolm's heart leapt to his throat. Noting the direction of the steps—away from the staircase—Malcolm shook off his tension. Probably a steward was crossing the floor to tend to one of the more incapacitated patients.

He crept along, deciding what to do next, when he heard someone coming from the west wing. Malcolm slid into the shadows of a recessed door, his heart pounding. He watched the central hall. A man came into view.

It was a patient, the intense officer he'd seen before lunch. The man crossed the landing and headed down the main staircase. Malcolm doubted that patients from the west wing were free to roam the house at night.

Once the man reached the front hall, Malcolm continued his search. There was nothing to do but to open each door and hope to heaven the occupants were sleeping as he sought his father's room. He should approach this plan in an orderly fashion, so he went back to the recessed door and listened. At hearing a soft snoring sound, he turned the knob. Malcolm entered, leaving the door ajar. No lamp lit the area here. It took several moments for Malcolm's eyes to adjust. He noted that the sleeping body was quite large—not the captain.

He left.

With stealth, he moved toward another door.

Just then, from below stairs, a ruckus erupted. A struggle grew apparent as two men argued. A chair crashed on the floor.

"Enough shame!" a man's voice cried drenched with vehemence. With a slap, skin met skin. "We've had it, damn you."

A call for help was cut off.

On Malcolm's left, someone behind the door rustled to action: feet hit the floor, followed by a heavy scraping noise. "Hang on, man. I'm coming. The bloody Hun."

It was the captain.

Malcolm threw open the door and groped for the light switch. He flipped it on. The dishevelled man standing in the middle of the room had his waist girded by a wide leather belt. A hideous chain ran to a brace fastened to the wall.

"Father!"

Before Malcolm got within arm's reach, he stopped, recalling the details of his father's night terrors.

"Father, it's me, Malcolm. I'm here."

Sunken eyes focused on him. "Malcolm?" The captain's features and shoulders drooped.

Malcolm approached. "Father, it's all right. I came on my own. I missed you so."

His father held out his arms. "My brave and brilliant son."

Warmth enveloped him. Malcolm's heart beat against his chest. He then realized a more significant pounding—footsteps racing down the stairs.

From the front hall, a man cried, "I'm calling the police."

Something else crashed and the walls shook.

Henry's voice, barking staccato commands, carried upstairs. Grunts and sounds of thrashing rose from the room directly below them. Moments later, Henry announced, "We have him secured."

A man near the phone at the front entry said, "They're sending over two policemen right away."

"Go on, son," the captain urged. "The fight is over. Go, see."

"Not until I can release your restraints."

"No. Go, see what's happened and report back to me."

Malcolm bounded down the steps. Once in the main hall, he turned toward the passageway that led to Smithers' rooms. Johnny stood in the doorway. Malcolm could see inside past Johnny. Henry and another steward stood near the restrained patient.

Henry said, his tone sardonic, "Now, what has got into you, Lieutenant Higgins?"

Somehow, Henry's attitude didn't surprise Malcolm. Higgins' words echoed in his mind. Enough shame!

Though seated and secured by straps to a chair, Higgins appeared calm, almost serene.

Malcolm nudged his way past Johnny and saw the medical superintendent sprawled on the floor, his head at an unnatural angle. Malcolm looked his question at Henry.

"Neck's broke." Henry sounded indifferent to his bluntness. Without a doubt, he wouldn't be missing Smithers.

Hours later, Malcolm and the captain were sitting at the kitchen table when Mrs. Hopkins entered from outside.

"Good morning, Captain, nice to see you down here." She nodded to Malcolm. "Jack," she added, her tone a question. "There's a Black Maria parked out front, I see."

The captain stood and explained matters. Smithers' body had been removed to the village surgery. "If I overheard correctly, the local inspector is waiting for Scotland Yard." He went on to say that Lieutenant Higgins was secured in a room upstairs for now.

Mrs. Hopkins, after hanging up her things and pouring herself a cuppa, sat and said, "It's a wonder we didn't have the storming of the Bastille before now, the Super was that tyrannical."

She turned to Malcolm. "This is a private facility, owned by Lord and Lady Hastings. The premises had been Lady Hastings' family home. I am sure they were unaware of the tensions here…since reports would have come from the superintendent himself."

Malcolm nodded.

Mrs. Hopkins took a pensive sip. The captain looked off, through one of the kitchen windows.

Male voices in the front hall rose and fell. The sound passed through the intervening rooms as a muffled buzz.

The cook looked at the captain and added, "There's a committee made up of the family, our MP and Dr. Miggins. I'm sure they'll get round to appointing a new medical superintendent soon enough."

"Scotland Yard is here," said a patient called Lieutenant Robbins. The man moved around the study like a gentleman at ease in his country home. This same patient had previously appeared as a gaunt man detached from the world as he sat in the dining room, apparently for hours on end. Whether the man's improved behaviour had anything to do with the end of Smithers, Malcolm didn't know and was too polite to ask.

"Not all rank and file here," the captain said from behind a newspaper. He was sitting in the same wing chair as at Malcolm's first visit.

Malcolm imagined that the situation *here* was anything but *rank and file*, if he understood the term correctly. Guildford Park House was an asylum for officers only, which often included those of the peerage.

His own family's status was respectable, apart from the captain's social awkwardness since the war. If not for the war, Malcolm had gathered that his father would have moved them from Stepney further north, perhaps to Newington Green. Aunt Jane had done so. The derelict condition of the Roberts' large house had developed only recently, a result of the family's loss of servants and the captain's condition. Malcolm had no idea what state the family finances were in.

Robbins turned and leafed through a book. "Since there's no question who killed Smithers, I'd wager the inspector has infiltrated the constabulary's realm because of the thievery going on 'round here; I'd mentioned the concern to one of the local police this morning. Forgot his name."

Malcolm's mouth went dry.

The captain's newspaper remained in its position. "What use are gold fobs and diamond cufflinks here? Mine disappeared soon after I arrived. I haven't had any call or desire to wear them."

Malcolm dawdled along one of the windows, keeping his movements restrained He hoped Robbins would continue talking.

"Maybe it's just the murder, then. I for one am happier about the loss of Smithers than upset over the loss of my loose change, though a considerable sum." Robbins replaced the book and slid out another. "Maybe the powers that be want to investigate whether Smithers' end came as a single crime of passion or the collusion of all of us. Maybe the local police weren't inclined to believe Johnny and Henry."

Robbins said no more on the subject. The captain appeared to be still studying the same page. With further enlightenment unlikely to come from the two men, Malcolm went to the kitchen.

In the main hall, Mr. Boggs, the admissions steward, crossed his path. The man's eyes darted here and there, preoccupied.

Unnoticed, Malcolm walked on toward the back hall. But the image of Boggs digging in the stable remained clear in his mind. Should he intrude on the investigation and ask to speak to the inspector? Police were police. He didn't relish the idea. Of course, PC Hawkins wasn't one of them, but still...

He pushed through the swinging door. "May I help dry the dishes, ma'am."

The smell of onions and scrubbed table tops filled the room.

"Oh, hello, Master Malcolm." Emphasis on his true name sat heavy between them.

He tried to read her feelings.

"Oh, yer don't need to work anymore, now that I know yer Captain Roberts' son. I should be miffed at yer for misleading me, if yer'll excuse me for sayin' so." Rather than anger, joviality carried on her contralto tones. Mrs. Hopkins beamed a smile. "But what yer did, seeking out your da, was a good thing. Nothing like a child's love." She wiped away a tear. "Would yer like a cuppa? I have some ginger cookies in a tin."

"Not now, thank you. I'd be grateful if I could help. I need to be busy just now."

"Well, if yer insist like." She waved him away to do the chore. "The clean towel is over there. Thank yer kindly."

He got busy. Mrs. Hopkins hummed while she chopped carrots.

The kitchen door creaked.

A male voice declared, "The, uh, inspector from Scotland Yard wishes to speak with this young man."

Malcolm almost dropped a plate. He turned. The voice belonged to one of the local police, a sergeant.

"The boy only arrived yesterday," Mrs. Hopkins protested. "His father is Captain Roberts, a guest here."

"Nonetheless, this fellow—excuse me, I mean this *Inspector*—is a thorough bas—, uh, stickler."

Malcolm set the plate in its place, dried his hands and then crossed the room.

"This way, lad."

Malcolm had not ventured into the office of the admissions steward, Samuel Boggs. The irony of the inspector choosing this room for his interviews added to the electric feel in the air. Had they learned what was buried in the stable? Did anyone else know about the location? The sergeant nudged him forward and closed the door behind them before going to a chair and picking up a notepad and pencil from the table. The Yard man sat with his elbows on Boggs' desk, studying a sheet of paper.

Though Malcolm had seen the inspector through the windows hours earlier, it now gave him pause to be before a policeman in plain clothes, nice clothes at that. Malcolm considered the man. Crow's feet fanning from the eyes and greying hair off his temples indicated that he was around the captain's age.

The man said, "I understand, lad, that you have been here a mere twenty-four hours, or thereabouts."

"Yes, sir."

"And that you were on hand to witness the unfortunate incident to some extent. Please tell me about what you can of the matter."

Malcolm's mind went blank. The man's eyes bore through him, as if to satisfy his assumption that Malcolm, a young interloper, could offer little of value. It felt like a dare. Malcolm closed his eyes to gather his thoughts. He then met the gaze and explained his observations in logical order. He described the suspect's cry about shame, how his father and others had been treated, and what he saw in the Super's room.

The inspector's cool eyes watched him without wavering. Malcolm also found it odd, even unnerving, that the inspector had not given his name or shown him an ID. He would do so with the adult witnesses, wouldn't he?

The inspector triggered a different type of vexation from that of Constable Hawkins and his cronies. Malcolm felt challenged not threatened.

Silence ensued.

The inspector resumed comparing other statements.

Malcolm wondered at a sinking sensation within. Was it disappointment? Had he expected to see more promise from Scotland Yard? Had he hoped for a higher level of...what? Capability? Brilliance? Decorum?

"You have nothing else to add?" The voice broke through his thoughts. This time, the eyes turned away—the man was dismissing him. The inspector shifted through his notes.

Malcolm cleared his throat and said, "I understand there is a concern over missing items here."

Both sets of eyes raised to focus on him. This time, with interest piqued.

Malcolm allowed some long moments to pass. "I did observe something else you may wish to know about."

"Go on."

He explained all he had noticed last night in the stable, the intensity of the shovelling, the location of the particular stall, and that the items evidently mattered very much to the culprit. He didn't mention what Robbins and his father had lost.

"I recognized the man in the stall."

"Well, speak up, lad."

"It was Mr. Boggs, sir."

The inspector listed off instructions to the sergeant, who was standing at the ready.

Just then, Malcolm wondered whether Boggs might be listening from the next room.

Cold drizzle filled the expanse between Malcolm and the Black Maria. As commonplace as the dampness was, the situation outside Guildford Park House felt surreal. The patient who had killed Smithers, Lieutenant Higgins, went into the vehicle without resisting the policemen.

Boggs was also taken into custody.

All but the Scotland Yard inspector wore dour expressions.

Malcolm didn't feel part of the common good with justice served. His father stood apart from the rest, detached from him again.

Samuel Boggs was anything but detached from Malcolm. Seething energy coursed from the man's glare. Had he overheard his interview? Had the police been sloppy with his account? Malcolm realized that he was the sole target of Bogg's anger.

A policeman shoved the handcuffed thief into the vehicle.

With unease, Malcolm wondered whether Boggs would be released. Or, if sentenced, for how long? Was some retaliation in store?

The Scotland Yard inspector and a sergeant were about to enter their motorcar.

Malcolm stepped forward.

"Um, excuse me, sir."

The Scotland Yard inspector turned, his expression unreadable.

"What will happen to Mr. Boggs?" Malcolm tried to keep fear from his features and voice.

Understanding lit the inspector's face. He nodded to the driver. "Excuse me, sergeant. This will take just a minute." He gestured for Malcolm to follow him. When he stopped just out of hearing distance, they were standing in ankle-high grass.

Cold mist clung to Malcolm's neck and hands.

The inspector said, "I should imagine you are wondering whether this man Boggs will be incarcerated for his thievery and, if so, for how long? How long will he be out of the way, am I right?"

"Yes, sir."

"Well, first of all, I expect he will appear before the Guildford Magistrates' Court. His crime is an either way offense, as we call it. So, I don't reckon the case will be bothering the Crown Court."

"Will I have to attend?"

"Unlikely. We have your statement. In this case, that should do."

"What might his sentence be?"

He studied Malcolm's gaze for some seconds.

Sporadic drops of rain plunked on Malcolm's shoulders and cap. An icy drop ran down the back of his neck. He wished they would tell him exactly what had been buried in the stall. Evidently, Boggs was working alone or was very loyal to his accomplice. How long would the man be locked up?

The inspector said, "Well—"

Malcolm then realized that this man never blinked during conversations,

"Seeing how this was theft without violence…and not a huge fortune, it might be five years."

Malcolm frowned.

"However."

The inspector looked up. His gaze scanned across the field.

"Since the victims were deliberately targeted…and since this was accomplished with some significant planning, it could be seven."

Hardly long enough for Malcolm's satisfaction.

"You could attend the proceedings, lad. Find out first hand."

"Um, I think not. Thanks." Malcolm looked down at the glistening grass and his wet shoes. "Thank you, sir."

The next thing Malcolm knew, the vehicles carrying their apprehended men were driving away and soon dipped from view.

Malcolm remained in his place, alone, with the image of Boggs' glare for company. Would the man reform or retaliate?

The answer settled in. Boggs would come after the stupid boy who should have known how to mind his own business.

Chapter Twenty-Six

Fire crackled and hissed in the study at Guildford Park House. The captain gestured for Malcolm to sit in the wing chair across from him.

His father smiled but said nothing.

Malcolm asked, "What do you think will happen to Boggs?"

"Robbins and I were discussing that before you came in."

Malcolm looked around the room. They were alone.

"Yes, he just went upstairs. Anyway, he tells me—his brother is a magistrate at London's Shoreditch Court—that Mr. Boggs' sentence will likely be seven years."

A sigh of relief escaped Malcolm's lips. It was better than five years, at least.

The captain added, "I have no idea what will happen to poor Higgins for his crime. He was driven mad by Smithers. That's my opinion, at least. Not sure what the point would be to send him to Brixton or the like. Being in an asylum is quite similar to prison as it is. Perhaps Broadmoor, but I don't see that there would be any harm in having him return here. Unlikely, though."

"Um, do you think I will have to go to court as a witness? For Boggs's case, I mean." The inspector had been sure he wouldn't, but Malcolm valued confirmation from his father.

"I couldn't say."

Malcolm looked away.

"Son, you are now above the age of responsibility. Your statement should hold. And if you are called in, I have confidence in you."

Malcolm's fingers tapped the arms of his chair; he studied the pattern in the carpet.

The captain said, "The good inspector nonetheless consulted me about your statement, as a courtesy, but it was an unnecessary one. Boggs gave himself away in the end."

Relief arose. He turned back to his father.

"You are old enough to obtain employment," his father added, "but you will be educated."

"Um, I can't think of that now, father."

Undeterred, the captain said, "You will be educated in accord with your potential, which, my son, is considerable."

Malcolm cringed at the idea.

"In fact, a friend of mine, a rather influential man both in government and academics, might even be of some assistance to you as regards your future. He was here to visit me a week ago. We had a nice chat about you."

A reply was in order. Malcolm nodded.

His father turned toward the lively fire.

Malcolm yearned for Stepney, for the life they'd had at home. He recalled a question.

"You had mentioned, Father, at our last visit, that, uh, a young lady had come looking for me. She'd come to our home, before you came here."

"Yes, a pretty thing with flashing eyes, lovely but serious."

"Had she indicated why she wanted to talk with me?"

"Yes. She said it had to do with the passing of your friend, the waterman."

"But she said no more than that? Left nothing for me?"

"No."

"Did she come alone?"

"Yes."

This was going nowhere. How else could he learn about her?

"Wait a minute," the captain said. "I recall now that she did join up with someone afterward, across the street. A man was waiting in the alley next to Drummonds' house."

That was disconcerting. Was she a minion of Julius Crocker?

"What did he look like?"

"Large. He stood in shadow, of course, in the alley. Let's see, I'd say it was late in the afternoon. Not that timing matters, I wouldn't think."

Well, Crocker, at least, was not large.

"Now that you bring it up," the captain continued, "It could have been a young man who is large for his age. I recall now that his shoulders were rounded. Young men who are taller than their classmates sometimes stand that way."

The blow hit Malcolm. He had to concentrate to keep any physical sign of it from his father.

The captain said, "Do you think she's a decoy? A troublemaker?"

"I don't know. Nothing to worry about, father. You've taught me to think on my feet, right?"

"You're one of the best, son." His brow furrowed. "But be careful."

Sounds from within the house murmured indistinguishably.

The occasional clang of Mrs. Hopkins' pots and pans as she prepared the next meal made for welcome normalcy. Bless the woman, Malcolm thought.

Malcolm broached the subject he most wanted to ask. "Will you be coming home now?"

The captain looked off through the window.

Outside, a bird began chirping.

Floorboards creaked above.

"No, son. At least not for some time yet. Smithers' approach has not helped. It was wrong." His hands folded before him, as if trying to keep his fingers from fidgeting.

"Having me at Guilford has at least protected Stepney's ladies of the evening." He snorted at this attempt at black humour.

Malcolm tried to smile but couldn't.

His father added, "I've heard some encouraging reports about other institutions." He checked his nails, fingers bent. Malcolm doubted that the captain actually registered their immaculate state. The man was searching for words.

"We'll be getting a new super. A friend of mine, the same one I'd referred to before, has assured me that there are those who are highly qualified and better trained. Better educated in the latest methods for treatment." We had discussed a possible transfer to another asylum. But now, with a new medical super on the way, we shall see."

Malcolm opened his mouth to say something. His throat felt paralyzed. Instead, he shifted in his chair.

"I need to give that a chance, son."

Malcolm nodded, his gesture unnoticed.

The captain's bleary eyes then met Malcolm's. "I have to. I'm sorry. It must be that way for now."

Chapter Twenty-Seven

Malcolm sat outside on a nearby rise. His muscles and chest eased in the surrounding silence. Ribbons of smoke rose from Guildford Park House's chimneys. He studied the place where the Black Maria had been parked, where he had talked with the inspector—and where Boggs had stared him down.

A gentle breeze carried the scent of decaying leaves.

Malcolm picked up a nearby twig. His fingers absently ran along its uneven surface. With both hands, he arched it, testing its limits. Bend, release, bend, release.

The captain had suggested he go out for a walk.

Malcolm jabbed the twig hard into the ground. It snapped in half.

His father's needs demanded more than he could offer, possibly even more so now, after all that had happened here.

He stared blankly off to the north. A dog in a neighbouring farmyard barked a short but congenial welcome to its owner. Malcolm smiled.

The morning sun hung low, clear of clouds, making the earth more vivid and satisfying, breathing hope into his nostrils and allowing Malcolm to take stock of his situation.

He would set aside his fear of Boggs for now. There would be time for that later. He would return to Auntie's flat and his daily routine. His father would eventually get better.

In the meantime, Malcolm would see whether Thaddeus Smith could be of use in warding off trouble for Limehouse. And, he would hold at bay, at least for the moment, worry over the clandestine activities of Wendell and Aunt Jane.

Above all, Malcolm would avoid contact with the Serbian girl. She sounded like trouble.

Chapter Twenty-Eight

Top o' the evenin' to you, sir."

Malcolm spun around on the walk in front of Merriweather Secondary and faced the familiar voice. "Jun, what's up?"

"A bit of good fortune came me way and I thought I might return the favour and buy a round of drinks—coffee, that is—at Jade's. And quick, like, before I spend it or get robbed."

Malcolm smiled, pleased at the generosity of this streetwise lad from Limehouse.

"Shall we hunt down Sid?" Jun offered.

"Sure, I was just heading to Stepney Green."

Malcolm and his mates settled in at Jade's with anticipation. Coffee was served to each of them. Darkness had already overtaken the Whitechapel streets beyond the mullioned windows. Jade had some candles lit. The atmosphere somehow made Malcolm's coffee taste even better. It was not yet Hanukkah but Jadocic Bojetu enjoyed the season of lights. Born into an Eastern Orthodox family in Belgrade, as Malcolm had learned, the proprietor nonetheless chose to observe the mores of the Jewish district.

Sid reached for the milk jug.

Malcolm said, "My family doesn't decorate for the—"

A whoosh of cold air and movement drew Malcolm's attention. A woman, no, a girl—*the girl*—approached. She gestured with her head for Jun to make space. He slid over while she situated herself next to him.

Words failed Malcolm as he read unspoken communication between Jun and the girl. A setup.

"I should have warned you about the slivovitz, Malcolm," she said with humor bright in her eyes, amusement at his expense.

Malcolm's lips pursed and he glowered at Jun.

"It's okay, Malcolm," Jun said.

The girl explained, "I asked Jun to arrange this meeting."

Sid's arm hadn't moved since the girl's arrival. It was extended mid-air, en route to the small milk jug. Milk forgotten, Sid set his hands on the table.

Malcolm asked, "How do you two know each other?"

"It's part of my territory, mate," Jun said.

The girl looked at Malcolm with a level gaze. "I am Katja Hasani. Joe Hasani, the waterman, was my uncle.

Chapter Twenty-Nine

"I'd have never thought—" Sid opened and closed his mouth.

"There must have been a funeral?" Malcolm asked, thinking how good it would have been to have seen Joe off.

"Just the family," she replied. A shadow crossed her features, as if she regretted not having sought him out for the occasion. Then her expression chilled, all sentiment ironed out.

"I want to find his killer." Self-possession became her as she got down to business. "Uncle told us quite a bit about you. He thought you had a brilliant mind, often said what a resourceful young man you were." Katja's tone indicated something unsaid. She held Malcolm's attention as completely as would a hypnotist. She proclaimed, "You failed *my* test, however." She cast a withering look his way, as though pitying such a foolish being.

"The slivovitz," she clarified. "I wanted to test your maturity. Utter failure on that count."

Anger flushed up his neck...but an intruding memory, like a paternal hand on his shoulder, tempered him. He could almost hear his father's voice. *A true man is honourable toward ladies, son.*

Malcolm silently cursed good manners. He took a moment to collect his poise—found it painful to ignore the quips he could have shared—and arched his right eyebrow by way of reply.

She added, "If you are going to play with fire in Limehouse—and help me find a killer—you can't ever let your guard down."

Malcolm lifted his cup; and with measured nonchalance, took a slow pull of his coffee, letting its warm flavour fortify his spirit.

A look of exasperation flashed in her eyes. "I've known boys to be slow when it came to words but I thought you'd be different."

"Miss Hasani," he envisioned himself as a captain or an MP, "why do you think insults will win me over?"

Without a blink, she considered her reply. "Because you loved Joe as if he were *your* uncle. Because you care about what's right. Because I have heard how well you can survive, moving around as you do in the East End despite being full of yourself and your gentrified background."

He wanted to laugh. He held back the urge for he feared it might turn into an insane peel of hilarity.

Just then, the din from the rest of the café saved him. Billy was clinking utensils behind the bar and that old diva hummed from the dark corner.

"Malcolm?" Katja's voice melted to something more civil and a slow blink restored charm to her eyes. "You passed this test; I baited you, and you held your tongue. Good." She leaned forward. "Will you help me?"

He took his time. "I've got a lot on my mind, Miss Hasani."

"Call me Katja, please. Will you help me...please?"

"You can't imagine what I have going on."

She squared her shoulders. "Let me at least tell you what I know so far. Perhaps you could advise me."

The sting from her disdainful tests still fresh, he merely nodded.

"A dock worker saw a man running from Shadwell Dock Stairs that night. For what reasons would a lone man run through the docks in the dark? Surely such a thing is more suspicious than not."

A number of reasons came to mind but he kept quiet.

"This meant little to him until he learned about my uncle. The worker, Harry Shippers, came by my mother's café to make mention of it, to complain how the Limehouse bobby just let the man run past. This man, he said, was lithe but awkward as he ran. The bobby just walked the other way."

"Oh dear," Sid said.

"I tried to get more detail but that was all Harry could say about it. But the timing, as I said, is suspicious. It seemed so to Harry, after the fact." She shrugged. "Uncle was a strong man. But no man's strength can withstand a sharp blade."

Silence settled on them.

Sid then said, "You're right. That's not much to go on."

"And another man found this." Katja slipped a water-stained sheet of paper from her pocket and slid it to Malcolm. "It was on the floor of uncle's boat. This man, I'm afraid I don't know his name, said it was found under the blanket there. Mum said he came to tell her that he was willing to keep Uncle's boat safe until she could arrange to sell it."

"Joe was well-liked," Malcolm said, his voice a whisper.

"It's probably nothing, but the man gave that slip to my mum, just in case. I imagine he couldn't read and wanted to make sure she had it…so she could decide whether it was important."

Malcolm examined the paper. It was an invoice for legal services rendered to the Stepney-Whitechapel Jewish Federation at Synagogue Poltava.

Sid slid closer and looked at it. "My papa is part of the federation. It looks like it has to do with a transfer of property or something to do with this address on Brick Lane."

Malcolm noticed some markings on the invoice and held it up. "I wonder what these markings mean, these numbers written below the address."

"I wondered about that too," Katja said.

"Might that describe dimensions?" Sid ventured.

"That would make sense but why a string of all digits? There should be some indication of north, south and that kind of thing, if it were. At least, I'd think so."

"Maybe it's just the solicitor's own calculations, or those of someone in the federation."

"I'd say the printing, though smaller, is similar to that of the clerk who wrote this out. I don't know why but, well," Malcolm considered the pattern, "what if it's a secret message?"

"Cor! A code, like in the war. That'd be brilliant," Sid enthused.

Katja's face lit with hope. Jun smiled.

"It's from JRC Solicitors on Jamaica Street." Malcolm's hands went cold and a pang thumped his chest.

"This invoice is from Julius Crocker."

Chapter Thirty

The older woman who had been humming to herself in the dark corner emerged into the candlelight and headed for the door. She fastened the hood of her black and red cape in place and left without a glance.

"Who's that," Katja asked.

"I wish I knew. She seems to be showing up everywhere I go lately." He turned toward Katja. "Hey, I saw her at your restaurant. You don't recognize her?"

"Her voice scared the daylights out of me. You're right. She'd been to our place, right after you left."

Sid ventured, "Maybe she was giving a kind of secret message."

Katja frowned. "For all to hear?"

"Secret nonetheless, to all but one…or a few," Sid replied.

Malcolm liked how Sid could get into the spirit of things.

"Should we trail her?" Katja asked Malcolm. He sensed a dare in her tone.

"No need to, mates," Jun said. All faces turned to him. "I know where the old dear lives. In Wellclose."

Malcolm said, "I'd like to know why she materializes out of nowhere—and so often. Coming to Jade's is one thing, but showing up at Katja's just as Sid and I were leaving?"

"I don't have time to lead yer there tonight," Jun said. "I've got a mission of me own to take care of, in Limehouse. But I could show you tomorrow."

"But I can't join you then," Katja said with chagrin. "We have a banquet to serve."

Malcolm wanted to point out that she wasn't invited but said, "We can't all of us go anyway, as if we are a parade."

Sid said, "I'm busy tomorrow too. Family stuff. Sorry."

Malcolm deflected the spark of envy and then looked a question at Jun.

"Meet me behind the music hall in Stepney," Jun offered. "The one off Cable Street, at, uh, half-past eleven."

"I'll be there."

"What about that invoice?" Katja asked.

Malcolm folded it and slipped it into his jacket pocket. "I want to work on those numbers. They could be nothing."

"Does your mum know the man who brought it?" Sid asked Katja. "I mean, does she trust him? It's a little fishy."

"She's a wise woman. She's had to be. I believe her instincts. She's not doubting the man that gave it to her. Whether or not someone else is winding us up, we'll—

"We'll just have to figure it out," Malcolm finished.

His hold on her approval might be tentative, but that earned him a lovely smile.

Malcolm added, "If this *is* something," he patted his pocket, "I'll get word to you somehow at your place, Katja." He nodded in Jun's direction to indicate—what? That he'd ask Jun to go? That he was too uninterested in Katja to contact her himself? Was he?

He left it at that.

Chapter Thirty-One

Even in Stepney, horse manure and debris had been regularly swept off the streets before the war. At least that is what Malcolm had been told. As a young child, the borough, the totality of his world, had lent orderliness and a sense of community to his bearings.

The offending horse nearby, attached to a beer delivery wagon, waited impatiently in front of a narrow alley and The Ugly Maiden pub. The animal snorted as Malcolm walked past.

If it were a summer's day, the droppings would be filling Malcolm's nostrils with their cloying odour. But more noticeable on this December morning was smoke from residential coal fires. The acrid scent tinged every sniff as he headed for Wellclose Square where he would find Jun.

The sky was grey as was the general streetscape. Small bits of dirty refuse lay in clumps here and there along the curb. A shiny Bentley rolled down the street, brightening the scene. A lady stepped from a dressmaker's shop. She was wearing a long fur coat and fine leather gloves. Malcolm touched the brim of his cap, and she smiled at the gesture.

After passing a number of buildings, Malcolm turned back to look. The Bentley had collected her. The car purred down the road in the direction of The City. What a contrast that lovely creature was to the woman he was going to observe with Jun's help.

The strange older woman, Madame Thibodeau, made for an interesting mystery, possibly a dark and dangerous one. He wanted to learn something about her. He did not believe in coincidence. His mind grappled with the different things she'd been in a position to overhear. She would have likely heard Jun telling him about Jack—not a big worry. She might have been in Jade's when Malcolm overheard Thaddeus Smith express his desire to write about the real world. He couldn't see how that would pose a problem. Where else might she have been lurking? Why?

Would she have been in Limehouse when Smith talked of the threat to the Chinese or when Malcolm had interrupted Jack's assault? She couldn't have been in Hong's. He would have noticed a Caucasian female, especially a flamboyant one. To think she might have been disguised as a man, whether British or Chinese, would be too fanciful for belief. The intrigue of it all, however, quickened his steps; and his mind shifted to a more down-to-earth matter: Jack Carrothers.

Malcolm had thought of himself as more genteel than the dishevelled Jack and remained vaguely disturbed at learning of the bully's higher station. Yet, people like Jack—like Crocker, and those who sided with him—held advantage. Lesser men and boys looked up to them.

Soon after entering Whitechapel, Malcolm noticed snowflakes appearing. His mood improved as he proceeded along Cable Street. He walked with more spring and strutted among the Sunday afternoon crowd. Jun should be waiting for him behind Gilley's Music Hall.

The snow had begun accumulating on the pavement by the time Malcolm approached the music hall. His steps crunched in time with the small orchestra inside as it accompanied some male singer. The melodic song was unfamiliar but its lyrics were no doubt bawdy. Discovering what he might learn was vastly more interesting to him than mere entertainment.

"D'yer want to be a hootchie kootchie dancer or somethin'?" Jun called out from between the garbage bins near the stage door.

"You ought to try it yourself. It's fun." Malcolm laid into his sliding, crunching steps, relishing the moves of his spoof dance. "Haroo!"

Jun fell in step beside him but moved with more dignity. "This way, then. Just up ahead and down Fletcher."

At the corner, Jun pointed toward the block of flats. "That fourth one, there."

"What do you propose?"

"I was thinkin'," he paused to read Malcolm's features, "that I'd look up some boys I know in the back ways. Ask a few questions. You could either watch for any comings and goings round her place, or go right up and invite yerself to tea."

Malcolm would have preferred to stick with Jun but was loath to show any weakness. He hesitated.

"It's like this, mate. I know yer know yer way round the streets, like, but me and you is different." He pointed toward the alley linking the square with the back ways. "That kind back there won't take to yer."

"So I just spy out the land here in the square, right?"

"I knew you were a bright chap."

"All right. When and where do we meet up again?"

Jun checked a clock tower Malcolm hadn't noticed.

"When the bells toll the hour, meet here. Does that sound...agreeable, sir?" Jun flashed a cheeky grin.

"Yes." Malcolm watched the waif slip away between buildings. He then turned on Fletcher, walking slowly, and took in details of the area. Midway down, he stood before a row of crumbling Georgian town homes, many of which had long been operating as rooming houses or divided into flats, one of which was where the woman reportedly lived. Only the most generous person would call this area respectable.

It was less crowded here in Wellclose Square, and he felt conspicuous. He spotted a recessed entry to a place called Skolnik's Dry Goods. As he approached it, he realized the shop was open with a few customers inside. The archway over the stoop was wide enough for him to remain and get his bearings in its shadow.

A cool breeze found him. With a dawning realization, he sensed someone's stare. He looked in the shop's bay window to his right and locked eyes with a pudgy brown cat.

"Don't you look so smug," he said, as vapour hung before his face.

The cat stared him down.

"If only you could talk."

Various dark concerns crept into Malcolm's thoughts like stray cats. He could more readily dismiss his pains: the loss of Joe, his mum, and his extended family. But worries over the dangerous, or the suspicious, characters in his life proved more difficult: Boggs, Jack, Crocker, and Aunt Jane.

A waft from the sewers brought him back. He resumed his vigil of the street and the building across. Who was this woman? What was her story? Possibilities niggled their way to his consciousness.

He waited, fearing that he'd have nothing to report to Jun.

Behind him, Skolnik's shop door jingled opened.

Malcolm jumped out onto the walk and turned to tip his hat.

"Hello, Malcolm," Madame Thibodeau said. "Would you care for a cuppa?"

Chapter Thirty-Two

Malcolm might better appreciate such overstuffed chairs and marble-topped tables were they to occupy a room thrice this size. As it was, only narrow pathways on the faded rug allowed a body to move. Dulled sunlight filtered through sheer curtains; it was an appropriate light for noticing treasures of the past. Dusty books and yellowed news clippings covered table tops and other flat surfaces. Hanging above the modest mantelpiece was a pasteboard print of The Grand Canal of Venice.

"Did you ever perform in Venice, ma'am?" Malcolm asked in hopes of getting a conversation going.

"Of course I've been to La Fenice, young man." She enunciated La Fenice in an exaggerated fashion, as if she were speaking of a royal personage with familiarity or even intimacy.

He noticed that she didn't say that she had *performed* there.

She gestured for him to sit across from her. Had the tea table not been squeezed in between them, he could envision the chairs in such proximity that he would have to work at not playing kneesies. He shook off a shiver at the thought. She lifted the simple Brown Betty teapot and poured for them both.

Concerned about the possible state of the milk, he declined and simply accepted a sugar cube.

"I suppose you are wondering," she began.

He examined her features, trying to figure out her game.

"Um, I'm afraid I wonder about more things than are good for me, ma'am."

She broke into a laugh, a laugh so free and healthy, it melted some of his tension.

She pulled out a wrinkled handkerchief from her sleeve and wiped her puffy eyes. "I will grant you a cheer for being ambitious, at least. And," she met his gaze, "if I may be so bold, I find that you must be the most circumspect young man I have ever run across."

He considered that for a moment. How could she know what his life was like? "Uh, thank you," he offered weakly.

"I never gossip. So, I cannot give you specifics. If you were an ordinary young man, I would offer you no clues whatever, for I would loath wasting information."

What on earth was she on about?

She regressed again, but this time into silence. One hand gripped the chair's upholstered arm while the gnarled fingers of the other went to her faux Faberge brooch. For long moments she stroked its smooth-looking surface.

"The hatred of foreigners by certain of our countrymen is disgraceful. It is also a very complex matter, sometimes laced with political shenanigans, certainly with fear, but sometimes...with something more personal."

"Um, I am afraid I don't understand the topic."

"You will."

The clock ticked. Were he not keen on getting answers, its sound could lull him to sleep.

"What should I understand by the *something more personal?*"

She reared up as if struck by the question, though her manner was not negative—more like a gambler's reaction had he just played a winning hand at cards.

"That, Malcolm Roberts, is what you'll have to figure out on your own. But look here." Her voice took on an eeriness that made the whole point dubious. "There you will find dirty work afoot. There you will find motivation—a will to meddle and destroy." Her rheumy eyes returned their focus on him. "There you find the motivation to kill."

Outside, the bells rang the hour, but he had much to learn.

She got to her feet with alarming decision.

Bemused, he added, "Um, before I go, Madame Thibodeau. I don't know how else to ask this. Well, actually, I wish to ask two questions."

Her eyes, still trained on him, were transformed with steely intent, as if to cast a spell or curse, one that would stay his mouth from babbling, as was done to Mozart's Papageno.

He willed himself onward. "How did you come to know my name?"

"I would venture to say that everyone who frequents Jade's knows your name," she said, too ready with the reply.

He added, "Um, also, I see you in many of the places I visit—and there is little pattern to my trampings. I find that odd, don't you?"

"I don't know what you're talking about, young man. I have only noticed you at Jade's. I haven't the energy to keep up with young ones, even if I had reasons to. Now, off you go."

Malcolm read something more in her than impatience with his impertinence. He smelled fear.

"You gave me some interesting things to think about today," he said, hoping to quell the irritation he'd caused and get her to say more.

"Yes, yes. I have seen much in my life. Now, it's your turn. Figure it out. Maybe, just maybe, you can save the East End from going up in smoke."

How could she know about that?

"Basta!" Her brows shot up. "Go."

"Oh, hi, Jun."

Jun waved off the courtesy. "While you was talkin' to the barmy Brunhilde, I was in fact able to do my own askin' around."

Malcolm grinned at Jun's personality, then asked, "First of all, how do you know anything about Wagner's Brunhilde?"

"Are you kiddin' me? You haven't seen Brunhilde's breasts? I mean her brass-brassiered breasts. Posters, my man. Gotta be a bit queer not to notice them."

Ignoring the jibe, Malcolm said, "Oh, posters. Anyway, what did you find out?"

"Madame's had a hard life. Never finished her studies as a young woman because her father cut her off after she eloped with a Frenchie. Her pa hated Frenchies. And this one was mixed with something dark. The boys didn't know if it were Pacific dark or Caribbean. Anyway, what they did say takes the prize—it were her pa that'd ordered her man's death. Nothing ever came of it in the courts. The stooges made it look like an accident."

Malcolm whistled in a low tone.

"Yep, my friend, Madame's had a hard life; no wonder she's a bit Bedlam."

They walked back toward Stepney.

The snow had stopped.

Jun said, "Hey, I can sneak yer a pint out the back of Donny Foon's, if yer feet can carry yer swell self that far wiv me. What d'yer say?"

Details of Madame's personal loss prodded disjointed notions in the back of Malcolm's mind. He needed to think.

"Thanks, Jun. Maybe another time. I must get back home, to my aunt's place, that is."

Chapter Thirty-Three

But life with Aunt Jane could disrupt time for reflection. He entered the flat only to learn that he had a dinner party to attend. There was little that could surprise him any more in her company.

He freshened up and changed and was expected to behave *like a gentleman* while Auntie and her friends enjoyed preliminary drinks.

The first surprise of the evening was that Wendell joined them dressed in tie and tails. No foreign garb or accessories. No pre-war leftovers. And it took Malcolm less than two seconds to deduce the cause. The ensuing party was to be at the home of *the snobby Harringtons* in Lord Curzon's honour. That in itself would likely make little difference to Wendell.

The *reason* sat in Auntie's throne-like chair sipping Champagne.

Sylla Le Feuvre's eyes, let alone the rest of the package, fascinated Malcolm, too. In one glance, those eyes could be coy, knowing, daring yet inviting. A stunning woman. And, for the moment at least, her countenance exuded a restrained interest in Wendell. Her right hand lifted for a touch of the gentleman's lips.

"Help yourself," Aunt Jane said, her tone dry and laced with meaning. She added, "There's gin or Champagne at the ready, my dear man. You know where they are."

Wendell kissed Auntie's hand and stepped sprightly to the drinks cabinet. He hummed as he opened the gin and poured a fair amount into a tumbler.

"Cheers, lad!"

Malcolm raised his ginger ale while sensing mild undercurrents of conflict next to him on the settee. Jane waved her glass cordially but then set it down. In a flash, she became the doting auntie and leaned Malcolm's way to begin fussing over his bow tie.

Wendell sloshed a drop of gin on his knee and uttered a mild curse as he sank in an occasional chair nearest Sylla. He might waste time and money, but Malcolm had learned that the man hated to waste a drop of his liquid spirits.

Jane brushed at Malcolm's clean lapels and said, "The Harringtons will be having one of those buffet dinners where we sit all around the place, balancing our plates. I do hope, Wendell, that a drop of gin is all you'll be adding to your ensemble." She turned to him and smiled sweetly.

Wendell was prepared to shrug off any offence; his smile for was Sylla.

Hoping to calm the waters, Malcolm said, "I didn't think young people, like myself, were included at dinner parties." He looked from one to the other for an answer.

Aunt Jane set upon Malcolm's tie, making sure it was straight.

Sylla began, "This is not your typical dinner, as Jane implied. It's more like a well-dressed picnic where we pretend to enjoy the musical recital while gossiping before and aft."

His aunt finally finished her fussing and said, "The Harringtons wanted their two sons from—oh, whatever military prep school they attend—to be involved. I believe they want their boys to get noticed by certain men of influence, particularly by Winston Churchill. Lord Curzon's presence, I'd guess, is a convenient cover. Ostensibly, the party is a belated congratulatory affair over the Cenotaph that he'd something to do with."

"You are wicked, love," Sylla said. "There will also be a few respectable military leaders and men of government." She checked the mantel clock, as if wishing to be on her way to mingle with such men.

"By having other younger guests—like you, my dear nephew— perhaps the Harringtons will appear less than brash." She gave him a wry smile and added, "Besides, I lied about your age. You do look older."

Wendell again lifted his glass in Malcolm's direction. "We have complete confidence in you, old man, and trust in your comportment." The encouraging words were followed by a slight glare that might have been a warning to live up to the notion.

The three fell into a silly discussion of Proust, banter bouncing about like a tennis ball, while Malcolm considered his mounting sympathies for his aunt's feelings. She was probably fifteen years Wendell's senior, but he'd noticed an obvious intimacy between them since joining the household.

Malcolm clearly recalled *the lecture* his father had given him last year, preparing him for adolescence. He worked at keeping the memory at bay as Wendell, Jane and Sylla talked nonsense amid delicate tensions. They were either oblivious of his awareness or were assuming their little performance might be of some future benefit to him.

Malcolm tried not to gawk at Wendell, but the man's enthrallment with Sylla elicited a mixture of embarrassment and awe.

Aunt Jane's husband had died at the Somme. Her efforts to maintain a stiff upper lip proved admirable, but Malcolm felt sorry for her as she tried to keep her hand in the game this afternoon.

Wendell asked Sylla, "So, with Lord Curzon as guest of honour, I shall assume we'll be graced with the company of Lloyd George?"

Malcolm wondered how Sylla would know.

"No, I don't believe so. I understand that the Harrington's disagree with his position on the Irish. They would have invited him, I'm sure. One must, in such a case, but I'd bet my baubles that the PM will have sent his regrets. I don't see how there could be any advantage to him in attending."

"Well, that shall make things a little less interesting. All we'll have for entertainment is observing the manner in which Churchill and Curzon interact. Too bad this isn't going to be a typical dinner round the table where we could all of us note the concentration of personae."

Jane's tone was dry. "In this setting, they'll have the freedom to avoid each other. That alone shall be amusing."

"Unless," Wendell stole his eyes from the younger woman and offered Jane a wink, "someone manoeuvers matters in hopes of some fireworks. I can't get enough of Churchill's barbs—aimed at others, of course."

"Do not instigate anything, Wendell," Jane said.

Sylla's finger traced the rim of her glass. "Curzon is still dreadfully miffed over Baku. He hasn't forgiven Churchill or Wilson, not one iota. But the dear Lord Curzon's arrogance can be—" Sylla interrupted her descriptive line just before it peaked with a quick glance Malcolm's way—it was *that look* adults gave when they remembered younger ears were present. She took a sip of Champagne and continued, her tone a step lower, "...uh, singularly interesting. I don't' think he's pompous, just arrogant. He simply knows his mind and deserves to be full of himself."

Wendell chuckled. "As a Foreign Secretary should."

Aunt Jane sat back. Malcolm noted less tension in her bearing. She said, "Well, he can be as arrogant or as pompous as he wants after saving Bodiam Castle from complete ruin. I was grateful to him for that."

The next thing Malcolm knew, they were up and heading for Wendell's motorcar and the Harrington's party.

Chapter Thirty-Four

Malcolm and his aunt crossed the marble floor surrounded by other guests. He wondered what one would call a room like this. A Grand Salon? A ballroom? He'd thought that ballrooms were typically upstairs, but, he chided himself, how would he know? This space was palatial with fluted columns trimmed in gilt and magnificent paintings and tapestries, each larger than Merriweather's blackboards.

His aunt turned from him like a butterfly spying an irresistible cluster of flowers. She joined a circle of beautiful people and was quick to respond to some witty remark. He heard her laughter behind him floating above the din, each staccato note clear and light.

Wendell and Sylla sidled off in the direction of the string quartet—probably so that their conversation could be more private. Malcolm then realized the convenience of their vantage point, ideal except for one pillar blocking their immediate right. He thought how much fun it would be to appear from around the column with a plate of pâté and a cheeky grin. It would unnerve them to no end. Images of disapproving frowns chased that idea off as he recalled Wendell's toast and backhanded warning to behave.

What were they up to? Were they flirting or planning a coup? Malcolm was so engrossed in the possibilities involved in their conceivable mission that he nearly jumped from his skin when a voice came through the potted palm at his elbow.

"Malcolm, look at the quartet. Don't look this way but listen."

He recognized Madame Thibodeau's voice immediately.

"It is vital that you appear as though we have never met. This is important. Do you understand?"

Malcolm kept his eyes trained on the cellist and feigned a cough in his hand. "Yes, ma'am."

"We can talk further some other day, preferably at my flat, if you insist."

"Yes."

"For this evening, ignore me as if I were a complete stranger."

"Yes, ma'am." He turned away from the fronds and went in search of a tray-bearing footman, trying not to walk into anyone as his thoughts whirled.

Moments later, his peripheral vision caught sight of the older woman approaching the same corner occupied by Wendell and Sylla. Malcolm stopped, hoping no one noticed his sidelong attention. There was no indication evident that the couple knew this woman. Moments later, Wendell escorted Sylla beyond the pillar while Thibodeau took a seat near the pianist. It soon became obvious that she was serving as the accompanist's page-turner.

"Ginger ale, sir?"

The footman's voice startled him as the well-balanced silver tray came round on his left. Malcolm felt a flush of satisfaction at being addressed as *sir* but wished this footman hadn't assumed ginger ale instead of Champagne.

Malcolm nodded his thanks and with drink in hand made his way to the room's far end. He hoped he was emulating nonchalance and positioned himself against the wall. He didn't care to have any further surprises from behind.

Beyond the milling guests, Aunt Jane stood next to the magnificent staircase. She looked elegant among a small circle of chatterers. Nearest her were their hosts, Mr. and Mrs. Harrington, to whom she was paying rapt attention.

At that moment, Malcolm became aware of two sets of eyes trained on him from the middle of the room. The taller of the young men whispered to the other. Their gangly bodies approached with an undeniable objective—he was their prey. Each youth was dressed in his military school best.

Both stood taller than Malcolm when they introduced themselves.

"Welcome to our home. I'm Alistair Harrington and my brother here is Miles."

Malcolm followed suit with the introductory chitchat but was feeling claustrophobic. Not only were these Harringtons hovering over him, the whole room seemed to be slanting his way. A number of gentlemen laughed too loudly over their drinks. It felt as if numerous bodies had suddenly closed in.

Alistair said, "We attend Walburn Military Academy. Where do you go to school?"

Malcolm dreaded this. "Merriweather Secondary."

Alistair pursed his lips, evidently biting back some insulting remark. Thank goodness this Harrington had the manners to hold a mean spirit.

Miles said, "My brother is captain of our rugby team. What do you play?"

Malcolm considered his reply.

"What is your sport, man?" Alistair pursued.

"Running." Malcolm couldn't help but smile at the sound of his answer. Images of his adventures in the East End flashed through his mind.

"You mean track and field," Miles said.

"Sure."

"What good is that?" Miles asked, less politely.

"Oh, you'd be surprised how advantageous it can be." Malcolm decided to take the offensive and added, "I'll be training for the Olympics when I enter preparatory school. I intend to beat the record set by the Flying Finn, Paavo Nurmi."

Their eyes widened. Could he be gaining credibility that easily?

Alistair said, "In addition to Lord Curzon, our guest of honour, we also have Mr. Winston Churchill among us tonight. Miles and I hope to be introduced to him. We intend to enter Sandhurst as he had done."

No reasonable reply came to Malcolm's mind.

Fortunately, the throng began moving from the room's centre. Mr. and Mrs. Harrington positioned themselves to make an announcement.

Miles said, "Hey, while everyone is lined at the buffet, why don't you join Alistair and me in the garden." He leaned in, his face flushed. "We've got gaspers." He patted his breast pocket.

"No thanks." He offered nothing further.

Each pair of eyes narrowed with disdain, and something else that Malcolm tried to decipher. Was it malice?

Chapter Thirty-Five

Malcolm stood among strangers in the buffet line. Although the minor Harringtons had indicated a diversion in the garden, they remained present, glancing surreptitiously but keeping their distance from him.

Evidently, the couple already dining with Mr. and Mrs. Harrington were Lord and Lady Curzon, both quite handsome. Aunt Jane was right: Lord Curzon displayed an air of pomposity.

Malcolm lost sight of Wendell and Sylla. Aunt Jane perched on the edge of a wing chair opposite an imposing-looking lady. The two engaged in what appeared to be cordial conversation, each still nursing their Champagne. Malcolm noticed his aunt's proximity to the Harrington table and imagined it to be intentional.

The gentleman next to him drew Malcolm's attention by saying, "Have you ever dined on kabobs and pickled onions, lad?"

"No, sir." Malcolm smiled acknowledgement at the inquirer before taking a closer look at the unusual items heaped on large platters.

The man began making his selections, heaping on rice on his plate and carefully selecting a skewer of cubed meat. He was paunchy, nearly bald, and smelled of exotic tobacco. "Persian and Indian entrees, these." He gestured to the generous spread. "In honour of Lord Curzon's taste for things Middle Eastern and Indian." The proffered smile fell flat.

"Ah, I see. Thank you, sir. What might you suggest for one unfamiliar with such things?"

The gentleman's face beam with good-natured interest.

"Those there are saffron rice cakes. And don't worry whether the figs, dates and sliced oranges are meant to serve as garnish. I suggest you enjoy them, as well." Malcolm noted the man's tone of authority.

The fruit did entice him, as did the fragrant rice cakes. Malcolm selected his choices. He vaguely noticed the gentleman's departure. But as the man approached the hosts' table, Malcolm couldn't help but stare. Without hesitation, the man took his place at the head of the long table opposite Lord Curzon. Whether he was a cabinet minister, a Harrington cousin or a bold intruder, Malcolm could not tell.

Chapter Thirty-Six

Malcolm went in search of Wendell and Sylla. He was lonely. Perhaps they would be open to intrusion now that dinner was served. He found them seated among the upholstered dining chairs near the piano. A handful of other guests were balancing their plates on their knees, conversing quietly. Four rows of matching chairs arced before a corner staged for entertainment. How on earth could a family own so many museum-quality chairs? Most of the diners appeared to be appreciating the music. Gentle pieces by Gabriel Faure flowed from the piano, melodies with which Malcolm was familiar. He'd learned a fair amount about classical music from his mother and her Victrola.

He was crossing the grand salon when an unmistakable sensation, a frisson of creepiness, spread through him. Someone was following him. Of course people milled about, but his intuition indicated something amiss. Without looking around, Malcolm continued on his way, happy to see an available seat next to Wendell, who slid his eyes from Sylla long enough to acknowledge him with an agreeable nod. Before Malcolm turned to sit, he looked up from his plate of figs and rice cakes to locate the two culprits, who should have been out in the garden smoking, but who were instead keeping him in their sights. Malcolm beamed a smile their way, showing that he was aware of their attention.

After he settled himself, Wendell and Sylla's warm welcome relaxed him. He hadn't realized until then how pent up he'd been.

"I approve of your gastronomic selections, old chap," Wendell said with a flash of white teeth and good humour.

Sylla leaned forward, her eyes bright. "You are doing so well, Malcolm. I could see you as a future emissary—or a spy. I hope you're enjoying yourself."

"Yes, ma'am." He silently cursed the flush that shot up his neck and undoubtedly reddened his cheeks. He certainly didn't possess a poker face. There must be a way to quell that reaction, and he hoped he would figure it out soon.

"It's a valuable asset to be able to blend in different situations," Wendell added, apparently blind to any flushed cheeks.

Despite the exotic fruits and rice cakes, it surprised Malcolm when he realized that his plate was empty. He could hardly recall the flavours. Amid the buzz of meaningless chatter and the bustling of footmen intent on removing plates, the background music, suddenly becoming stentorian and percussive, demanded attention. The recital would soon begin.

Mrs. Harrington silenced the vast room by taking her place as Mistress of Ceremonies. She began explaining the program, but Malcolm's attention shifted to the positioning of individuals. In the semicircle, it was as if he were watching a play unfolding before him. But he couldn't decide whether or not it was macabre.

Madame Thibodeau came round the piano and returned to the hard-backed chair next to the piano bench.

Malcolm slid his eyes from her and spotted the Harrington boys who were taking seats near the guests of honour, Lord and Lady Curzon. Mr. Churchill and the woman who had been talking with Aunt Jane during dinner—evidently Mrs. Churchill—settled in the row behind the Curzons. While most of the expressionless faces watched the MC as she spoke, Malcolm noticed across the way a gleam of mischief in Churchill's face. It looked as if he were plotting some schoolboy prank on the politician in the front row.

It wasn't until after Mrs. Harrington sat down and the pianist began that Malcolm spied his aunt off to the side, looking down, her fingers fidgeting. Why was she looking nervous?

A melody soon captured his attention. The music was Russian. Malcolm's mother had loved the genius of Rachmaninoff. He didn't recognize the piece specifically, but the music likely came from that composer. He closed his eyes and basked in beauty and warm memory and imagination.

He envisioned lovely but haunting faces. The young ladies of varying heights, stood at the edge of a hazy yellow field. Ukrainian wheat? The saffron of Central Asia? The grain didn't matter. Ever-so-clearly, the features of Russia's grand duchesses came into view. Their eyes smiled at him.

Olga had been the one for him. Marie was prettier. Anastasia, though closer to his age, held no appeal. He marvelled at the power of facial expressions captured in photography. The whole world, including Malcolm's mother and her ladies maid, had fussed over the Czar's family photographs as they had appeared in magazines and papers, especially since the massacre. Even in those staged portraits, Olga's charms transcended from magazine pages to Malcolm's dreams.

As a precocious eight-year-old boy, he'd realized that she was special. Over time, as he entered adolescence, he began to understand his attraction, an attraction that was as unattainable in life as in death.

The music and memory held him fast until an unexpected key change jarred him. The dreamy faces of the grand duchesses changed. Lovely features began contorting into expressions of utter horror. Genteel ladies slaughtered by the Reds. Malcolm's eyelids ripped open, his body jolted in his seat. He breathed in slowly and guessed that Wendell would have assumed that he'd just woken from a lulling sleep.

Without moving his head, Malcolm took stock of his surroundings. Everyone's attention was on the performance. He took comfort in the privacy of thoughts, even the troubling ones.

And troubled, he was. How could civilization survive so much unrelenting distrust and violence?

Applause broke out and Malcolm sat up straighter. Though he clapped, his concerns moved from things Russian to the potential tragedy close to home. A heinous crime, just as bloody, would be soon unleashed in his own part of London, if he and Smith could not stop it.

This time, Katja's face visited his thoughts but in a more elusive fashion.

More applause. Malcolm realized he'd missed the introduction of the next offering. Evidently, the next piece was to be sung.

The woman in the Chinese gown positioned herself near the curved bow of the piano. Her serious expression foretold high drama. Conversations ceased.

The accompanist began with a spectacular chord; then the woman's voice catapulted like nothing he'd heard before. Some of his mother's Victrola discs had been operatic, but the energy of this somewhat alarmed him. *What could she possibly be singing about?*

Some notes came as shrill but with purpose. What had sounded like a call to arms then tempered and dripped with sentiment.

Principessa Lo-u-ling were the only words he could snatch from the line. He could tell that it was a lament. *Must be about a dead princess.*

The nature of the lyrics took a turn and the volume rose.

Just then, the performer lifted her right arm and pointed toward the centre of the audience while singing an accusatory vocal line. *Straniero!* Whatever the meaning, he realized with a start that she was pointing at the guest of honour, Lord Curzon.

Tension filled the room.

The music then settled down but soon rose with even greater intensity, lifting the tones to a piercing call, as if this character intended to impale someone. Malcolm looked around, half expecting glass to shatter or possibly for the audience to flee. Most looked enchanted. A few gentlemen began studying their shoes or hands. He turned back to the singer.

Her diatribe then rose to a new level, a magnificent one. Malcolm's head tilted back as if blown by a wind. With wide open eyes, riveted to the performance, he felt every hair follicle on his arms tingle.

The spell fell apart with the jarring applause. Malcolm breathed in and then looked around for a footman. He needed a drink and he wanted Champagne.

Wendell leaned his way and said, "That aria was one of vengeance."

"Indeed," Malcolm said, sounding breathy.

Wendell folded his program and slid it in his breast pocket but not before Malcolm saw some writing scribbled on it.

Wendell said, "Evidently, Turandot is a princess of ice who wreaks vengeance on men on behalf of some maltreated and now dead relative. Should be an interesting plot once Maestro Puccini finishes it."

"When it plays in London, I'd love to go."

Malcolm realized that Sylla had not returned. He surveyed the large room.

"Where's Sylla?"

"She had to leave." Wendell's tone indicated that there'd be no further explanations as to why or where the lady had gone.

A gentleman approached and cleared his throat by way of announcing his presence. Had he just clicked his heels?

"Master Malcolm, if you would be so kind as to follow me, a gentleman wishes to speak to you."

Malcolm arched up his brows at Wendell, for guidance or salvation.

Wendell said, "Off with you, Malcolm. It sounds important. I imagine you should feel flattered rather than apprehensive."

The man said, "My name is Krupp, and your aunt will accompany us to the gentleman. Shall we?"

The sight of the minor Harringtons brought on a wave of relief. Their evident jealousy indicated that Malcolm was about to be granted something desirable, in their esteem, at least. What could it be?

Malcolm followed obediently.

Chapter Thirty-Seven

Malcolm ascended the stairs and felt the hard gaze of the Harrington boys endeavouring to skewer him. It was an exhilarating sensation, as if predatory animals at the zoo had singled him out but were rendered impotent by constraints.

The man to whom he was being taken must be important. Mr. Harrington would hardly allow the use of his study otherwise.

Aunt Jane whispered behind him. "The man we shall meet has held various cabinet positions and will no doubt hold others. I shouldn't need to tell you to watch your manners—but watch your manners, my boy."

Malcolm looked at Krupp for any possible reaction. If the man had heard Aunt Jane, he gave no indication but marched on up the stairs.

Malcolm slowed to let his aunt come alongside. He took her hand, then switched to holding out his arm as escort. Her fingers were cold.

On the first landing, they followed Krupp down the hall. The Persian carpet was so thick, the three progressed without a sound.

Krupp knocked at the first door on the right. After a muffled reply within, he opened the door.

Malcolm barely noticed Krupp's departure and the closing of the room's door. The *important man* behind the desk was the older chap who had introduced him to the Persian cuisine. The gentleman stood, albeit for less than two beats, in deference to Jane's presence.

"Come, sit." He motioned with his free hand; the other held a glass of amber liquid. The man sat back, suggesting that there would be no handshaking. Despite having assisted Malcolm at the buffet, a distinction in their classes was duly made clear. Yet, there was no ill-will in his eyes.

Jane said, "Mr. Churchill, this is my nephew Malcolm Roberts, Captain Roberts' son."

Her introduction felt unnecessary. If Malcolm had been summoned, who else would she have brought? Nonetheless, Churchill rewarded her with a slight smile and nod.

His steady gaze then settled on Malcom. It was cool, intelligent, and curious; but its power came from purpose. The man's face was otherwise not special, not handsome like Lord Curzon's. And now that Malcolm faced him head on, he realized Mr. Churchill was not as old as his receding hairline and fleshy features had first indicated. But his air of confidence offered more assurance that all was right with the Empire than Malcolm had ever felt before. This awareness of privilege, sitting before this man, sent a chill up the back of his neck.

Scents of whisky and tobacco wafted across the desk.

When Churchill's features relaxed, so did Malcolm.

"I met your father, young man, back when we were both of us stationed at the Front. We were of different regiments, I should say, and most of our interactions were within the confines of a pleasant but ordinary pub some distance back from the action when we were both of us off duty."

Malcolm had no idea what was expected from him. He nodded acknowledgement.

A gleam in Churchill's eyes indicated approval.

Aunt Jane's hands fidgeted on her lap. She wanted to smoke, Malcolm knew. But she sat ramrod straight and her attention did not waver from Mr. Churchill.

"Your father's heroic achievements were numerous. I was honoured to have made his acquaintance, and I'd like to think that he had enjoyed my company as much as I had his."

Something stirred inside Malcolm. *Was honoured?* Had something happened since he'd visited his father? Was he dead?

"I took myself to East Horsley and paid the captain a visit not long ago. He is quite proud of you. I hope you know that."

Relief flooded Malcolm's body.

Churchill's features took on intensity.

A clock ticked somewhere in the room.

Malcolm lowered his gaze.

The man said, "I'd be pleased to help you, young man."

The phrase went past Malcolm like a rugby ball sent wild. He concentrated on recalling each word and its emphasis.

"Me, sir?" Malcolm's voice came as a squeak. Could this man of government possibly know about Malcolm's hunt for Joe Hasani's killers? He'd never even told his father. Would Mr. Churchill help him with such a thing? Would it force Malcolm to talk with the police? Official interference might make that inevitable.

"I can guarantee you admittance into Harrow, if you wish. And then the Royal Military College."

Churchill's head tilted a fraction. "Despite your grades." He smiled. "I know enough about you to realize that you are more able than Merriweather's scholastic records indicate."

Malcolm almost asked him how he knew but caught himself. An inner voice held sway.

"Thank you, sir," he replied, his tone still high. He tried to relax and lower it. "I am grateful to you, sir."

He had no interest in boarding schools. Despite the unorthodox life with an aunt whose clandestine activities troubled him, he preferred that to having no home at all. He certainly didn't relish the idea of a military career.

Churchill read him.

"What have you thought you might like to do with your life?"

"Journalism, sir."

"Ah, I see. Well, time will tell. My offers will stand. We may meet again."

The interview was over. Churchill stood and nodded to Jane.

"Thank you, madam."

She mumbled an inconsequential reply.

The door mysteriously opened by Krupp as he and Aunt Jane approached. Before leaving, Churchill said, "Take care of yourself, Malcolm."

The inflection caught Malcolm by surprise.

"Yes, sir. Thank you, sir."

Perhaps the man knew some of Malcolm's secrets after all.

Chapter Thirty-Eight

"But it wasn't me."

The intensity of Sylla's voice arrested Malcolm's attention, pulling him from his warm pillow and the verge of sleep. She spoke quietly, but urgency in her tones carried down the hall from the parlour.

"I would gloat over the fact had I murdered Julius Crocker, but someone beat me to it."

In one fluid motion he was up out of bed and tiptoeing to his door.

"Wendell thinks it was the Secret Service Bureau," Aunt Jane said.

"You mean the SIS."

"Ah, yes. That's right. You know Wendell: if he's not in the past, he's in some other realm. But still brilliant, poor dear. The SIS would be what he meant to say. He's surmising someone from that department may have been involved."

An icy silence filled the flat, growing louder and stretching on.

With a shiver, Malcolm realized that they might have sensed his eavesdropping. How could they?

Aunt Jane finally said, her tone dramatic, "Tell me, when do you expect to return to Paris?" She was changing the subject on his behalf.

Footsteps and whispered low tones receded. The door to Aunt Jane's study clicked shut.

He returned to his bed, his mind racing as fast as his pulse.

Crocker was dead, murdered.

Apparently, neither Aunt Jane nor Sylla were guilty, nor Wendell, for that matter. He'd like to believe that was true.

Who were the SIS? Why would they want Crocker out of the way? The notion that governmental departments directed assassinations shook him.

How did Wendell know? Auntie had said *Wendell thinks it was*. So, it may or may not have been them. He'd like to allow relief to settle in. With Crocker gone, there might be no threat to Limehouse. But, then, what was yet niggling at him?

Was it a possibility that Auntie, Sylla and Wendell were not through with whatever it was that bound them in purpose?

He pulled up the covers. Now there were two murders. Was Joe's death connected with Crocker's?

It was going to be another long, sleepless night.

Chapter Thirty-Nine

The next evening followed on the tails of a long day at school. Throughout Jones' lecture on Constantinople, Malcolm had disciplined himself with effort not to doze or daydream.

The view beyond his bedroom window was dark. He sat at his desk. A small mound of newspapers sat off to the side. He had combed through them, looking for any news of Samuel Boggs' day in court and his forthcoming sentence but found nothing. The case involving the patient Lieutenant Higgins in the murder of Mr. Smithers got smallish mentions in two newspapers. There was nothing more to be found.

The green-shaded lamp illuminated various sheets of paper that now held Malcolm's attention. Instead of doing homework, he studied the sketchy numbers Katja had pointed out on the receipt. He'd wracked his brains over them a couple of times since and had written out different keys, attempts to break the code. He'd had just enough success to vex his nerves. Nothing new stood out this evening. He shook his head and allowed his gaze to instead settle on the two parties listed on the receipt: Poltava Synagogue and Julius Crocker.

"Yer not wearin' me spectacles, then?" Adelaide stood at his open door off to his right. How long had she been there? Her declaration carried accusation and hurt, and it shot through his core.

"Oh, uh...silly me." He scanned the top his desk. Pulled open a drawer, then another. "Ah, here they are." He placed them on and beamed through the scratched lenses. His smile said, *Don't you know how absent-minded I am?*

"Well, there you go." Her gaze slid to his paperwork. "What are yer doin'? It doesn't look like school lessons." On the plate in her hands sat a lumpy brown muffin.

"Uh, just my own ciphering. Little exercises...to entertain myself."

Her shoulders relaxed. "You've been holed up here since comin' in from Merriweather. Ignoring yer tea I laid out for yer in the kitchen. Here, I brought this for yer. Wanna cuppa, too?"

"Uh, right. Sorry. Thanks for the muffin. I'll get up in a bit and get my own tea."

She set the plate on his desk next to the receipt from Crocker's office. "You cipher on someone else's chit?"

What should he say? She was considering the slip. Malcolm took it and placed it on the far side, as if it were unimportant. "It's nothing. I found it in Whitechapel. Someone must have dropped it. Just curious how solicitors bill for their services."

She shrugged and limped back to the doorway, then turned to face him. "Yer want to be one someday? You'd make a fine one, I'm sure." She shifted her weight to leave. Her eyes brightened as she turned away. Was it from satisfaction? Whether it was from the crumb of acknowledgement he'd just paid her or something else, he couldn't say.

Quiet filled the room.

The numbers stared up at him for long moments, divulging nothing.

His window revealed black nothingness.

A nudge of guilt distracted him. He'd gotten sloppy in his manners with Adelaide. He was not a snob, and she deserved better. After the plaguing questions surrounding Joe's murder and Crocker's intentions were settled, he would concentrate on being more considerate.

He returned to the mysterious numbers.

20 1 11 5 x 5 3 20 7 x 15 6 x 10 3 21 3 16 11 x 20 15 14 9 7 8 20

After he'd first studied the pattern—after he'd had some time alone with the receipt—beginners' luck had seemed to strike. His ego had soared as he'd caught a pattern, after he'd thought to align the numbers with the alphabet. The first and last word became clear: *Take . . . tonight.*

Then nothing else fit.

The muffin smelled dubious, and he moved it to a far corner. What were the *x* markings all about? If the markings weren't for property dimensions, as in a treasure map, they could be for mathematical purposes. But what of the spaces?

Just then, a shiver went through him.

"A change in the code," he said to the room.

He shifted the papers on his desk. Where was his alphabet?

He leafed through a half-started book report, lifted his blotter, opened the desk drawers.

Adelaide must have thought it was rubbish. Why can't she leave things alone?

He grabbed a blank sheet of paper and scribbled out his letters along its bottom. After aligning it with the numbers—at the first *x*—he shifted the digits by one, praying that he wouldn't have to work with a Chinese or Cyrillic alphabet for any of these numerical segments.

A hint of motion beyond his open door drew his attention from the digits. Aunt Jane swanned down the hall away from him, as if having been at his door. He hadn't heard her come home, let alone approach. Had she been standing close enough to see his papers? Would there be a reason for her to have recognized the receipt?

Images of her with Crocker coming out of The George played through his thoughts.

He tried to concentrate on the possible numerical patterns but the image of Aunt Jane prevailed.

His stomach grumbled. He frowned at Adelaide's muffin.

He couldn't allow his mind to lose focus.

You can do it. Concentrate. Concentrate on the digits…double digits…spacing, the letters.

He took a deep breath and then shifted the alphabet by two digits after the next double space. Ticking off the digits, the second word appeared: *care.* He wanted to cry out, to hoot, but he focused on the next segment.

It was only two digits. He shifted the letters right, then left. Nothing made sense. He tried again and resumed the same alignment he'd used for *take* and *tonight.*

Of.

Take care of 10 3 21 3 16 11 tonight.

He was on to it. His fingers trembled as he worked it out.

Take care of Hasani tonight.

Malcolm had to see Katja. He got up from his desk. Entering the parlour, he found Adelaide rather than Aunt Jane.

The girl turned from stoking the fire. "She's in 'er study, on the telephone and can't be disturbed."

"Could you please let her know that I won't be here for dinner?"

"Neither will she." Shadows crossed Adelaide's face, but he couldn't contemplate her feelings at the moment.

"I don't know what time I'll be back." He grabbed his jacket and cap from the hall closet and dashed out of the flat and down the stairs.

On the main level, Mrs. Doran opened her door.

"You're going out," she said with some alarm. "Be careful, young man. I realize you're no stranger to dark streets, but please be careful."

"Thank you, Mrs. D. I will. Good night."

After he shut the home's heavy door, his feet tapped down the front steps and out onto the pavement along Newington Green. The park across the street stretched dark with night shadows while dim arcs of light at regular intervals marked the quiet neighbourhood.

He breathed in the cool air with relish, allowing it to stimulate his thoughts, and decided to walk rather than take the underground. He found the bowels of London transportation to be noxious and the commuters, rude. His destination was only a few miles south.

Katja's eyes will shine with admiration when I tell her of my discovery, he imagined. He had more than adequately passed this test.

He turned at Mildmay Road with his footsteps sounding a victorious cadence on the concrete. It was thrilling to know something vital that the police and Smith did not.

A brilliant bit of code breaking, he thought. His boyhood dream of sleuthing, like the character Detective Joe Phoenix, felt attainable. He could become an investigator…or a newsman like Smith…or a police detective—*no, not a policeman.*

His pace slowed.

Yet, other than a connection with Crocker's office—*big surprise, that*—his revelation didn't really tell him anything substantial or beyond what he knew before. Anyone from Poltava could have used the invoice for the message. And finding it right in Joe's boat—it could even have been planted there to throw off any investigation.

In a jumble of seconds, he sensed more than dark thoughts pressing upon him; he heard rushing footsteps and then a whoosh. Bright twirling lights flashed in blackness. The side of his head hit the pavement. He lay sprawled out. He marshalled his senses but his limbs paid no heed. Hands grabbed his arms and hoisted him off the pavement. Restraint shifted and, with increasing strength, gripped him in a choke hold.

Another man came round. A stranger. Then Malcolm saw the truncheon. The man swung it back and then hard into Malcolm's gut. Pain and panic sucked out what breath he had.

The man stepped in close.

"Yer gotta learn not to meddle, boy. Yer can't help the yellow fools." The man smelled like a dockworker. He then stepped back and slapped Malcolm's face with his bare hand.

"This is a warning." His other hand raised the weapon and nudged it up against Malcolm's nose. "If yer don't mind yer own business, this here'll beat yer brains out next time."

The hand with the truncheon swung back.

"No! Please!"

It struck Malcolm's gut again.

Malcolm went limp in the grip of the thug behind. He then landed hard in an alley. He heard garbled Yiddish and retreating footsteps.

Then nothing.

Racking coughs brought back his senses. He forced himself up on his elbow and spat. With dullness of mind and throbbing pains, he pushed himself up to a sitting position.

Pressure welled up from somewhere deep and coursed up his neck. Every facial muscle grew taut while raspy sounds rose from this throat.

"Muh...Muh...Mummy, Mummy, Mummy."

The inner contortion strangled his words. Heaving sobs unleashed. His breaths came jaggedly.

"Mummy, help me...help me."

He fell back against a brick building and stifled another sob. With whirring thoughts, his mind relived the violence. He ached for his mother's touch.

Shame followed. It hissed in his head, *The dead cannot help you. No one cares. Curl up and die, you pathetic boy.*

Malcolm picked up his fallen cap and struggled to control his thoughts. On the battlefield, the captain had no mother to console him. None of the men had. He tried shaking his head, to fling his devils away. A whisper of ease arose. Self-loathing retreated. Pain held fast.

With care, he breathed, regulating his lungs.

It took long moments to gain control.

A man walked past the alley, without noticing him. Humming tires rolled down the street, heading toward Newington Green.

Click, click, click. Careful footsteps approached with the sound of a lady's shoes.

"I saw it all from across the way," the woman said as she stood before the alley. "Do yer need help, young man?" The scent of perfume wafted his way.

She came closer. "I'm sorry I didn't call out. I, uh." She stopped. Through the dimness, he could see that her gaze was soft, compassionate, that she had at one time, not too long ago, been lovely. A woman alone after sundown. She must be a prostitute, he reckoned, a higher-class streetwalker. No wonder she hesitated to call for the police.

"Can yer get up?" She asked. "Shall I try to find a doctor?"

"No...thank you."

"You're bleeding."

"Yes. I think, uh...but I think I'm all right. Thank you, ma'am." He tried to get up with measured smoothness, as though he was fine, but dizziness made him stumble forward. She stepped in and held his arm, steadying him.

He smiled at her. "Thank you." He walked past and out onto the walkway. When he took a cautious deep breath, the woman's light perfume lifted his spirits—hints of normalcy.

He must get to Katja's.

He touched his cap's brim. "I'll be off. Good night, ma'am."

"Take care, young man."

He wanted to say *you, as well, ma'am,* but he kept going, limping in the direction of Whitechapel.

He considered the incident with each step. They must have been Crocker's men. Yet, no one could possibly know that he had figured out the secret message.

But Crocker was dead.

He had never before been interested in political ideologies. The possibility of a pogrom in Limehouse changed that. He began to wonder at Crocker's motivations when warm droplets of blood rolled down the side of his face. He wiped at it. Gritting his teeth, he walked on.

He turned from Mildmay and looked around, listening. Another purr of tires ran over worn cobbles. The sound diminished and he watched the vehicle's tail lights glide away down Boleyn Road. Nothing else could be seen lurking about. But, of course, hidden vantage points were more numerous than streetlamps.

The two thugs had done their deed. They would be drinking in a pub right now, enjoying their blood money, no doubt.

Malcolm spit some more blood and used his handkerchief to wipe his mouth. He touched the side of his head with it and blotted the sticky wound.

By the time he got to Wentworth Street, dinner hour was past. He approached the restaurant. Would Mrs. Hasani be rolling her midlands about for the entertainment of her clientele? He opened the door. A different pall hung in the air. He stepped in. The stage was empty. But the café was not.

Worse than the pain in his gut was that caused by the sight of Katja leaning across a table in deep conversation with Jack Carrothers. His broad back was stretched forward. She was holding his hand.

Katja looked up and spotted Malcolm.

He turned and walked out. Was she Jack's stooge? What was she playing at? Had she herself created the message? It was a distinct possibility.

"Malcolm, wait?" Katja cried, her voice piercing the sooty Whitechapel air.

His instinct was to run from the humiliation and betrayal, but he hurt too much; he hurt all over; and part of him didn't care, didn't care about anything anymore.

"What happened?" She blocked his path. "Who did this to you?"

She grabbed his arm.

"Ow!" he protested.

"Why are you upset with me? Because of Jack? I hope that's not why for I don't want to think of you as a fool, Malcolm."

"What do you know about him?"

"Excuse me, but what do you know about him?"

"That he's a bully who attacks helpless Orientals, that he's a part of a gang, a gang that's up to no bloody good. And that his tough guy act appeals to you," he challenged.

"I'd slap your face … if you weren't bleeding and bruised. Come. We should talk."

He stood there, his thoughts muddled.

"Come."

She took his hand.

Chapter Forty

Inside the café, Malcolm looked around.

"He left," Katja said, her tone and face unreadable.

Familiar comforts of the warm café, its aromas, seemed to be reaching out to wash away his anger. Just then, try as he might to hold back, uncontrollable shivering and fatigue took over. This, in front of a girl, would normally infuriate him. But the overpowering need for consolation won out.

Mrs. Hasani approached. "You are in shock. Come."

In the back rooms, the two cleaned him up, fed him and did not push for further answers after he waved off his experience as nothing.

He trudged back to his aunt's in the still of the night without having told anyone about decoding the message.

A chill, colder than winter's breezes, ghosted through his clothing. It rose from the smooth limestone beneath and behind him. Atmosphere was fickle. Abney Park Cemetery was no exception. It held no comfort now.

He tried to cast off the image of Jack with Katja. Why could he not control his thoughts?

Beyond the cemetery, buildings stood in silence, their windows dark. Most folks would be asleep.

Pain shivered down his leg. His head throbbed.

His mum could not help him.

Malcolm got up with some difficulty and walked away.

Chapter Forty-One

At the end of the school day at Merriweather Secondary, Malcolm passed through its halls and down its stairs to leave. Joviality and mundane conversations surrounded him but in the same disconnected fashion as did traffic on the Thames.

Ships had international destinations, workers a common goal. But on the docks, separated by water and space, isolation was what Malcolm had most often felt—until he'd met Joe.

Here, he had known his fellow students since shortly after the death of his mother. Schoolmates these many years, a lifetime of sorts, yet he was alone. Just as well today. He looked a sight with scabs and bruises on his face.

Lockers slammed, a free-for-all ensued with the tossing of someone's cap and general youthful vigour filled the air. Air that he shared, emotions that he didn't.

He'd reached the main door and out onto the pavement along Mile End Road without anyone noticing him, for which he was grateful. He was in no mood for silly chitchat.

"Malcolm!"

That voice was a different story. He turned back and saw Katja elbowing her way through the crowd.

"We have to talk," she said with authority. He smiled at her self-possession despite his feelings; and there was a hint of affection in her eyes. "Jun is waiting for us at Jade's."

"That's assuming a lot." He kept walking.

She kept abreast, her intensity relaxing possibly due to the fact they happened to heading in the right direction together.

"I will go only if Sid joins us."

"Fine."

He knew it was Sid's habit to loiter in Stepney Green in hopes of meeting him for some adventure. As the two approached the park, Sid stood open-mouthed, gawking at Katja's presence.

En route to the coffeehouse, Sid filled the awkward silence with boyish chatter.

Once they were settled with warm coffee mugs between their chilled hands, Katja got down to business.

"I know Jack has done some awful things. I caught him bragging about a pretty awful assault behind our restaurant one day."

Malcolm held his tongue but his expression must surely convey his feelings: *And you like him?*

She considered Malcolm's demeanour, took a quick sip and set her cup down. "If you only understood his problems, you'd be more generous."

"Is it your habit, Katja, to take on lost causes?" He regretted his words before he finished.

"You are testing my patience, Malcolm."

"I'm sorry." And he was. "Forgive me."

Her shoulders relaxed.

Sid watched in breathless awe at the interchange; he hadn't even sipped his coffee and was wise enough to keep out of the fray.

"I thought you'd have more faith in humankind. You did appear to have some sensitivity."

"I'm sorry. Tell me why you believe Jack is redeemable." He wanted to add *and why don't you believe he will destroy Limehouse?* Instead, he lifted his cup and held it just under his nose.

He took a hot sip. It was difficult accepting that he could misjudge a person like Jack.

She explained a few details about Jack's home life.

"He lives where? Near Regent's Park?" He was so surprised at Jack's station, the respectability of his residence, that Katja's mention of an abusive father escaped him for the moment. "What's the address?"

She frowned. "I don't know his bloody address, just the area and its...status."

He glared his disbelief.

She said, "There was no reason for him to tell me his address and he certainly had no call to take me there."

Malcolm shrugged.

"Anyone can suffer tyranny in the family." Katja gave Malcolm a withering look. "However, the nouveau riche are often ripe for abusive behaviour, in my opinion. They don't have generations of decorum to fall back on. More is at stake in their social climb."

"How do you know about these things?"

"My cousin is in service in Mayfair; she has seen a lot."

Jun appeared at their table, as if he'd been standing in the shadows. Katja slid over. Jun sat down.

"As I'd said before, Malcolm," Jun beamed with confidence, "I can tell yer exactly where the bloke lives."

Chapter Forty-Two

What could a young man from near Regent's Park have against the Chinese?

He entered Highgate. Jack's father was in Trade, but he evidently held a more than respectable position in society. The family was gentry.

Images of Jack dressed as a poor East Ender ghosted through Malcolm's mind: his hulking presence behind Crocker's building, his assault of that Chinese family in Limehouse, and stalking him in the warren of slums. Had Jack really tried to kill him?

What could be fuelling Jack's xenophobia?

Fear? But the Chinese weren't taking away any jobs in which Jack could possibly be interested.

Revenge? Katja had said that Jack was an only child. He didn't have a sister who might have been abused by a Chinaman.

Mr. Carrothers was a successful tea merchant, dealing more in teas from India and Ceylon than those from China. India tea was popular and not likely to be overtaken by China's. As far as he knew, the British Empire had enough tea drinker's to accommodate the various imports. Or was there something about the tea market Malcolm needed to discover?

Communism? With the family's commercial success, how could Marxist ideals hold any appeal?

Jack's connection to Crocker's group didn't make sense. Granted, a young man could, and often did, rebel against his father's ideals. But why resent a comfortable future?

Chapter Forty-Three

Malcolm recognized the sound, though not from personal experience. The unmistakable snap came from the garage behind Carrothers' house. He expected to hear someone cry out but stillness remained unbroken.

He stepped closer. Before he could get to the open door, another piercing whack sent a chill through his body.

A man's voice said in an even, intense whisper, "If I ever catch you showing disrespect again, I'll give it worse than this."

Malcolm was careful not to step on any gravel and give his presence away.

The same voice said, "My man has served me loyally since before you were born."

Inching to the doorway, Malcolm peered inside and saw an older man standing below a single light bulb and re-buckling his leather belt. On the ground lay Jack curled in a foetal position, whimpering through clenched teeth.

"I will instruct Wong to inform me if ever you show him anything but deference. Chinese or not, he is more of a gentleman than you'll ever be." The man walked away through the garden toward the house.

Malcolm turned from the door and stood still, listening. The sound of restrained sobs triggered pity and shame.

He picked his way back along the alley.

A dog barked tentatively from nearby. The sun had set, melding dark sky with low-lying shadows. Isolated arcs of man-made light marked the neighbourhood. Malcolm walked on, feeling numb.

Chapter Forty-Four

Katja was late.

Vicky Park stretched her sodden skirts in all directions away from Malcolm's vantage point. He sat within sight of Victoria's beauty spots, the primary one being the Burdett-Coutts drinking fountain. Its soaring cupola of pink marble and granite held his attention. From his bench, he could barely make out the clocks that were mounted on the shiny slate roof, each facing in a separate direction. Even more obscured were the marble cherub and the tiled drinking fountain within. It had been a gift to East End residents, providing the poorer ones with clean drinking water, as well as something for the soul. Her ladyship had believed that everyone deserved to look upon beauty.

Baroness Angela Burdett-Coutts. Malcolm liked enunciating her name. Surely, every facial muscle and relative nerve was utilized in producing the sounds.

His gaze swept across the grounds, past the three-story townhouses across the way, with their arched windows and mansard roofs, past the Hebrew cemetery and then toward Regent's Canal where a light fog was slithering in from the Thames.

In his mind, Satie's Gymnopedie played hauntingly, a contemplative melody that well-accompanied a solitary individual prone to musical musings.

His mum had sometimes played the record to calm him when he, as a toddler, was fretful.

After she died, he would go to her room and play the music, mostly on Sundays—until that day when he picked up the black disc from the machine and smashed it in the fireplace.

Cool damp settled on his shoulders. The tomb-like air was keeping most folks indoors. It was the first day of the holidays. Normally, Malcolm would be thrilled to be off school for so many days. But, in the midst of today's dreariness, he had to take care of business.

The only other person loitering in the large park was a man sitting in one of the semi-domed alcoves. These small pavilions were made of ornate limestone left-overs from the Old London Bridge.

A few people moved about their business on Gore Road. But no one would be able to hear his anticipated conversation with Katja.

He recognized her figure as she entered the park from the west where Regent's Canal and Hertford Union Canal joined. She'd already come over the old footbridge and was sauntering along the side of the pond. Despite crossing a damp and uneven lawn, she moved with grace and at a pace that indicated no haste to meet with him.

When she came within speaking distance, Malcolm stood, an action that brought a smile to her face. He thought it a dubious expression, as if she might be mocking his manners.

After an awkward greeting, she sat at one end of the bench, he the other, angling toward her though she chose to face straight ahead.

"Jack is not a bad person," she challenged.

Heat flushed up his neck. "I have seen him lash out against innocent and gentle people." He slapped the back of the bench. "I felt his anger up close when we wrestled. And later, Sid and I both experienced his wrath when he chased us."

"Have you never taken out your anger on someone else?"

"No." Had he? No. He had sulked; he had cried in his pillow; he had avoided others. Then he recalled smashing his mother's 78s. He cleared his throat.

"But you feel passionately about things," she said, "like helping that Chinese family."

"See," he said with accusation, "you know about his assaults."

She turned to face him and her eyes softened. "But, I realize that when you intervened you never intended to hurt Jack, only to stop him." She studied him, as if seeing him for the first time. "Have you never hurt anyone?"

He frowned. "Not with violence." He forced away memories of his failings and held his ground.

"Well, Jack didn't have the loving mum like you had. I know you lost her, but at least you had a mum for some years. Jack's had died giving birth to him, and his father has always blamed him."

She hesitated as she chose her words. "Over the years, Mr. Carrothers became dependent on Wong, his butler, preferring his companionship over that of anyone else. Jack was never good enough."

Malcolm sat up. "Well, I don't know anyone who has a close relationship with their father. Sid doesn't. In fact, I can't think of anyone who does," he chastised himself for the repetition, "and they don't go around assaulting others over it."

Again, her eyes warmed. "There's more to it, and, well, we are all different. You have to try to see that his actions are born from desperation. I believe he simply needs to be trusted and loved.

A sceptical harrumph escaped Malcolm's lips, surprising him, but he added, "Can't he see that he is not helping his situation? Who could trust a bully?"

She stood. "Enough of you, Malcolm. Just go and sulk away your life."

Katja stormed off, leaving Malcolm speechless.

Chapter Forty-Five

Jack evidently did not come to Jade's for the coffee. The large youth advanced to Malcolm's table. Jun and Sid instinctively got up and went to another booth.

"I would like to talk with you."

After Jack sat across from Malcolm, Billy approached to take orders, looking wary. Jack waved him away and then pulled out an onyx cigarette case—the quality of which surprised Malcolm as much as the fact that he carried one—and proceeded to light up.

A puff of grey-white smoke rose above Jack's face, Jack said to Malcolm, "I understand you know the Docklands pretty well."

"Somewhat."

An attempt at a flamboyant smoke ring failed. "What do you know about getting work on ships?"

Malcolm understood and was nonplussed at the surge of compassion he felt. He knew next to nothing of the subject.

He sat back. "I've observed comings and goings, loading and unloading. What do you want to know?"

"I need you to swear to secrecy on this. Do you?" The youth's fingers began to tremble. Jack left the cigarette to dangle between his lips and set his hands on his lap.

Malcolm caught the wide-eyed looks of Jun and Sid from across the room. It would be difficult not to tell them about this.

"Yes," he replied. At that moment, Malcolm knew he would help Jack.

"I, uh, want to see the world." Jack straightened. "I thought that getting work on a ship might be the ticket."

Did Jack know that Malcolm had observed his beating? He thought not.

There was no question that Jack was strong enough to handle the hard labour. And if he didn't especially like life on the seas, he could start a new life at any of their ports of call. India? Australia? The idea had merit.

Malcolm wanted something from Jack, however.

Lacing his voice with implication, he said, "Tell me about the meetings at Crocker's."

"They were stupid," Jack spat the reply on the table between them.

Malcolm considered the lad's features. Jack's eyes held no malice for him.

"What do you mean?"

"I was one of those stupid men," he puffed another stream of smoke, "naïve and ready to be manipulated."

A question surfaced in Malcolm's mind, but his nod encouraged further explanation.

"I owe a lot to Katja." Jack's gaze was resolute, as if he was not to be questioned about their relationship. "Those meetings and my shenanigans in Limehouse fed something dark that I didn't understand. It was like opium.

"Katja and her mum have helped me." Instead of elaborating, he pulled a slow drag, held in the smoke for long moments and then released it, aiming it up and away from Malcolm. The expression on his face indicated that the topic of Katja was closed.

Malcolm's attention returned to an ongoing concern. "Were there any women attending those meetings?"

"Yeah, one."

"A lady or a woman?"

"A lady dressed like an ordinary woman. She tries to blend in but doesn't. At least she didn't fool me."

Chapter Forty-Six

"Malcolm, could you get the door, please?" Aunt Jane called from her room. "Adelaide's out for the count with her nasty cold."

"Yes, ma'am." *One more paragraph first.* He tried to read quickly but succumbed to the narrative's magnetic pull and lingered. The book on China proved to be more interesting than he'd imagined. Why couldn't Old Jones teach like this?

"Don't keep them waiting, Malcolm. I suppose it's supper."

He slipped Smith's business card between the pages, crossed the room and opened the door.

"Jun!"

"You're in for a treat, mate." He held up a paper sack. It was dappled with grease from something aromatic inside.

"From Donny Foon's?"

"Yes indeed, my friend. Eggrolls, half a dozen."

Aunt Jane called from beyond her door, "There's money on top of the drinks cabinet, Malcolm. It includes tip and train fare for the deliveryman. Now there's a good lad."

Malcolm smiled at Jun and said, "Auntie's going out and her maid is ill and having only broth. Can you come in and help me take care of these?" He took the bag and paid Jun.

"Wish I could, but I 'ave to get back, and I'm trying to outdo Kou in deliveries this week." Jun tipped his cap. "Jade's on Sunday?"

"Okay," Malcolm said. "But if I can't, where should I send word? Foon's or the other place?"

"Behind Foon's." Jun smiled and then bounded down the stairs two at a time.

Malcolm closed the door. He half wanted to dash out and keep Jun company on the evening's deliveries. Instead, he walked down the hall and tapped on Adelaide's door."

She blew her nose by way of reply.

"Would you like an eggroll?"

"Ugh, no." More nose honking. "But thank you."

At the table, Malcolm dipped his eggroll in the mixture of tomato sauce and jam he'd made, a concoction he'd learned from Bryn when sitting in Wendell's kitchen.

He read on, careful not to soil the book. Good food and reading material helped keep thoughts of Katja, Jack and Aunt Jane—along with all undercurrents related to them—at bay. He hadn't thought much about his father during his busy days. Bedtime, on the other hand, brought on a host of worries. In the wee hours, sheer weariness induced a few hours' sleep.

The chapter's narrative, however, was fast becoming stilted as it dealt with the difficulty of China's accessibility, its vast uncounted population and its recent possession of Eastern Turkestan.

Unfortunately, he'd not come across much to help him understand the country's current political situation. If only he could find a book like this written since the war. He tried to think like a member of a Western government as he read on, but couldn't.

"I'm glad to see you enjoying those eggrolls," Aunt Jane said from the doorway. This time, she was rather elegantly dressed.

He dabbed his lips with a napkin and smiled. "They're a treat. Thank you, Auntie."

She made a small production of showing no interest in his reading material. He imagined she checked his room whenever he was out and about. If she hadn't, she would surely remark on the topic.

"Don't wait up for me, love." She whipped open the fan in her hand and held it before her rouged lips while arching her plucked and painted brows. The fan was Asiatic with delicate tree branches painted on it.

He wanted to laugh at her attempt to mock a fashion plate pose but only managed a weak smile.

"Yes, well, the cabbie awaits down below." She blew him a kiss and left.

After reading through increasingly irrelevant chapters, Malcolm set the book down and walked into the parlour. He turned off the lights and crossed to one of the front windows.

Across the street, and a few yards into the park, something gave him pause. The faint glow from the coal end of a cigarette brightened and faded in a slow rhythm. The dark figure faced Auntie's flat. Malcolm judged the silhouette to be male and stocky...and the man was unaffected by the fact that Auntie's cab had taken off toward The City.

Chapter Forty-Seven

From beyond the mouth of the Thames, the world's greyness brightened.

Malcolm had arrived before dawn as amber arcs of light stationed like sentries marked the Limehouse warehouses. Luminous reflections undulated along the waterway. The damp air smelled brackish with hints of effluvia, rotten pilings and tar; it was full with the hum of activity, punctuated by the occasional thud or clang. The Docklands.

Malcolm stood on the quay edge above where Joe used to moor his boat and faced the dock belonging to Lambert & Sons. Preparations for a ship's departure were underway. On deck, a leading seaman was providing Jack Carrothers with a lesson in some kind of nautical knot tying. Malcolm couldn't see well enough to know which type. He could identify a bowline and a jug knot, but not how to manage either one. All he had learned from Joe was the value of the Flemish coil.

Memories of his conversations with Joe flowed in and out like the tide.

I bet your mum was a real lady, Malcolm.

Um, she sometimes had a few ladies over to tea. Her laugh was lovely.

His mother's face appeared in his mind, a quick flash before receding to its abyss.

Pearls—she often wore ropes of pearls to tea.

You were there for the ladies' tea? Joe had smiled, his jab good-natured.

Mum wanted Nanny to bring me in for a short visit. I suppose she liked to show me off. Mum was cheerful at those teas. She was kind, kind to everyone.

I think you carry on some o' that kindness, lad. Feel good about that.

Malcolm retained more appreciation for Joe than he'd ever revealed in those days. Now, he not only grieved over Joe's death, he regretted not having shown more interest in his friend. He couldn't think of a time when he displayed interest in Joe personally. He knew nothing of Joe's family, which was why the appearance of Katja had surprised him. Back then, he'd been more curious about life on the river and had asked a lot of questions about that. It was Joe who had once, and only once, brought up his feelings about the Old Country.

Malcolm turned his attention back to the ship's deck. Jack appeared to be in good hands. Lieutenant Commander Wilson and his crew did not run on tyranny, he'd learned. As the ship pulled away, Jack looked across and his gaze locked with Malcolm's. The youth then gave Malcolm a salute full of recognition and gratitude. It was brief, for Jack was visibly keen on learning from the seaman, but that moment, the look on Jack's face, would forever be etched in Malcolm's mind.

Malcolm stood there, enveloped by loneliness, barely aware of the activity around him. He remained stock still until Jack's ship was out of sight.

Malcolm walked through Limehouse toward Stepney. He viewed its inhabitants with admiration. Many beat the odds, surviving poverty and crime. Most stood strong in the face of the East End's stricken spirit.

He approached the Tube station sign.

Shoulders of other pedestrians jostled his while the crowd descended steps to the platform. The underground commute and its sensations blurred with his brooding. The next thing he knew, he was climbing the stairs near Regent's Park.

Malcolm rang the bell at the front entrance. If the house wasn't imposing enough, the door was a study of British upper class: oversized, ornate, shiny black with a substantial brass knocker that was shaped like a gargoyle's face.

He tapped the grotesque head against the brass plate twice and marvelled at Jack's incongruence. The youth had merely pretended to be an Eastside ruffian in order to release his own pain—that was why Malcolm forgave him: they both understood domestic vexation, though Jack had the more difficult lot. At least Malcolm had some sense of belonging. The captain was mentally distraught. He had an understandable reason for self-absorption. Malcolm could now admit that his father loved him more than he did any other friend, let alone a household servant.

What about Jack's father?

Malcolm could understand a labourer's reverence for the ideals of socialism and communism. Mr. Carrothers made no sense.

The image of Jack on board arose, followed by that of him on the floor of his garage, his face taut with pent-up misery.

Malcolm let the knocker fall again.

A bird chirped in a tree. Someone down the block crossed the street. He waited.

The heavy door opened silently. The butler's Asiatic eyes assessed Malcolm's social position. The servant was strikingly handsome. His hair shone as black as a lacquered cabinet. And he was disdainful. To his credit, he hadn't relegated Malcolm to the rear entrance.

"I have a message for Mr. Carrothers," Malcolm said, "from Jack—uh, from his son."

Nothing, no expression whatever crossed the butler's face. His gloved hand took the sealed envelope. The odd thing was, Malcolm thought—in addition to the absence of polite acknowledgement—the man never lowered his eyes. His defiant gaze remained on Malcolm. The door closed.

Chapter Forty-Eight

Neither the cheery yellow walls of Aunt Jane's kitchen nor the smell of coffee could help Malcolm's mood. The room succumbed to the grey morning light. Drabness blanketed the back garden below the kitchen window.

Adelaide had been merrily humming when he came in for breakfast, but she was quick to sense his disposition. After washing up a few things in the large enamel sink, she thought of something else to do down the hall; she excused herself and left.

He was supposed to take his meals in the dining room, but it had no windows, or occupants. Aunt Jane had apparently come in late from one of her mysterious haunts. In some subliminal way, he picked up on the household rhythms even while sleeping. If you could call it sleep.

He appreciated the dining room well enough when it was full of interesting dinner guests. But here, he could look over Mrs. Doran's flowerbeds, which would be coming to life in a matter of weeks. In a vague way, the view nurtured hope.

Adelaide's voice down the hall broke into his thoughts. At Auntie's bedroom door, low tones of interchange hummed through the flat.

Malcolm looked around the room. There was memory within a kitchen: the consoling presence of Cook at his own house, a kindly woman who cooed a lot over him when he was a toddler—until she had fled the household.

"Do yer need me to warm the kettle again, Malcolm?" Adelaide stood at the door, her plain face creased with concern. "Yer haven't touched yer tea or anythin'. Are yer feelin' all right?"

"Thank you, Adelaide. I am fine. Just groggy yet." He took a sip of his tepid milky tea. "It's fine."

"Oh, I forgot to lay out me scones, made fresh this morning." She turned to the oven and removed a plate heavy with burnt-looking scones from the top shelf.

Malcolm had detected early a deficiency in Adelaide's baking. He'd noted Auntie's pointed hints on the subject. He'd also sensed indications lurking between the lines of the maid's complaints. *She hardly eats anythin' at home. I swear the lady lives on coffee, cigarettes and gin.*

Not wanting to hurt the girl's feelings, he took a scone from the offered plate and almost dropped it on the table. *What did she use in her recipe—powdered lead?*

He smiled his thanks, hoping she'd leave before he had to take a bite.

She waited, watching expectantly.

He brought the thing near his mouth. It smelled fine. He bit down and met resistance. He tried again.

Her expression fell.

"Did I forget the baking powder again? Tough on the teeth, is it? I'm sorry, Malcolm. I think I over-baked them, too. "

He couldn't think of a thing to say.

She said, "Well, the bread's all right, if yer want some with your porridge. Bought it from the baker yesterday. The porridge is good, isn't it?"

"Yes, thank you." He hadn't touched it.

"Then, if yer'll excuse me, I'll get back to me work."

He beamed a look of gratitude. She turned and shuffled down the hall.

He took a small spoonful of porridge. It was bland, but he swallowed it manfully.

He wondered at Madame Thibodeau's connection to the situation at hand, if there was any. Something in her history troubled him, something more than her personal loss.

Rage? Expressions of rage? Surely the most debased things could warrant such hatred, things like rape, murder and assault. War involved such things.

Some of the victims who had survived the Great War would never recover.

Would the influenza have spread had there been no war? Would his mother still be alive? The captain would be sound, no question there.

But Madame T's hardships came from another source: intolerance.

At that, a snippet of memory drifted through his mind, opaque like the smoke from Aunt Jane's cigarettes. It was a man's voice. *The world has gone mad, completely mad.*

The opium den! Some unknown man in the grips of the narcotic had said that. Was it so? Each of Malcolm's concerns came alive like a swarm of gnats, all wanting a piece of him.

"Basta!" Malcolm cried.

Adelaide's shuffling in the parlour came to a stop, but she said nothing.

He said it again, with care and a low tone, as if feeling the sounds in his mouth. "Basta." He didn't know what it meant, but he liked the way Madame T had said it when she had wanted him to leave.

Rage. Intolerance. Fear.

Malcolm slapped the table top and cast off the pesky gnawings of uncertainty. Like his da, he would keep forward, he would go over the top of the trench, he would prevail.

Chapter Forty-Nine

"Take that look of pity off your face or I'll do it for you," Katja demanded.

The harshness of Katja's tone neither surprised him nor dampened his spirits any further. What surprised him was his transparency. Malcolm thought he was doing well at hiding his feelings. The cluster of hovels surrounding a public well made up Joe's neighbourhood in Shadwell. No cobbles covered the alley or courtyard. The residents kept the mud at bay by paving the place with whatever bit of hard refuse they had no other use for, such as damaged bin lids, broken crockery and worn shoe soles.

Malcolm faced her, allowing his feelings to show. He loved Joe and knew the man had little means. But his wisdom and goodness had been superior to that of most in Malcolm's circle. He couldn't muster any words.

Her tone softened. "He was proud that he had his own house rather than an airless room in the tenements. A good thing, isn't it?"

Despite himself, Malcolm smiled at the thought of Joe being house-proud. He nodded his reply.

"That's his place." She led the way, passing a thin girl with scabby knees who was pouring water into a pitcher.

Only one door and one window serviced the front, but the place wasn't without appeal. Everything was in good repair and there were real curtains in the window. Katja unlocked the door.

Before stepping in, Malcolm noted some of the neighbours standing about. Evidently, they recognized Katja. All stayed put, silent, as if paying their last respects.

Stale air filled his senses with smells of a working man. Palpable, as if Joe would return from a short errand any minute now. The house consisted of one room with a small bed in a corner, a table and chairs under the window. It had a dresser—and a bookcase. Malcolm crossed the room and allowed his gaze to linger over each spine.

"Not many watermen read, let alone in two languages," she said. "He could have gotten a job of importance here were it not for prejudice."

Works of Plutarch, Dickens and Wordsworth leaned against one another. Above them were spines lettered in what must be Serbian. Her words sunk in.

"Prejudice?"

"Don't you know anything?" she said. "Everyone blames the Serbs for the bloody hell that developed after Sarajevo."

"Oh, right." A twinge of nausea arose. He should have been more interested in Joe's lot in life. He'd give anything to be able to change that.

He would take the time now. He slowly scanned Joe's books again. If only he could talk with his friend about such treasures.

"I could stand here all day." Hearing his thoughts voiced aloud startled him.

"I thought you should see where my uncle lived. We'll be cleaning out the place soon. It won't bring much, but Mama already has someone interested in renting it."

"Thank you. Thank you for bringing me here."

"You're welcome." She looked around. "I sure wish this place could speak. Mama and I went through it after the funeral in hopes of finding some clue as to what led to his murder. Nothing."

Malcolm ached to see the killer, or killers, brought to justice.

"Hey," Katja said, "look at this." She retrieved a small object from a wooden box next to Plutarch. "Must've come from one of his customers." She held up an earring. "I think it's onyx. And look at the painting on it. So delicate. See? A Chinese lantern."

She dropped it into his palm.

"Not valuable, of course," she added, "but lovely."

The painting on such a small surface was expertly done.

"Mama says I can have a jeweller make it into a pendant." She admired it. "Onyx is nice. So shiny. Funny how something so black reflects light."

He handed it back. *Yes, like answers in the least expected places.*

She said, "I'll let you have one of his books, if you like. I'd let you take them all, but Mama says she intends to sell them. Can't get much for used books but she is a business woman. And, well, that's how she is."

Malcolm reached for Plutarch's *On Sparta*. The cloth-bound book and the fore edge of its many pages bore slight stains from the oils of touch. Joe had never spoken of Sparta or Plutarch, but he had spoken enough of historical things that Malcolm found it easy to believe his friend had enjoyed this book. As a last minute thought, he flipped through its pages for any markings.

Nothing.

"You looked through everything for clues?"

"Everything, yes," she replied. "There are sixty-four books on those shelves."

By a gentleman's standards, that number was nothing. But for a Thames waterman, a treasure. Malcolm noted the pride in Katja's eyes.

He hated to leave. He wished to sit at the table and pore over Joe's books, but it was getting late, and he knew Katja would be needed at the café.

She was waiting at the door, and Malcolm was taking a final look around the room, when something caught his eye.

"There's something under his pillow," he said to her. "May I?"

"It's just a cosh. For protection. Mama keeps a knife in a drawer next to her bed."

Malcolm turned back the pillow and picked up the dark baton.

"It's not just a cosh, Katja. It was meant for the Limehouse Constabulary."

"What do you mean by *meant for?*"

"Usually, I'm pretty sure, the constable's name is on the truncheon. This has the crown and the constabulary name but that's all. It's new. No fading of finish, no dents."

"What of it?"

He was not prepared to say, but he was pretty sure of its significance.

Chapter Fifty

It was mid-day. From across Fleet Street, Malcolm spotted Thaddeus Smith coming out of *The Telegraph* building, a brown paper sack in one hand, a closed brolly in the other. Malcolm trailed him for a block and a half, then crossed over to come up alongside him.

"Did you imagine that I didn't see you, young man?" Smith's tone and curve of mouth proved ready for banter.

"I could only hope. May I join you?"

"You already have."

Malcolm walked with the newspaperman.

"Mr. Smith, have you ever had to report on a court case?"

"Why, do you expect to be caught on this fine Wednesday afternoon by the attendance officers?"

"No." Malcolm expelled a burst of exasperation and humour. "Merriweather's teachers are in some kind of a meeting in the auditorium. We were let out early." He trotted to keep up with the man's strides. "Have you reported on any court cases for the newspaper?"

"I wish I had."

"Oh, um, in any case, do you know what kind of sentence a thief might expect?"

"What are you on about?"

"There was a situation in Guildford that I'd like to follow up on, but I can't find anything in the papers."

"You could telephone the local constabulary or the magistrates' court."

"Um, I could." How could he explain his hesitation?

"Ah, but you're thinking of *The Telegraph*. Yes, there are several telephones. I don't understand your shyness—you are anything but. I suppose you'd like me to make the call for you."

"I'd really appreciate it."

"All right, then, but you'll have to be willing to run the odd errand for me someday."

"Understood."

Malcolm explained what he knew of Boggs' case and why he was hoping for a long sentence, all the while wondering whether Smith was paying close enough attention.

They came up to Lincoln's Inn Fields, a pleasant park that needed more benches. The snobby nobs didn't want too many commoners peopling their square, evidently. Three benches were occupied with nannies in earnest conversations. A very plump woman dominated the last. Malcolm followed Smith toward her.

"Good day, Madame," Smith said. He sat without asking and scooted in next to her, leaving a few inches for Malcolm at the end. He nodded for Malcolm to sit. The man's wink indicated a plan.

Malcolm obeyed.

"I do hope you don't object," Smith said to the woman, leaning so as to nearly rub shoulders, "to my lunching on some sardines and herring, Madam. I have such a short time before I must return to my desk."

The woman harrumphed and left. Smith slid down and pulled a sandwich of cheese and pickle from the brown sack.

Malcolm was about to ask about the fish and caught himself in time. He would hate embarrassing himself before this clever man.

After a shared chuckle and Smith's first bite of lunch, which he munched away at for long moments, Smith said, "I have news."

Smith took another bite of his sandwich.

The man must chew a hundred times before swallowing.

Malcolm looked off across the green, controlling himself with effort. Instead of heaving another sigh, one which was aching to be released, he took interest in a man walking a dog. The animal dawdled with indecision much like Smith was doing with getting to the point.

A butterfly alighted on a nearby shrub.

Smith's features drew together, poised to finally present some revelation.

"A shipment of truncheons went missing."

"As I'd thought," Malcolm said.

The man with his dog crossed from the park and then disappeared around a corner.

Malcolm asked, "How did you learn that…and what about the cricket balls?"

"I took a desk sergeant out for a pint after his duty."

"Did he know about the cricket balls?"

Smith savoured another mouthful.

"No, just that a case of new truncheons was stolen before reaching the Metropolitan Police Station there, about two months ago."

Malcolm nodded. Darker clouds advanced on the park.

After polishing off his main course, Smith opened a jar and sipped at what must be tepid tea. "I tried to get information from the River Police about your friend's murder but got nowhere."

Malcolm grunted.

"Except that they think the waterman got knifed off the boat and then was put inside and sent off to drift. It would have to have been that way, I imagine. Throat slit and all."

"Yes."

"They, whoever *they* are, must have wanted the man to be found, perhaps to serve as a lesson for others."

"They? Not he . . . or *she?*"

"Well, we don't know, do we?" Smith replied. "I only said 'they' because it would be awkward manoeuvring a dead man into a boat."

Part of Malcolm wished Smith would be more considerate when talking about Joe's death. Oddly, the frank expressions distanced the pain.

After long moments of silence, Smith excused himself, got up and headed back toward *The Telegraph*.

Malcolm remained on the bench. Intermittent raindrops pecked at him. Joe must have been involved in transporting the stolen goods. Very likely he'd had no idea the stuff was stolen. But maybe he had known. Images of the new truncheon at Joe's home nagged him.

A hard rain commenced, washing over Malcolm and disguising the fact to any would-be passers-by that tears streamed down his cheeks.

The rain had moved on and Wednesday's sunset cast the sky in pink-grey hues. Its final moments conveyed both generosity and unease while Abney Park lay in deep shadow. The chill from the mausoleum's limestone seeped through Malcolm's damp jacket and clothes. He doubted whether he could explain his need to come here.

In tune with the silent dead, not a sound came from the place. There was no wind passing through skeletal branches. No birds chirped. Not another living soul...except for the owner of the two Asian eyes peeking over a headstone.

If Jun didn't wish to be seen, he could have hidden more cleverly.

"Come," Malcolm called.

Jun rounded the block of granite and approached warily.

"Why did you follow me here?"

"I didn't plan ter. I mean, I came round lookin' for yer, that's true enough. Then I saw yer trudging along like yer boots were made o' lead. I almost called out to yer, but changed my mind. Then yer entered the graveyard."

Jun took his time considering the place before returning his gaze to Malcolm. The arch of his brows asked the question.

"This is my family's mausoleum. My mum's in there." He jerked his head back in gesture.

"Cor, I didn't know yer were a nob. Yer family's rich, then. Gotta be."

"Oh, I don't think so. Not now, at least."

Silence hung for some moments. Malcolm's gaze travelled over the effigies that had become so familiar, so close he could take them for granted, like family.

He said, "Even if my father were wealthy, money means nothing."

"Money? Nothing?" Jun's elfin frame jolted, as if he'd just heard blasphemy. His lips puckered this way then that as if his mouth were tasting the words he'd next say. "I, uh, I guess it can't help a hurt heart."

A well of surprise turned Malcolm's head to scrutinize his new friend. Malcolm shook his head. What did he know of Jun's family situation? Or their living conditions? And yet, this youth had the sensitivity to notice Malcolm's pain. Jun was wise for his years. Life on the streets could make one wise in some ways, he well knew. But where had Jun's kindness come from? Malcolm felt it rude to pry about the lad's family.

"Jun," Malcolm struggled with his question; he settled for frankness, although indirect, "are you happy? I mean, generally, most days."

"Hm. I'd have to say I don't think about whether I am or not, I guess. But, I ain't sad."

"What about disappointments?"

"Yer mean like when a nob stiffs me of a tip?"

"More than that. From people you know."

Jun considered this. "I s'ppose if yer don't expect much from yer regular folks yer better off."

Malcolm wanted to digest that, but an undertow pulled his thoughts back to Joe's involvement with stolen goods. How could he agree to that? Malcolm yearned for those moments of feeling secure in Joe's company, of sensing dependability.

He sat in darkness, heavy emotions almost overwhelming him to the point of forgetting his manners. His friend had sought him out and been sensitive to his feelings.

"Thank you for coming by, Jun. I'm going to have to give some thought to what you said—to your words of wisdom."

Chapter Fifty-One

Sid met Malcolm in front of Merriweather Secondary after class. Their plans involved a small adventure in lieu of tea, in lieu of coffee at Jade's and in lieu of buckling down with their school lessons. They headed for Fleet Street.

"By the time we get there," Sid said, suddenly uncertain, "Smith might be done tapping out his ditties and gone home. We don't know where he lives."

"I'm putting my money on the pubs. Bachelors, especially curious ones like Smith, aren't the type to retire early."

"Sounds reasonable. Only problem is, which pub. I saw a slew of them last time."

"I've got my ideas. We'll see."

"Or," Sid added, "he could be at one of those secret meetings."

"Possible, but I think those are held later." That thought brought to mind Aunt Jane's late-night absences. But the focus now was Smith and the subject of Sylla.

Shadow had overtaken the business district by the time Malcolm led Sid around a corner near *The Daily Telegraph*. Sid's stride and bearing revealed a confidence he'd lacked on their first visit.

Malcolm strode up to the building and entered. Not surprisingly, the same hooded-eyed-thin-moustached man was there, keeping guard.

"We're in the process of closing, lads."

Malcolm frowned. The man had called them *gentlemen* previously.

"We just want to see Mr. Smith again, sir. We know the way."

"Sorry, but we can't have you up there when we're securing the building. You'll have to call again tomorrow."

"Could you tell us whether or not Mr. Smith has left for the day?"

"I couldn't say. Now, be off."

Out along the pavement, Malcolm felt a similar lack of welcome. Well-dressed businessmen swarmed the area.

Gawking, hesitant youths only served to annoy those whose momentum was interrupted, which meant everyone surrounding Malcolm and Sid.

Some men headed for the underground stations, some hailed cabs, but many filtered into the different pubs.

"How are we ever going to find Smith in this crowd?" Sid asked.

More and more windows began springing to life. Few establishments had the need to draw drapes. Witnessing such a metamorphosis in a respectable part of London dazzled Malcolm; it was like seeing the many facets of a gem as each refracted light.

The smell of various tobaccos wafted from the ever-opening pub doors, a heady scent. With his adulthood nearly in his grasp, he found the surrounding camaraderie fascinating. It was easy to imagine the anticipation these gents must be feeling for conversations both convivial and beneficial.

But he hesitated, unsure of himself, of how to begin the search for Smith now that he stood here. Sid's impatience became palpable after Malcolm had led him up the street for several blocks and then down for several more. What had Mr. Smith said about these pubs? Or was it something said by Smith's companion in Jade's so many weeks ago?

In front of them, a number of men turned down an alley. Malcolm came up to its entrance to see the attraction. A pub. It was situated off the main street, as Jade's was, only with a lit sign above its door and a higher-ranking clientele.

Sid said, "I'd like to try that pub. Ye Old Cheshire Cheese. Do you think the cat is there?" Sid caught himself. "A picture of it, I mean."

"I don't know whether the place has much to do with books by Lewis Carroll, my friend.

Sid then pointed to a nearby by establishment. "The Tipperary looks jollier. Shall we try that one?"

Malcolm considered it and then looked up and down Fleet Street again. Fortunately, Sid had not seen The Punch Tavern. He imagined his friend would expect to see a Punch and Judy show there.

What had Smith said?

Men of government hold much more interesting conversations than those of commerce.

Not as colourful as a workingman's pub.

Ah, a time and place for everything.

Smith would likely choose to eavesdrop or interact where political conversations prevailed rather than fiduciary ones.

Strains of music caught Malcolm's attention. Down the street to his left, at the next corner, a busker was playing a violin.

"Come on, Sid."

The thin young musician looked more approachable than any of London's men of means. And Malcolm needed help. He produced a copper and sixpence from his pocket. Instead of dropping them in the open instrument case where a few coins were strewn, he kept the money in his open palm before the musician.

"Excuse me, sir."

The violinist looked at the coins and stopped playing.

"Forgive my intrusion. That was a lovely piece of music, but could you kindly tell us where Pump Court is?

The young man pointed his bow in the direction opposite the Punch Tavern.

"Just a bit farther along and to your left, my friend."

Malcolm nodded his thanks and dropped the coins in the case.

"Onward, Sid."

Strains of "Rule, Brittania" floated merrily behind Malcolm as he and Sid carried on.

In a matter of moments, Malcolm spotted the Pump Court Pub. Its two front windows were of bevelled glass. Malcolm checked the surrounding buildings. As he had thought, the area was full of establishments relative to law, chambers of this and that barrister. None of the names were familiar to him. Although Malcolm wasn't quite sure of the distinction between barristers, solicitors and such, he doubted that the late Julius Crocker would ever have attained enough prominence to set up chambers here.

Malcolm approached the pub, stood at one of its windows, and scanned the room. Oak panelled walls, brass light fixtures, and a haze of smoke. Some men were already in evening attire, as if bracing themselves for, perhaps, a long and late night at the opera with their spouses. Most were in business suits, of good quality. The general decorum was relaxed and cheery.

Just then, he spotted his quarry inside, sitting alone in a corner with studied disinterest.

"Come."

Sid followed Malcolm into the place. Malcolm dismissed flutters of self-consciousness due to their school clothes, which could only spotlight the incongruity of their presence.

No one paid more than a cursory interest. He assumed sons of such men might occasionally come to collect their fathers, sent by impatient mothers, perhaps waiting to attend some evening function. It was early for that sort of thing, but nonetheless, the notion helped him feel invisible.

Malcolm and Sid approached the journalist.

"What do you have?" Smith asked, his voice low. He looked neither agitated nor pleased by their appearance at his table.

"Um, have you had opportunity to look into Crocker's murder?"

Smith's mouth formed a crooked smile. "I asked the question."

Malcolm wondered at the man's coolness, but then realized he and Sid might be interfering with Smith's objectives here. He knew enough to speak softly.

"Sorry, but this might be important. Have you learned of a Sylla LeFeuvre?" Malcolm hated betraying her. But he wanted to further the inquiry and hoped, were it possible, that the lady could be eliminated from his mental list of suspects. He felt he should also ask whether Smith had checked into Wendell's background, even Aunt Jane's, but couldn't utter the words.

"What do you have besides questions, Malcolm?" Smith's face remained bland.

The words stung. Sid paled. It occurred to Malcolm that this interchange might be under someone's surveillance. He kept himself from looking around. Why else would Smith be acting this way?

Malcolm held the man's gaze and in a low tone said, "I overheard Miss LeFeuvre discussing Crocker's death. She'd said that she hadn't been responsible, but it sounded to me as though she could have been; she seemed disappointed, as if someone else had beat her to it."

Smith nodded and said in a hushed tone, "Do you know anything about Mata Hari, lad?"

"Of course."

"Well then," Smith continued, "There's an idea. If your Miss What's-her-name is such a person, one could look for such clues in the lady's whereabouts and associations. For example, I am aware of her enough to know that she resides in Paris, or is reportedly known to. The question is: with whom is she staying while in London? The home of a lover, or a *supposed* lover? That would be a clever choice. Or, were it true that she is here by design, to do the bidding of some minister connected to foreign affairs, she could be housed at a discreet government-owned residence, such as at Berkeley Square. Not the smartest choice in my opinion, but whoever said brilliance sits to govern? I'd think a busy hotel would also serve well."

Smith sipped his glass of brandy.

Malcolm was aware that Smith had not asked them to sit. Was the rudeness a matter of necessary subterfuge? Maybe not. Malcolm admitted his own naiveté in expecting this man to treat him as an equal.

Smith continued, "The supposed lover would be the best option, I'd say. Such a residence could be anywhere; her insidious motives—were that the case—could be cloaked in mystery. Were she to be followed from social events by suspicious characters, such a location would offer nothing."

A lifted inflection, followed by an overly casual sip kept Malcolm riveted.

"But no one asks me." Smith produced a wan smile.

"Well," Malcolm began. He felt crestfallen and couldn't understand why. At least, not exactly why. "We'll be going. Thank you." He turned to leave.

"Oh," Smith called, "I found out about your Mr. Boggs."

Malcolm spun around and met his gaze.

In that brief moment that Malcolm had turned away, Smith had produced a gold toothpick, which he began using, prodding around his uppers—stalling for effect. He finally extracted the implement. "Seven years. As you'd been told was possible. That was his sentence."

Gratitude and relief muddled Malcolm's thoughts. "Um, why, thank you, Mr. Smith." He nodded and turned again to leave.

Smith cleared his throat and said, "Of course, prisoners have been known to escape now and then." He chuckled.

Malcolm, sensing Sid in tow, kept on toward the door and stepped out into the night.

Chapter Fifty-Two

Morning sunlight glistened on the still dewy lawn. It had been almost a week since finding Smith at the Pump Court Pub. Two evenings ago, Malcolm had overheard Aunt Jane mention Sylla's departure date from London.

Sid complained, "If she's at all as brilliant as you say, she'll spot us in two seconds."

"I don't care anymore." Malcolm noted the acerbic tone in his voice but shrugged it off. He didn't care. Not much. He hadn't slept well for weeks, it seemed, and it was getting to him. Twice he'd let down his guard. Like the time he let slip his thoughts in front of Katja at Joe's place. Normally, he weighed everything before he spoke. Now, his thoughts sometimes lumbered into being or they mixed together like the dubious ingredients in Adelaide's baking.

More than once, he'd thought of escaping London like Jack had done. If only he weren't so blasted curious.

Berkeley Square was the stateliest setting he'd inspected thus far. It was the farthest part of the West End he'd ever been to. If he weren't so tired and out of sorts, he could sit here and bask in the clean loveliness, but focus was needed.

"Do you think we look silly?" Sid asked. "Two boys, sitting on a bench, reading the newspaper as if we're old military chums with nothing better to do?"

"As long as you're dressed appropriately and do nothing to call attention to yourself, people will usually pay little attention to you—I mean that in general. It's like hiding in plain sight. I've experienced it myself."

Malcolm looked over his paper and gazed at the address where he thought Sylla was staying. Smith felt certain of his facts, that the chosen residence might be one owned by the SIS, a not-so-discreet choice to house its various "guests"—those individuals that the department employs for the greater good of His Majesty's government.

"I don't know what we can accomplish other than verify that this woman exited the building." Even Sid was getting cranky.

They both could use a new diversion, Malcolm admitted.

"If she comes out at all, she's either going to get into a motorcar or walk right up to us and ask what we're doing."

"We might note whose company she keeps. She might stroll somewhere that matters. And it is the only way we can verify Smith's claim that she is a guest of the SIS."

"And you think she was used by them to assassinate Mr. Crocker?"

"She told Auntie that she hadn't done it, but people lie, especially those involved with government."

The townhouse was the only one of red brick while the others in the row were of limestone or white-painted brick. Though only three windows wide, its glossy door, decorative appointments and four stories were elegant, like the woman herself, that is, when she wasn't committing crimes or being outrageous. Malcolm liked her and did not want to think of Sylla as a killer. It would add to her mystique were she a spy, one who learned and shared important information for the Empire. A warmth spread through him as he realized he himself was, after a fashion, a freelance spy.

A bird alighted on shrubbery nearby and began to chirp, a sweet sound. The sun's rays began warming him.

Then an impressively long and shiny motorcar pulled up to the redbrick residence. As soon as it came to a stop, a footman appeared, escorting Malcolm's quarry, Sylla Le Feuvre, down the steps. She never disappointed. Today she was wearing a gorgeous fur coat and turban. And she was leaving—leaving London or at least the SIS residence. Another footman came out carrying four suitcases, two gripped and two pinched under his arms. Then another descended with a large suitcase and three hatboxes.

The first footman opened the rear door for her while the luggage was being arranged in the boot. Before getting in, Sylla looked across the park and locked her gaze on Malcolm. He couldn't make himself raise his paper. He half expected her to wave or send out the hounds…but he thought she smiled. He couldn't be sure with the distance between them, but he sensed goodwill and, maybe, amusement.

Before the motorcar pulled from the curb, the three footmen bowed to her. Not surprising. He felt so inclined.

The vehicle glided along and rounded a corner.

"Come on, Sid. We have to find Smith."

"Yer lookin' for Mr. Smith?"

Malcolm turned and found a janitress leaning against a recessed door frame. She had opened it without a sound. Behind her was one of those rooms necessary for the building's maintenance. A spiral of lazy smoke rose from the cigarette in her hand.

"Yes, ma'am. Any idea when he might be back?"

Sid stood by, silent.

She stepped to the large sink and turned the tap, extinguishing the smoking weed before tossing it into a bin.

"That's the big question 'round here. Nobody's seen him for days."

"Perhaps he's down with a cold or helping a sick relative."

"His boss hasn't heard from 'im. That's what we've heard, Maggie and me. Mr. Sigmore even sent one o' the clerks round to Smith's flat in Hackney. We hears the landlady hadn't see 'im neither. It's one thing not to come to yer own 'ome, if yers know wot I mean, but another to miss work. Maggie and me is thinkin' someone didn't like his nosing round and dumped his body in the sewers or the river, all the same, really." Her expression sagged with regret. "Oh, I hope you're not his next o' kin. In any case, I didn't mean to be disrespectful. He was a nice un, Mr. Smith."

Malcolm frowned at the past tense. "I'm sure there's a good reason. He's probably . . ." His words died out. He conjured up a brave face but a knot began twisting inside him.

"Let's go, Sid."

Chapter Fifty-Three

Katja opened the cafe's back door to Malcolm's knock and said, "We need to talk." She stood at the threshold with a large knife in hand and blood splattered across on her apron.

Alarmed and intrigued, he followed her into the kitchen. No one else stood among the sinks, stoves and large tables.

She whispered, "We need to talk where we won't be overheard."

Beyond the door to the dining room, someone was clinking glassware in a wash tub, humming a doleful tune.

Various parts of what had once been a lamb now lay strewn over the butcher block. He'd wondered while waiting at the door what all those hacking sounds had been about, glad that the bludgeoned bone and flesh was not human.

Katja held the large knife as a daintier girl would hold a parasol.

He considered the implement with its wood handle secure in her grip, the blade greasy. "I suppose you should set that thing down, then." He nodded at the weapon.

"Oh, well, yes." she looked at the kabob preparations, placed the knife next to some smaller meat chunks and wiped her hands on her apron. A whole line of knives hung from a rack at the table's end. Further down the table sat bowls mounded with different vegetables. Onions, peppers and something he didn't recognize lay cut to size, ready to be skewered with the cubes of lamb.

A savoury aroma came from one of the ovens. Despite the arresting smells of Hasani's café, the serious look in her eyes moved Malcolm to respond in kind.

"I know just the place." He turned to leave.

"Wait. I need to ask Ludovic to take over here."

Outside, smells of soot and sewer dominated. Their route wended its way along Whitechapel. In no time it became Old Montague Street, an ancient cobbled stretch. A general hush lay over its pedestrians. Everyone appeared to be more anxious than usual. Here, voices could carry. Confidential talk would have to wait for the destination Malcolm had in mind.

Having a female companion produced unprecedented sensations, he realized. Her long dark hair, gathered back and held by a ribbon, baring the smoothness of her neck, attracted him, not to mention the shapeliness of her form under a smart jacket and skirt. He became conscious of his stride, confident, manly. He hoped she would notice. Never had a girl fascinated him so. They had a block to go before reaching the Brady Street Jewish Cemetery.

Birds could be heard from the cemetery's shrubbery; their chirpings sounded pensive, as if they were discussing the brevity of life.

Malcolm came to a stop at the graveyard's gate.

"Here?" Katja peered in through the gateway into the quiet surroundings. Skeletal branches stretched to heaven.

On the largest monuments and gravestones, Hebrew lettering bespoke a culture that was at the same time foreign and familiar to Malcolm.

"Malcolm, we don't even look Jewish."

"This will work. Let's find a grave site that's out of the way. English lettering, preferred, of course. In case our presence is noticed and we need to mention a name."

Malcolm welcomed the smells of earth and moss. The foliage muted city sounds beyond, which would also absorb to a degree conversations, if mourners were to appear. At present, the place was empty.

"We don't even have any flowers. That would have been a good idea. You should have told me this was your destination."

Accustomed to her prickliness, he offered a wan smile. "They'd only question us if we were carrying sledgehammers and shovels. No one bothers people in cemeteries, especially people mourning before a tombstone."

"Okay," Katja said, ready to take charge, "Let's go over there where the gravestones are humble. That area looks a bit neglected, we're less likely to be disturbed there."

He followed her. After some deliberation, she began to kneel.

"Don't kneel."

"Why not?"

"Better to sit on this bench."

She didn't argue. He liked the delicate scent wafting from her hair, nothing like the bold type worn by Aunt Jane. A flash of desire to stroke Katja's hair surprised him. He resisted and studied their "late relative's" burial place.

The flat gravestone had Hebrew lettering at the far end. Close to Katja's feet, the etching in English told the briefest story: Ira Skolnik, born 1895 in Whitechapel. Died 1915 at the Somme. Malcolm wondered whether this Skolnik was related to the rabbi at Poltava Synagogue.

Bringing himself back to practical matters, he asked, "Should this be your relative or mine?"

"He was only twenty years old." She whispered, uninterested in the question. "How sad."

A ripple of unease ran through Malcolm. His father could have been killed in France—so, so readily. With all of his own upheaval, self-pity and guilt, Malcolm had overlooked the obvious. He could at least look forward to visiting the captain now and then. And maybe—hope burned raw in his heart—just maybe his father would work through his shell shock and escape from those night terrors…and come home.

He finally told her about the decoded message. She offered no enthusiasm but stared blankly at the gravestone.

A few birds huddled in a tree nearby; this time their chirpings sounded as if they were discussing his failures.

Katja said, "We have to break into Crocker's place. We're not getting anywhere with finding Joe's murderer."

"Hey, what about that message?"

"So what." She softened and touched his arm. "Sorry, you were brilliant with that, really, but who killed my uncle and why? We need more information. And we might find something of interest in the offices of that man." She looked off toward the birds and then added, "But the police will surely have cordoned off his place until they find his killer. They'll have a constable on duty."

"Maybe. Maybe not. We'll have to check it out, of course."

"Maybe not? Oh, I see. Didn't you say that he might've been bumped off at the direction of the Foreign Secretary? Then maybe not, right?"

"I never said 'Foreign Secretary' per se. But I have reason to believe that he might have been assassinated for the greater good of

Britain." He didn't want to mention Sylla's possible involvement. It felt disloyal.

"Did you learn that from your newspaperman friend?"

"Uh, no, and he's disappeared. He too might have been done away with, but I think he's gone to ground. If he doesn't appear after the Chinese New Year, then, I'll accept that he's gone for good."

"So, how did you come up with that idea?"

"I'm a good listener." He stole Sylla's line with pleasure. It made him smile.

"You and your secrets. We have to work together. Are you in?"

An old woman shuffled through the gate and headed to the opposite end of the cemetery.

Katja raised her brows at Malcolm. For long moments, the two sat in silence. Malcolm even feigned the act of praying.

The woman said a few words to her lost one. Her right hand reached out and rested on the top of the upright tombstone. Her other held a handkerchief to her mouth. She turned to leave. Before exiting the gates, a sob escaped her.

It unsettled Malcolm. Whether mothers, wives or sisters, women mourned deeply the loss of their men. Just then, a frisson of alarm ran through him. Chinatown might soon lose any number of men in the planned pogrom. He envisioned hundreds of Chinese women weeping among debris and cinders. And that event, timed for Chinese New Year, would be upon them all in short order.

Malcolm wiped his damp hands down his trousers.

An elbow jab in his side brought him back to the present. His companion silently nodded toward the crying woman who was passing through the gate and out of the cemetery. Katja's eyes agreed with his over the woman's pain.

Malcolm opened his mouth to speak of his mounting concerns over Limehouse. The number of fatalities could be horrendous. Then he decided not to discuss that with her—not now, at least.

Instead he answered the question. "Of course I'm in. Why would I change my mind?"

"Shall we go tonight?"

"No, in broad daylight, on Saturday. Less suspicious that way."

"Well, night or day, what about the police if they are there? How do you propose we get past them?"

He stood and smiled at her chutzpah. He was expected to come with up a solution. "Oh, I bet there are no constables on duty there. If it was an assassination ordered from the top, they'd have no reason to waste manpower at such a place just for show. Now, if I'm wrong and we find one or two constables stationed there, then we'll work out some other tactic. First we check it out, then we proceed one way or another."

The smile she beamed his way lifted his spirits higher than any other occasion he could recall.

After dusting off the seat of his pants, Malcolm asked, "Any word from Jack?"

"No." She looked down as her feet picked their way in the ankle-high grass.

Thoughts of high adventure on the seas, followed by a slew of conceivable dangers, crossed his thoughts until something caught his eye.

A name...on a flat gravestone.

Esther Lever, born 1901 Whitechapel. Died 1920 Limehouse.

Chapter Fifty-Four

It was good to be sitting across from Sid at Jade's. It felt as if months had passed since, though it had been only a week and a few days.

Before getting down to business, Malcolm asked, "How was school today?"

It was Thursday and Mrs. Shapiro allowed Sid to have his tea with Malcolm. She'd even given Sid some money. Although Malcolm was not actually welcome at their home, he sensed a growing acceptance from Sid's mum. She manifested appreciation for how he'd saved her son from the bullies at Mile End. Perhaps she has even noticed some improvement in her son's bearing, his confidence. Malcolm would like to think so.

Sid replied, "Morris Silverman had to go to the schoolmaster's office today. Everyone said he got a whipping. Hope he did." Sid's eyes lit with mischief.

Two men dressed in suits talked good naturedly at a table in the corner. Their conversation had something to do with economics. Their demeanour brought Thaddeus Smith to mind. Malcolm wondered whether Smith was carrying on his investigations incognito or not. The alternative would be dreadful. He reined in his thoughts.

"About Esther," Malcolm prompted.

Sid replied, talking around a bite of muffin, "Yes. I haven't heard a word of gossip about Esther. Only that she'd moved away some time ago to help a relative, an aunt or something, in Liverpool, I think."

"It sounds like the kind of thing parents would say when their daughter has to birth an illegitimate baby."

Sid shrugged. "Well, I only know not to bring it up when I'm in Lever's bookstore. Mum had said not to. I thought it was just because they missed her. Then I thought it might be because they were out of sorts for having to take on the chores Esther had done all those years." He took a sip of his coffee.

"Surely, someone in Whitechapel would know what happened to Esther and be willing to talk about it."

Sid considered this for some long moments. "Batya Schuller!"

"Go on," Malcolm encouraged.

"She was our neighbourhood yenta, a real busybody. She moved to Soho last year, and I think it was to get away from Whitechapel. She'd probably upset a lot of people with her meddling. Mum had nothing to do with her. The woman's niece lives a few doors away from us. I bet she'll know where in Soho. That is, if you really want to learn about Esther Lever."

Chapter Fifty-Five

A hint of motion drew Malcolm's attention down the alley. The prowler was either unaware or uncaring of his attention. Stealth fascinated Malcolm, as did determination. Two buildings away from where he sat, a wary rat scavenged among the rubbish.

The amount of debris was meagre compared to the smelly mound that had sat neglected behind Markov's. Malcolm's flesh crawled at the memory of hiding under rotting cabbage and unthinkable detritus that had soiled him with rankness. And poor Sid.

Malcolm considered Sid's spirit, which caused a smile to stretch wide. He recalled all that was brave, noble and loyal in his waif-sized friend.

He couldn't imagine life without Sid.

The smile faded. A vague problem began gnawing away at Malcolm's contentment. He had to admit that he was largely responsible for Sid's welfare. They were playing dangerous games. Could Sid's small frame have survived the beating Malcolm had taken the other night? Malcolm wasn't much taller but he was heartier. His attackers had clearly meant the beating as a warning. Neither he nor Sid could expect any mercy were they set upon by thugs who meant business.

Katja popped her head out the café's kitchen door, returning Malcolm to the matter at hand. "Ready to snoop?"

He needed to keep Katja from trouble, too. His mouth opened to speak, then closed.

"You're not getting lily-livered on me now, are you?" she challenged.

"Of course not."

The determination in her features brooked no argument. They would be out of the public eye once they got into Crocker's building. What harm could arise there?

"Let's go, Miss Hasani." Malcolm set off in something close to a march.

"What are you two doing there?"

The woman standing on the back step of Feldman's Timepieces spoke more from curiosity than challenge. She wore an apron over her drab outfit. Wisps of grey hair escaped all round her dusting bonnet.

He'd thought they would have the alleyway to themselves by coming just after dawn. He'd forgotten about charwomen.

Katja said, "My mum sent me to tidy up Uncle's Julius' place before she meets the estate agent here."

Malcolm smiled at her inventiveness. The neighbours would know—especially the charwomen—that Mr. Crocker had died under mysterious circumstances at The Midland Grand Hotel. That much had been in the papers. Word on the street said the man had been poisoned, Malcolm had heard. Crocker's neighbours would likely also know that the police had searched the place already as routine procedure. Life moved on. Of course the building would need to be readied to go on the market. The question was: would this charwoman know Crocker's relatives? Malcolm had no way of knowing whether any of Crocker's relations had already done just that. Or whether they might arrive like buzzards while he and Katja were snooping around.

The woman wiped her nose with the back of her hand and turned back to her duties in the clock shop, shutting the door behind her.

Katja pulled a key from her pocket and inserted it into the lock.

"Blast," she whispered. "This usually does the trick."

"Is it your habit to break into places with a skeleton key, Katja?"

"You never know when you'll need something like this. Mum uses it when necessary on the rooms she lets out. Not to worry. I'm an expert at this." She replaced the key with two metal implements.

He could think of no other purpose for them except picking locks.

Malcolm began to sweat. The operation took more than the casual turn of one's wrist. She got down on her knees and peered closely, head tilting, ear listening as she fiddled. His gaze swept along the alley and up along buildings. Only two windows. One with the shade down. The other blank.

Click.

"After you, sir," she said as she stood, her tone fairly dripping with satisfaction. Her tools plunked together as she dropped them in her pocket.

The back room had one wall of shelves stocked with office supplies, but he saw no crates of weaponry.

"No cricket balls in sight," he said, "and I'm sure he wouldn't have them in the front offices. Either the police took them—if they were here at all—or Crocker has them stored elsewhere."

The floor overhead creaked. Katja's eyes widened in alarm. Slow, deliberate footsteps crossed a space comparable to the room they stood in.

"Are you sure he's dead?"

"He probably has a tenant in the flat upstairs."

"What if it's a relative of his?"

"We'll be in trouble, if they check on us."

"Is it against the law to be in someone's building if we don't steal anything?"

"I'm sure of it."

They passed through the open doorway to the front offices.

"Wait, let me look for cleaning supplies, just in case," Katja said. She went back and Malcolm followed.

"Maybe in this closet?" She opened it.

Malcolm looked over her shoulder, relieved to see no dead bodies or hiding detectives. He released the pent-up breath he'd been holding. He didn't know what he expected to find here, but trespassing made him nervous and nerves clouded his reason.

"Here we go," Katja said, her tone calm. "Now, I'm all set in case we're discovered. I'll walk around with this feather duster."

The first room was large with an elegant table and six chairs.

"This must be where he meets with clients, when he's reading a will or something. If he does that sort of thing."

"Did," she corrected.

"Right."

The walls of book-laden shelves and tall file cabinets seemed oppressive despite the breadth of floor space. There was no window. Malcolm would hate being behind closed doors here for any length of time.

"Where on earth do we begin?"

Malcolm scanned the walls of books. His previous task and discovery in Joe's modest library paled compared with a hunt among all these. Trying to imagine a villain's analytical prowess, Malcolm decided to investigate the file cabinets' contents.

"Why don't you work your magic on those cabinet locks?"

She nodded with bright eyes. The lock for the first set of drawers gave in without a tussle. The next proved otherwise.

Footsteps bounded down the stairs beyond the west wall. Was the tenant going to check on things here? Would he have been someone close enough to Crocker to have been given a key?

Malcolm's pulse thudded, sounding as loud to him as the descending footfalls. But Katja's attention remained riveted to her probing. The lass had a cool head.

The lock for the second set of drawers finally released with a click. Katja beamed with satisfaction. Her smile fell when someone's knuckles rapped repeatedly against the front window pane.

The person had no key, then. That took the edge off Malcolm's worries. Could he and Katja wait it out and remain unseen in the office?

Katja turned, picked up her feather duster from the table and said, "Follow me." At the office door she added, "Oh, and roll up your sleeves, quickly."

He obeyed and accompanied her into the front rooms. A gangly figure, wearing a city suit and bowler peered through the window. His mouth opened to insinuate something.

Katja spoke loudly through the glass, "My mum sent me to tidy up." She did a half curtsy and waved the duster as if it were a small parade flag.

The man's mouth clamped shut. His eyes darted his question to Malcolm.

"My cousin," Katja supplied. "He came to keep me safe." She smiled and held the man's gaze.

The tenant shrugged without a word and ambled down the street, hopefully en route to his job and not to the Metropolitan Police.

Combing through Crocker's files became tedious. Malcolm forced away his discouragement. Katja was a drawer ahead of him at the next cabinet.

He completed the top and moved on to the next drawer. *Fairchild…Farris.*

"Hey…maybe." Malcolm rescanned the file headings front to back in the drawer. "I might have something here." Each file heading had a client's last name followed by a first initial. Midway along and sandwiched between *Feinstein* and *Feldman* was one marked CC.

"This is odd," he said as he removed it. He sat at the table and opened the file. Katja took the seat next to him.

"A bunch of news clippings," he said, then realized he was stating the obvious.

Katja didn't mock him but took the handful that he offered her and began reading.

Silence pervaded as two sets of eyes pored over details. On the third clipping, Malcolm saw a name that disturbed him. Leeds. What was it about the name of this city that knotted his insides? A conference for the Communist party should in itself catch his eye. A call for unity. But why did Leeds sound familiar?

His aunt. She'd mentioned having to tend to business there. Why else would she go there? Malcolm set the article aside face down on the desk.

Katja said, "Here's one from last January, about the communist party in Italy, just established in Livorno. Are the Bolshies popping up all over, I wonder?"

Malcolm's voice cracked as he said, "Do the Bolsheviks and these communist parties in other countries have the same ideals? Do they help one another? I sure wish I could find Mr. Smith. He'd know."

She scanned another. "This one is about Spain, from last April. Its communist party came into being this year, as well."

He read, "Mongolia declares independence from China," he read. "Says nothing about communism, but he has it here for some reason." Malcolm scanned another. "Ah, here we go, from July, China now has its communist party. Well, I'd already heard that from Smith."

Her tone now matter-of-fact, Katja held another clipping and said, "Tbilisi, Georgia, now occupied by the Bolsheviks."

The next one fascinated Malcolm. "This yellowed one is from 1914, the only older clipping here." After moments of silent perusal, Malcolm said, "I'll share this bit that's taken from a speech given by Benito Mussolini about changes in Italy back then.

The nation has not disappeared. We used to believe that the concept was totally without substance. Instead we see the nation arise as a palpitating reality before us! ... Class cannot destroy the nation. Class reveals itself as a collection of interests—but the nation is a history of sentiments, traditions, language, culture, and race. Class can become an integral part of the nation, but the one cannot eclipse the other.

I wonder if Crocker admired this man. Crocker certainly aspired to have some kind of importance in Britain. I'd love to know what he was actually thinking."

The last one took Malcolm's breath away. It wasn't just the advert for Croft and Sons, manufacturer of croquet balls and mallets, *made from the best Jamaican ebony*. It wasn't even the clear reference to the company's pride at being the supplier of truncheons for the Metropolitan Police Force.

He tilted the advert toward Katja and pointed to the hand-written notation: *arrange river transport*.

Chapter Fifty-Six

"Yo-ho! Malcolm!" Sid called from down the street.

Malcolm was trying to decide whether to enter Lever's bookshop. He wanted to learn about Batya Shuller.

Mrs. Lever might be a likely receptacle of local gossip.

Sid approached. Malcolm's stomach sank. How was he going to get rid of Sid without hurting his feelings?

Running the rest of the way, Sid came up to him in front of the shop window.

Malcolm could see Mrs. Lever nestled at her table, illuminated by a shaft of light from the front window. Her pudgy hands held a tea mug to her lips while reptilian eyes watched them from over the rim.

"Hey," Sid said in greeting. His smile lifted cheeks that were rosy from exertion, but his eyes were already busy deciphering Malcolm's demeanour. "What's up? A new development?"

"Uh, nothing, really." Malcolm gave a parting glance at the book seller's wife and moved on. Images of Sid's bludgeoned body galvanized his pace.

Sid worked hard to keep up. "Where are we going?"

Malcolm's mind went blank. He kept walking.

Sid came abreast and kept up until a small group of seamen, dressed in pea coats and caps, rounded the corner in a rush. They parted round Malcolm while Sid fell back nearly becoming lost in a current.

In the next block, Sid again came abreast. "What's the matter with you?"

Malcolm wished for a good lie. Nothing.

Sid grabbed his arm with a jerk and pulled him into an alley. He then pushed Malcolm up against a building. The boy's breathing grew deep and fast.

"You're not leaving me out of this."

"Wha—"

"I get you. You took a bad beating and now you think I can't handle one. You want to act like my big brother. You're not. We're equals." Sid glared at him.

Malcolm's resolve wavered, but then, flashes of his recent assault coursed through his mind. He felt the panic afresh, as he had then; and its electrifying surge echoed in his body.

He looked into Sid's waiting eyes. No fabrication would work with Sid. They knew each other too well. He needed to walk away. He stepped out.

Sid landed a punch in Malcolm's gut and the small fist knocked the breath out of him. A whack to his right shin stopped Malcolm cold. Sid closed in on him, and his sudden fury unleashed itself with quick jabs, and yet, at the same time, their grappling played out in a slow eerie way reminiscent of a nightmare.

Malcolm gasped. The slap against his left ear stung worse than the punches. He reached to grab hold and restrain the lad. But Sid leapt into his grasp, encasing him with arms and legs and cursing. They went down hard onto the cobbles. A jolt like lightning flared from Malcolm's elbow and shot up his arm.

They thrashed and rolled together on the worn cobbles, rolling and scrambling deeper down an alley smelling of urine.

Then, they stopped. Sid sat up across from him dishevelled and smudged and breathing heavily. Malcolm sat up and studied the dissipating energy and the anticipation in his friend's eyes. The expression said, *have I earned the right now?*

Laughter escaped Malcolm's throat.

Sid chuckled in reply, then said, "Is that understood, mate?"

Malcolm felt his stretching smile. He allowed a few beats while catching his breath, then said, "Understood, old thing."

He sent Sid home to get details from Mrs. Shapiro of where they might find Batya. Having been entrusted with a mission, Sid took off, heels kicking back as he ran.

The morning still allowed an opportunity for Malcolm to venture into Limehouse. There was one culprit he had to flush out from hiding —if the man hadn't been murdered already. And who knew whether any of Malcolm's enemies might be on hand, lurking along Pennyfields, watching from the opium dens? For that matter, how was Malcolm to know whether or not Mr. Thaddeus Smith had joined up with that lot?

Chapter Fifty-Seven

The front windows of Hong's Teahouse glinted in the day light. Dampness from a daybreak cleaning remained on its sills, as well as the front walk. Hong took pride in his humble place, even if he was gruff with guests.

Dampness also hung in the air, smelling of the nearby river and muting the shuffling of Limehouse's pedestrians. Everyone along the walkways moved with purpose.

Malcolm's hope of finding Smith among the crowd was half-hearted, fed more by the lack of any other option than by expectation. After a careful look through the glass pane, beyond which only three Chinamen sat slurping their pale tea, he made his way across the street, located a recessed door that seemed rarely used and squatted on his haunches in Oriental style. It was the first time he'd tried this posture, one that he'd witnessed here; and he was proud that his legs were toned enough to handle it with grace and only a little pain.

His father had extolled reconnaissance work, and that was what Malcolm had in mind. Slim chances didn't bother him. A pang of instinct fed Malcolm's belief that Smith had gone to ground for his own purposes, to write that winning story and instinct counted for something. Smith was clever and ambitious.

Malcolm's attention was magnetically pulled toward an out-of-place figure, a pleasant distraction. The young woman looked West End with her graceful walk, smart low-waisted dress and fur stole. She'd slowed her pace and held his gaze, possibly more from curiosity at his odd sitting position than from any particular attraction.

What was she doing in this part of Limehouse? He'd like to know, or at least imagine, her story for being here, but he turned his head away.

A moving picture show with Lillian Gish had created a bit of a stir. Apparently, not a few British females, abused by the men in their lives, had become intrigued with Chinamen as a result, preferring them as prospects for marital bliss under the impression that they'd find more gentleness.

Malcolm looked back in the girl's direction, but she was gone.

Just then, discomfort in his thighs sent a tingling sensation that spread and intensified, as if he'd come under the care of a mad acupuncturist. Even his breathing became shallow, forcing him to admit defeat and change his posture. He tried to stand but in the process gave way to gravity and collapsed, landing abruptly on the doorstep.

Malcolm looked around for any observers ready to deride. No one noticed him.

In scanning those within his view, he wondered whether Smith might be in disguise, like he had done when infiltrating Crocker's meeting. He considered the faces of passers-by.

Was Smith being fanciful in his theory that political manipulation was threatening Anglo-Sino relations? Was his need to accomplish something significant in his journalistic world so strong that he had concocted this motive from nothing? For certain, a growing number of troublemakers were planning an attack. Each would have their own reasons. The reason must lay with the group's leaders. What drove Crocker and now his replacement?

What if Smith was just winding Malcolm up? What if he were actually the leader now that Crocker was dead? That could explain his disappearance. Smith could have far more in mind than a career with the newspapers. He wanted to taste the real life. Was he drawn to power? Was his need for dominance a desperate thing, like the command of opium to its users?

No, Malcolm had heard Smith speak of his goals as he eavesdropped on his conversation at Jade's. Smith's aims were literary. His sincerity sounded harmless, at least.

A brackish breeze fluttered against Malcolm's face. Fewer people were bustling about. Malcolm squinted against the brightness of the street as the sun reappeared from behind some clouds.

A vague notion came more clearly into view, warming him inside. He realized why protecting Limehouse held significance—what drove him to bother with all this. Aside from wanting to prove his mettle, aside from thwarting the agitators so that no harm came upon the Chinese, there was something additional.

He wanted to—even if in small measure—improve Britain's reputation as a civilized country. No, it was something broader: he wanted humanity's reputation cleared of reproach. After all the brutality of the war, he yearned to see a lesson learned.

Silently, he chided himself. Who did he think he was? Didn't matter. He could not quash his feelings.

Malcolm again looked out over the scene before him.

It was then that he spotted Smith.

Chapter Fifty-Eight

"Mr. Smith!"

Smith took off.

Malcolm ran in pursuit.

The newspaperman's head bobbed ahead but his short stature proved troublesome. Malcolm could only catch glimpses of Smith winking through the mass of Asiatic tunics. At any corner or alley, he could lose track of the man.

"Mr. Smith...huff...It's me!"

Smith kept to the gridiron-network of Chinatown's back ways. The man was clever. Malcolm imagined him judging every niche and corner, his lead assured by the throng. What was up with him?

A clearing opened up and Malcolm sprinted through. He closed in on Smith by half a block. Then the man disappeared around a corner in the next stretch. Malcolm dashed around a waddling fat man, keeping the corner in sight. Just then a cascade of rice escaped a sack carried by a boy, creating a ruckus right in his path. The boy wailed. A gaggle of Chinese women moved in, shushing and clucking as they bent to help.

"Sorry. Sorry," Malcolm cried as he leapt over the spill and jostled the crying boy.

Malcolm darted around the corner and found himself thwarted at the seething intersection where the two India Dock Roads converged. He got held up by the steady flow of chugging lorries and motorcars. Then, like before, he spotted his quarry on the other side of the road.

He pressed his lips together and took off between two vehicles. The angry blare of a horn jarred him. He lost sight of Smith.

Malcolm came up on the other side. All he saw were strangers. Finally, he saw Smith running along Three Colt Street. Was he heading for the Limehouse station? Malcolm's heart leapt at the opportunity this might afford.

He kept his gaze on the building with its raised platform that hugged the viaduct ahead. Smith entered. Yes!

Malcolm sprinted.

He skidded to a stop as his feet hit the lobby floor. He'd have to buy a ticket to get up to the platform. Smith must have done so. He was nowhere in sight. Malcolm eyed the attendant at the stairwell. No getting past him otherwise. Two people waited at the ticket window. Malcolm's fingers tapped tattoos on his thighs. The one customer turned from the window, leaving just one woman before Malcolm could pay his way. His right foot tapped the floor. He looked around again and in two bounds checked the water closet. Vacant. Smith must be above, waiting for the train.

Palms sweating, pulse beating, Malcolm waited while the old woman dug around in her purse for the fare.

Finally, she lumbered off. He stepped to the window.

"To Blackwall," he announced as he shoved his pennies under the window.

The rushing sound of the approaching train and its clanging bell above ratcheted up his pulse. The entire building echoed with its reverberating presence on the tracks. He must hurry.

Malcolm grabbed his ticket, passed the attendant and bounded up the flight of steps.

Up at the top, he looked around. One last passenger, the old woman, was just stepping aboard. Malcolm's feet pounded along the platform. He passed the news kiosk, then a girl waving to someone on board, and jumped into the last carriage.

His breath came in fits and starts as he gazed about at the seated passengers. Dark hat, flat cap, woman, woman. No light hat. Smith must be in one of the other cars. The train lurched forward and began swaying in quick jerks. Malcolm grasped the metal pole nearest him, too excited to sit. It was impossible to see clearly into the next compartment, let alone the one after that. He would have to jump out at West India and then Poplar.

Outside, something caught his attention. He turned. As the train rattled off from Limehouse, Smith stood waving goodbye to him from the side of the kiosk.

Chapter Fifty-Nine

"Wow, Smith is a pretty clever man, to pull one over on you." Sid's inflections carried no barbs. He'd never disparage Malcolm. His enthusiasm over Malcolm's tale had his eyes looking off over the crowds on Soho's Dean Street.

"I'm just glad he's alive."

Malcolm had been to Soho only once before. He took in its details with pleasure, fascinated by the variety of establishments. Delicious aromas wafted from an inviting Café Moscova, making Malcolm's stomach grumble with yearning.

Fleet Street had its businessmen. West India Dock Road its labourers. Dean Street attracted an interesting blend, many of whom appeared to be intellectuals from the Continent. Some would cast them as anarchists, he imagined, bespectacled young men with drab clothes and worn shoes. But there were also women of different classes present and, no doubt, for very different purposes.

A young man with Ashkenazi features dodged another's gesturing hand and bumped into Malcolm. He excused himself and kept on.

Malcolm scanned the upper floors, many of which held flats, and said to his friend, "I'd read that Karl Marx once lived on this very street. Long before the war. His family was poor, I understand."

Sid appeared unimpressed, as if his attention remained on that train platform and on Smith's crafty manoeuver.

An odd feeling came over Malcolm; it soon signalled alarm.

"Stop. Look here."

He directed Sid's gaze to a shop window nearby. Hoell and Sons. It wasn't the lovely violins displayed within that drew him in. Juxtaposed upon the clean pane and moving in shafts of shadow and sunlight, pedestrians carried on with their different paces. Malcolm scanned the crowd behind him to see whether anyone's eyes were trained on him, or on Sid. Was someone following them? Who could possibly know of their mission today? No one. Across the street and a slight distance down, a man was facing a cobbler's window. Surely, there'd be little there to interest a window shopper. Was the stranger watching them in the reflection in return? No. Not at the moment, at least, for his attention was focused too low.

"What's going on?" Sid's voice sounded breathy.

"Not sure. Maybe nothing. Just keep looking over this window display while I make sure."

Sid obeyed.

In order to appear natural, Malcolm busied himself with studying the shop's contents. Evidently, Hoell sold and repaired stringed instruments. However, there was one odd duck among the merchandize. At the end of the window display, near the entrance, a bookstand exhibited a publication entitled *The Finished Mystery*. It didn't appear to have anything to do with music. He guessed it was put there as a conversation piece, possibly with religious intent. He wished the mysteries in his life were finished.

Back in the reflection of the street scene, the stranger was now engaged in conversation with the cobbler, who'd come outside. The two talked as if they were old chums. Malcolm welcomed the relief this brought. He turned and looked directly up and down Dean Street. The imagination could create a mystery out of each and every individual.

He shrugged. "Let's go, Sid. Guess I was being silly."

"Can't be too careful." Sid looked around. "Looks fine to me, though. St. Anne's Court is just up there." He led the way.

St. Anne's Court was not unlike Stepney's alleyways, narrow, dark and ancient. But it smelled better. An intoxicating scent pulled Malcolm's attention to a curry shop. He stood off to the side and took a moment to enjoy the aromas while considering the passageway. Evidently, it connected Soho's Dean Street with another neighbour-hood. The alley was cloaked in shadow by three-storied buildings on each side with a number of people were passing through.

"We want The Morris Arms," Sid announced. "Batya Schuller's niece didn't know the number but said it was about midway down."

Before moving on, Malcolm considered the faces in the crowd, looking for anyone who might quickly turn away or in some other way appear suspicious. Reasonably satisfied, he nodded to Sid.

Many of the buildings contained rooms to let. Few offered architectural interest.

A recessed door in need of paint stood ajar with a small plaque-like sign in place of a knocker. Malcolm, with Sid in tow, wended his way through the throng.

"This is it," he announced. "It's a boarding house."

Sid came abreast. "Not sure what to do. I got us this far." He looked to Malcolm with raised brows.

"It says to apply at the ground floor flat. We'll have to ask which room is let to your yenta."

Malcolm nudged the door open and stepped into the modest foyer. Pale green linoleum covered the floor. The hallway had two doors on the right and a scuffed wooden staircase on the left. Mustiness filled his nostrils.

He stepped forward and looked up through the banisters as if the stairway would produce the former Whitechapel inhabitant. Nothing. He smiled at Sid and then knocked at the first door, unsure whether the two doors were for the same flat. Floorboards from within creaked, a bolt slid and clicked. The door opened. Two eyes squinted, as if incredibly near-sighted. An old man's suspenders hung loosely over a grey undershirt with stains down the front. An unpleasant but familiar odour met Malcolm.

He forced a smile and said, "We've come looking for Batya Schuller."

"Is that so?"

"Her niece sent us," Sid offered, his eyes bright and looking satisfied with his quick fabrication.

The man's pinched, rheumy eyes stared blankly, as though tired of squinting for details he could never see.

"Last floor, last door." He bowed his head and turned partly away.

"Thank you," Malcolm said.

The door closed in Malcolm's face.

He and Sid climbed the stairs. A floorboard creaked from behind one of the doors. Otherwise, tomb-like silence hung in the air.

The first door along the top hallway stood open. A pile of putrid rubbish lay in the middle of the room.

"Poor Batya," Sid whispered. "Not a pleasant building."

Malcolm could think of a lot worse near the river but said nothing. Compassion for the poor often niggled at him as it did now. But the matter at hand demanded his full attention. He looked at Sid and then knocked gently on what must be Batya Schuller's door.

No response.

"Does she work?"

"Too old," Sid said under his breath, "unless she's watching someone's baby or something."

"Maybe she's at the market."

"She'd have little to spend. Most shoppers would be back by now, I'd think."

Malcolm knocked again. After a few moments he turned to Sid and grimaced his frustration. What had he expected? It was silly to have imagined that this old woman would be found, sitting at home and ready to share Whitechapel's secrets at his bidding.

Sid nodded for Malcolm to step aside. "Maybe she's afraid." He knocked and called, "Mrs. Schuller, it's me, Sid Shapiro, Sophie's son." Sid tried the knob and opened the door.

"It's me, Sid." He looked inside.

Sid's audacity both shocked and pleased Malcolm.

His friend stepped backward, his face blanched of all colour.

"She's dead," Sid's voice squeaked. He cleared his throat.

Dumbstruck, Malcolm said, "Are you sure?"

"Her head's been all bashed in."

Chapter Sixty

"What should we do?" Sid hissed.

Malcolm tried to ignore the shriek of his nerves. He breathed in slowly and said, "Walk out calmly and then run for the tube."

He could read the questions crossing Sid's features, the same questions that were racing through his mind: Was the landlord's acuteness and sight good enough to describe them or recognize them later? Had they said where they were from? Would he know that Batya had moved from Whitechapel? Would the police search for them there? He couldn't chance the police.

Sid nodded, as if they'd just discussed each concern.

They moved with caution down the stairs. Each step groaned or creaked. A chair scraped the floor from behind a closed door. Followed by silence. Then a raspy cough erupted from deep inside another room on the level below.

On the main floor, Malcolm studied the landlord's door. It was shut, thank Heaven. He glanced down to check whether he could see the man's foot shadows in the space between the floor and the door. All was dark. His heart pounded his chest while he tiptoed onward, Sid close at his heels. The front door tried to give them away; its relentless whine seemed to fill the entry and rise up the stairwell and into every room.

Outside, he met a wall of sound. But he tried to casually note faces in the milling crowd. Sid's face was still pale, his eyes wide.

"Look smart, Sid, and keep up."

He turned right toward Dean Street. He wanted to sprint, to run all the way home, but as a disinterested throng enveloped them, he forced himself to dally on the way to the tube station.

Neither spoke. Malcolm felt ongoing panic, but it was beginning to calm down. He breathed deeply and kept walking.

Before ducking down to the platforms, Malcolm stepped aside and searched again for any indication that they were being followed. Nothing. He leaned against the wall of a building to take his time and check again. Sid stood at his shoulder.

"What do we do about Batya?"

Malcolm took stock of their surroundings. Pangs of guilt hurt his chest. He should disconnect from Sid. Go it alone and keep his friend from harm.

"Uh, Sid." A keener pain shot through him, blurring his convictions. Malcolm couldn't affront Sid's dignity. And he'd never be able to pull off a lie. His words caught in his throat.

"What?"

"Nothing."

A pretty lady in well-tailored clothes passed by, as did a number of less well-dressed people. A spectacled lad kept pace while reading a book. Two businessmen went past deep in conversation.

Finally, he felt composed. He remained alert to the street scene, masking his interest with passivity.

"First off, old thing, we leave your yenta to be discovered. I think we're in the clear. A nearly blind landlord is the only witness to our presence there. He heard no violence during our visit. The man might even be totally blind for all we know. If I were blind and strangers came to my door, I'd put on as if I could see somewhat, for my own safety."

"Okay, we're in the clear. Now what?"

"We find out why someone wanted her dead. I can't believe it was random. Can you?"

"You're right." Sid studied his dusty shoes. "There's too much going on. Crocker's dead. Your friend Joe. Esther Lever. And there's that business brewing over at Limehouse." Sid frowned, as if sensing the dismissal Malcolm had considered. "What do we do?"

Light raindrops began pecking at hats and the stretches of open street before them.

Malcolm turned up the collar of his jacket and looked Sid in the eye. "We get the gossip on the gossiper, my friend. Plain and simple."

They bounded down the steps to the underground. Malcolm's thoughts shifted from one option to another with each jarring step: Mrs. Lever, Mrs. Shapiro, Madame T, and then a few others he hadn't talked to in months. The names repeated, changed order.

The problem at hand: one needed to be especially cautious when talking with a gossiper.

Chapter Sixty-One

"Welcome to our home, Malcolm," Sophie Shapiro said, turning from the kitchen sink. Apron on, sleeves rolled up, she stood ready for any task within her domain. Her forearms would do a dockworker proud, Malcolm thought.

Sid closed the back door behind Malcolm. An awkward silence fell while Malcolm formulated his reply. Sid's lips pressed together tightly, as if he feared saying anything wrong.

Malcolm took another step in and wiped his feet on the coarse rug.

"Thank you, Mrs. Shapiro." Should he say something like, *May this house have peace?* He should have asked Sid about their customs. In his excitement, he'd forgotten to look for the mezuzah. Would it have been a courtesy or an affront for him to have touched it? She watched him with neither approval nor disdain. After silently chastising himself for being dim-witted, he added, "What a cosy kitchen."

"Yes, thank you. Now take a seat at the table while I put the kettle on."

She busied herself with routine while Sid took the chair next to him, his face flushed, his eyes bright. Yet he looked the question: *How is this visit going to play out?*

Malcolm shrugged.

Sid said, "My papa is at the synagogue. We've got two hours before he comes home. He's studying Torah."

Mrs. Shapiro dealt Sid a threatening look. Sid's face burned red. His first words had placed him on bad footing before his mother even joined them at the table.

Malcolm looked around the room. It was a proper British kitchen redolent of the turn of the century. Though that was only twenty-odd years ago, his family home had the more modern enamel gas stove, as did Aunt Jane's flat. The Shapiro home still used a cast-iron cooking stove. And from the evidence in this one room, the house had not been converted to gas, let alone electricity. Setting any inconvenience aside, he found the oil lamps to be charming. With the tea things nearly ready and the commencement of a hummed melody from Sid's mum as she worked, Malcolm felt the muscles in his neck and back relax.

Teapot, cups and accessories appeared before them. Malcolm's pulse picked up again. Any moment now, Sid's mum would take her place at the table. How would she respond to the questions?

A flurry of thoughts suddenly crisscrossed, and Malcolm feared he would babble like an idiot. Mrs. Shapiro would get impatient with the poor, stupid boy; he could imagine it all clearly. She would then declare that their tea was over and pack him off where he belonged.

Under the table, Malcolm's fingers tapped tattoos on his legs. Tea was all very nice, but Malcolm was anxious for solutions.

She turned from a cupboard with a plate piled with something delectable. Malcolm discerned the item's quality from Sid's eager face. Whatever lay hidden beneath a clean linen towel, it had Sid's mum smiling too.

Mrs. Shapiro took her place, glanced around the table with satisfied approval and then whipped the cloth off the plate. Some type of dinner rolls gleamed before them. Malcolm knew enough to recognize that the appetizing shine came from an egg wash while baking. A yeasty scent wafted his way.

Mrs. Shapiro talked a bit about their family's history in the Old Country and how she'd come upon this and that recipe.

"These," she gestured to the rolls, "are from yesterday's baking." Her inflection carried a tinge of apology.

Malcolm bit into the supple bread roll. Much of his tension melted away like butter as he savoured the chewy texture with its wholesome, yeasty flavours. This baked goody may be a day old, but it was not to be compared to Adelaide's muffins, which had death-dealing density even when fresh from the oven.

Malcolm's worries about initiating a conversation about the late Batya Schuller proved unnecessary. Word of Batya's unfortunate passing had been buzzing around Whitechapel since the morning papers, and Mrs. Shapiro erupted with more information once they had each polished off their first roll. Sid had, of course, explained beforehand the nature of the concerns. And, as far as Malcolm understood from their arrangements, Mrs. Shapiro believed that he and Sid simply wanted to understand life—how and why such awful things happen?

"Well, Batya was a walking encyclopaedia of everyone's sins. It's a wonder someone hadn't bumped her off years ago."

Her bluntness didn't shock Malcolm. He found it interesting to observe her features glow as she began to prattle about the gossiper.

She rambled on about how Batya knew of an English woman who had married a Chinaman, *to everyone's disapproval.*

"I've seen it happen more than a few times," she expounded, "especially round Limehouse. It's not like these are ladies who worry about Society, mind you. But families of such women don't wish for these unnatural unions to become public knowledge."

Malcolm balked at her words but said nothing. He then smiled and nodded, hoping for more details.

"Then there's Rabbi Skolnik's son. He'd gotten in with a bad lot of boys—well, young men, a bit older than you, Malcolm. After one of their late night drunken revelries, Batya said that it was he who had beaten a woman of the streets nearly to death. She'd lost her front teeth, poor thing. It was dreadful. Even if the woman was out there for unspeakable reasons, she doesn't not deserve to be mistreated and especially not injured."

She looked off over Malcolm's head. "That might have been the reason old Batya chose to move up to Soho. One doesn't get on the bad side of a young man like that, or that of his father." She clucked her tongue and mumbled, "Not far from the tree."

Sid's brows flew up at the fountain of information. He turned and smiled at Malcolm.

Malcolm took a second roll.

"Batya had earned a reputation years ago as a busybody. And, not only that, she came to my door more than once looking for a hand-out.

"Oh, and then there was the baker's wife down in Shadwell. Batya relished telling the stories of how the woman turns into a monster, a candidate for Bedlam, at her time of the month."

Mrs. Shapiro coloured at this, realizing too late that she'd said too much, especially while conversing with young lads. She hurried on to another instance.

"Old Batya even had it in for our coppers. She had learned from her homeland not to trust those in authority. I don't know those details from her past, but it wouldn't surprise me one bit if I heard that she had been trying to blackmail a policeman or even the magistrate, that is, if she'd ferreted out something incriminating."

She sat back and concluded, "Maybe that's what it was all about, then."

Malcolm's mind was spinning with all of the possibilities. "What? I mean, which?"

"Any and all. May she be at peace now."

Chapter Sixty-Two

"Go home, Katja," Malcolm said for the third time. If he couldn't dismiss Sid, he had to at the least keep this girl from harm.

She ignored him, increased her stride, and led the way from Pigott Street across a pathway to Gough Walk. In the dark, he could barely see her, but he felt her determination.

"I won't have you do this alone, so don't bother to argue," she snapped.

A clock tower had struck midnight a few blocks back. Malcolm wished Sid could have escaped through his bedroom window tonight, but Mrs. Shapiro's keen hearing and suspicious nature ruled that out. Jun was on duty at the opium den. It had been sharp-eyed Jun who had mentioned the building and its after-hours use. Katja, upon learning all this, volunteered. The clandestine gathering would likely be the last before evil rained down on Limehouse.

The gas lamps along Gough Walk were remnants of an earlier age. Like Pigott Street and many in the East End, they had not been updated. And in this neighbourhood they were few and far between— as they had been in the days of Jack the Ripper.

Malcolm walked alongside Katja. There was not much to say. They'd gone over their mission. Dressed in old clothes from the mission store as Smith had done, they hoped to sneak in and learn what they could. And that was that. What else could they plan for? Each of them emitted a palpable energy from focused intent and fear.

"That should be the alley that leads to the back of the Whittaker Building," she whispered.

"I wonder if they'll have it guarded."

Malcolm and Katja approached with careful steps. He imagined he could feel Katja's pulse racing as he felt the nearness of her warmth. They turned into the alley. At its end, a splotch of yellow light from an open door cast a geometric glow on the cobbles. A wooden chair sat empty next to the entry at about three meters from where they stood. Voices, one in particular, could be heard inside.

"...till I give the command, I expect order."

A mixed buzz of murmuring came from a crowd of what might be two dozen men. Whoever was speaking did not have complete support.

"A disorganized mob can accomplish its aim by its sheer numbers, but an organized one can do much better. And we want to really show them, don't we?"

The murmurings indicated more agreement. Malcolm took a wary step closer then another. Unsure whether it was worth the risk to enter and join the gathering, he paused. He could hear well enough in the relative safety of shadow. Only a dim sheen of light reached them and on into the street. Katja came alongside, brushing his shoulder.

"Now," the voice continued, "this side of the room has been chosen by the late Mr. Crocker and myself to discharge the cricket balls."

The speaker's voice struck a familiar chord, alarming Malcolm, but he couldn't put a face to it. He listened for tones of Wendell's voice and then Smith's but came up short.

"...side of the room, the truncheons. Both groups will be equal in leading our cause to glory."

The familiarity of the voice troubled and excited him. Who was it? He took another step and had caught something in the enunciation of the speaker's 'r's when a large silhouette of a man came out through the door. The man's stance changed. He'd spotted them.

Malcolm grabbed Katja in his arms and backed her against the brick side of the building and kissed her with passion.

Her lips parted and somehow his tongue was there exploring her mouth. Was this how it was done? She moaned. Katja was a quick lass, she caught on to his ploy in a flash.

Malcolm never lost sight of the danger, but his heart thumped in his chest and every fibre of his being came alive.

"Hey! You two. This is no place for that," the man cried. "Be gone with yer."

Malcolm turned, grinned at the guard, and clasped Katja's hand. He led her away as would a lad in love.

Just before they were out of the alley, Katja, keeping in character, giggled.

They fled back to the darker streets of Whitechapel.

Malcolm led her down a side street and turned back across the pathway that lay in utter darkness before stopping.

"That was brilliant, Malcolm!"

Did she mean his idea or his kiss?

"You saved us." She added.

Idea.

"Where did you learn to kiss? Am I your first?"

Kiss.

He smiled and again directed her away from lamplight. "Who hasn't seen Rudolph Valentino?"

"So, I am the first," she declared.

He stopped. "And I am not?"

She slapped his face.

He grabbed her shoulders and said, his tone urgent, "This is not the time for pettiness. That man could have realized our game."

"Who's being petty?"

He fumed.

She turned to him. "Sorry."

He checked around, saw no one, and walked on.

Katja kept pace with him. After a block's distance, she confided, "You're not the first, but it was very sweet."

He said nothing for the rest of the way.

After seeing her home, he stormed to the tube station. He didn't care if she'd been kissed before. She'd probably kissed Jack plenty of times.

Malcolm took off in a run. Anger of another kind inflamed him. He didn't want such blasted yearnings.

Love could go rot in the grave.

Chapter Sixty-Three

"I'm off to the ball." Adelaide's presence at the kitchen door surprised him as much as her declaration. But that was nothing compared with her appearance. Her lips were rouged, her eyelashes done up with whatever women did to them—and she was wearing jewellery.

Malcolm, sitting at the table before his evening meal, remained speechless.

"Okay, in truth, I'm just going out with me girlfriend, to that club in Soho: Hell's Belles. Do you like me rags?" She held out her arms, which were draped with a gaudy wrap. Its vivid print had bits of red that clashed with the burnt orange tubular, low-wasted dress, unless she was aiming for the burning bush effect.

Malcolm finally gathered himself up to be polite. Standing by the table, he chastised himself for not crediting Adelaide with more than he had. For a young woman with a club foot and humble position to attend a popular club where all the Bright Young Things go to be seen was a brave thing.

He smiled at her with warmth. "I hope you have a marvellous time."

"Thank you. Well, I better get going. I'm to meet Mildred at the Holloway tube station in a few."

He'd never heard her speak with flare before. He made a mental note about the value of fashion. That, and getting out about town, must do wonders for the spirit.

A bit of sparkle winked from her earlobe. He stepped closer. Her right earring looked familiar.

"Um." He took another step. It was shiny black with a Chinese lantern painted on its front.

"Oh, I know they don't match. I'm starting a new trend, I am. Should become the latest rage any minute now; they will call it The Adelaide Look." She touched the other one, which consisted of a splotch of garnets set in some dark metal.

"This came from me auntie. She lost its mate in the House of Horrors while at a fair in Brighton years ago."

"Um, the black one's a cracker," he managed.

"Lovely, isn't it? Chinese, or made to look Chinese." She evidently mistook his interest and blushed.

Vexed at his clumsiness, he felt heat flush up his neck. Then an alarm went off in his head. The mate to the Chinese earring could be the one he saw at Joe's. Such trinkets were plentiful, but Malcolm didn't like the coincidence.

As if covering the awkwardness, Adelaide touched the lacquered earring. "Got this one from Madam, after she'd lost its mate. And this snappy wrap was a gift from her. Wasn't my birthday or anythin'. She's kind-hearted, your aunt, and generous. I'd do anythin' for her, I would."

Adelaide's eyes darted at the clock on the wall. "Gotta run, Master Malcolm. Ta-ta." She twiddled her fingers and turned.

The clock chimed the hour, but he didn't count.

Adelaide left the flat. The uneven clomp of her descending steps resounded in Malcolm's gut. He dashed to the sink and retched.

Chapter Sixty-Four

Malcolm entered Tower Hamlets Cemetery as arranged. Although the smattering of Christendom's cold stone saints represented an ideology distinctly different from that seen in the Jewish cemeteries, and although not as opulent as Abney Park, a similar pall hung in the air. He was in the consecrated section, he surmised. Within the spacious grounds, handfuls of people stood in silence, as if mirroring the images and idols.

He spotted Katja. Standing straight ahead by several yards, she looked up from checking her watch. She was wearing a burnt orange coat with a matching hat. Her gloved hands pressed together and her right foot swivelled in jerky uncharacteristic movements.

He wasn't late, but something felt amiss.

She smiled as he approached. Her cheeks were pink from the cold.

"Come. This way." She moved stiffly down a walk leading toward the north.

He followed, wondering at the mixture of messages conveyed in that mere breath of moments. What had he expected? He assumed that coming together before Joe's grave would foster a closer bond. They each loved him in their own way. Had she not realized until now that sharing time and space at the site would feel intrusive? Was that it? Or was it something else entirely?

She pointed to the headstone.

A flood of emotion welled up inside, surprising him. Joe Hasani's name laid bare, inscribed on a slab of limestone. Malcolm fought down conflicting feelings as thoughts of his mother's grave arose. He focused on Joe, his friend, his mentor.

Let me tell you about the streets, lad. Walkin' round in the East End is no time for daydreaming. Keep alert. Take stock.

Joe cared. That hardy body now lay beneath this mound of earth. Finality disturbed Malcolm with a fresh surge of pain.

He sank on his left knee to place the flowers in the cast iron cup at the stone's base. Dirty leaves dusted with snow hovered in its bottom. He stuck his fingers in and cleaned out the cup, then set the flowers there.

Katja waved her hand over the gravestone. "My mother is proud of this."

Malcolm studied the marker. Much simpler than his mother's but just as significant.

Katja then pointed off to the north. "Over there is the paupers' grave."

"Paupers?" A shared grave?"

"Yes. Don't you know? That's where they bury any number of those in the same grave. A public grave."

He wanted to ponder this revelation but something in Katja's coolness held his attention.

"I thought you deserved to see my uncle's resting place." She straightened. "Thank you for all you've done." Her tone rang with dismissal.

"Done? We've more to do. More to learn."

"Our time for grief has past. I no longer care to pursue the matter." She stuck out her hand to shake away the entire issue.

No words came to mind. He sucked in air to speak. His mind went blank. The light in her eyes changed. They narrowed but held his gaze with defiance.

Cold air rushed into Malcolm's lungs. "You know who did it." He stepped closer.

She stepped back.

"You know and you're not going to share it with *me?*"

"No. I'm done with it. That is all."

He noticed something stirring from behind her. It was a man. No, a youth, one taller and possibly older than he. The youth looked familiar. It was Jack's companion. The one who had assaulted the Chinese family and chased him and Sid through Limehouse.

He nodded the lad's way, his tone challenging Katja. "You know *him?*"

Her stance wavered. She then said, "Yes. Now leave, Malcolm. Thank you, but you and I no longer need to discuss my uncle's death."

Malcolm repeated, "You know who killed him."

The youth came up and stood just beyond Katja's shoulder, ready to fight if she gave the word.

She said, "Come, Bart. We're done here." She took Bart's hand and turned to leave.

Malcolm cried, "That's wrong. I need to know who killed Joe." He jumped in front of the pair.

Bart brandished his fists.

"Wait, Bart." She jabbed her finger at Malcolm's chest. "Yes, we know who. And I've come to understand you, Malcolm. You would only interfere. Leave it."

Malcolm's body tensed, the muscles up his back and down his arms were taut with rage.

"Come on, Bart," she commanded. The two walked on toward the street.

Malcolm's knees locked. He watched them go. His voice faltered. "Katja?"

She looked around, checking the distance of other mourners, and replied, her voice intense, "We will manage it in our own way. Now, go save Limehouse or whatever else you care to do."

Katja and Bart walked on and rounded the gateway, disappearing from sight. A truck rolled past on the street. Someone coughed at the far end of the cemetery.

Malcolm stood, still and cold as a statue.

Chapter Sixty-Five

Malcolm's classmates filtered out of the room, and Old Jones gathered up his paperwork. Malcolm vaguely noted the methodical placing of this here and that there, a file slipped into the old leather satchel, a brushing down of his jacket. This was how Old Jones prepared to leave for the day. Every movement measured. One would hardly guess that the man was anxious to get to his tea. But Malcolm knew otherwise.

He had heard the talk last term near the front steps. As Jones walked down the street, a cluster of boys leaned in together for a gossip, as if they were old biddies. *There 'e goes. Off to that Mrs. Kramer for his tea. Did ya know she's a widow who'd married a German before the war?* Malcolm had not lingered to hear any more of it.

He glanced up and caught Jones shaking his head in disdain as he gathered his satchel and crossed the room to leave. There was no comment made. Both were accustomed to the strained relationship. Jones viewed him as a hopeless dreamer. Having given up hope that Malcolm would progress, he passed by without a word, as if he couldn't bear to waste any more than he had in class. The light switched off. The chalk-dusted shoes clicked away on the hard floor, down the hall.

Greyness filled the space beyond the window. Over the street a light fog blurred the details of the brick buildings, making them look sombre rather than pitted and soot-stained.

He checked the clock. Should he head for Stepney to see whether Sid could join him for a cuppa at Jade's? He loved Sid, but the idea of mustering up enough spirit to discuss all that had transpired with Katja left him exhausted. Outside, clouds and fog made it feel later. Or had time passed? He checked the big clock again. It was time to leave.

The hallway was empty.

On the front steps, damp air met Malcolm's face on the front steps. Its tingling felt as annoying as walking into strands of spider webs.

The image of Adelaide waiting with the kettle hot on the stove and a plate of deadly scones on the table nudged him away from the tube station.

He walked on.

Katja had chosen to hold Bart's hand. Malcolm recalled kissing her in the alley. Though play-acting, he had enjoyed her lips against his.

Fog billowed across the narrow streets from the river. Malcolm changed course and headed west. He wouldn't pursue Katja. He'd leave her be. But his feet took him toward Whitechapel. *Just a bit of a stroll. Easier to think than having to talk with anyone.*

Could he have ever gained Katja's esteem? She'd been attracted to Jack. And now to Bart. It was like some of the women he'd read about in his penny dreadfuls—attracted to bad boys, thugs. Katja would never have fully approved of him. There was something about him that she would have always viewed as weak. Kindness? Or ... maybe ... no, he cast the matter aside. He'd leave those concerns in the gutter here.

He hardly noticed the mews to his right, situated behind the old inn, now a flophouse. Next, the abandoned warehouse. A true-to-life house of horrors, according to some. What PC Hawkins had done to young Jiggs in there was deplorable. Malcolm tried to convince himself that most policemen were not monsters. But the other constables had sided with one of their own; they had and would again choose to support a fellow officer over a street urchin. The day after Jiggs had reported an unwarranted beating by Hawkins, the constable had sought the boy out, brought him here and gave him what for, an assault more savage than before.

Bloodlust. Those lesser men who needed to feel powerful thirsted for it. That was PC Hawkins.

According to a friend of Sid's, Hawkins had afterward left Jiggs bleeding and barely conscious in the abandoned place.

At least Jiggs was staying in Islington now. That is, if he were still alive. There'd been no word for months.

Policemen were not to be trusted. He walked on.

The next block of homes worked its way back into respectability. The street lamps were losing their battle with the fog.

Thoughts of Katja returned. Katja and her flashing eyes. He half wanted to see her approach through the mist. He quashed the yearning.

At a corner, Malcolm listened carefully before crossing a street cloaked in mist. Footsteps but no vehicles.

He walked on and entered a narrow lane of modest homes.

Behind him, footsteps came closer.

Malcolm continued on.

Behind every window, drapes were drawn against the coming of night.

"Stop, lad," the voice commanded.

Malcolm turned. It was PC Hawkins. The man's right hand gripped his truncheon. Slowly, he began tapping it in his other hand.

"What are you up to, lad?"

"Nothing, sir." Malcolm's stomach lurched but his senses remained on guard. *How to be done with this? To run would antagonize him.*

"I'm glad to see you, sir. This fog can make a person nervous." He forced a smile.

The tapping continued.

"It's handy for those up to no good." The man stepped closer.

"Well, if you'll excuse me, sir, I should be getting home."

"You've done enough gadding about, sniffing for trouble. I've seen you."

"I just enjoy the East End, sir. It's my home."

Malcolm turned to leave. Hawkins grabbed his collar and hoisted him off his feet. The pressure on his throat robbed him of air. His cry cut off. Then pain from a blow of the truncheon seared his hip.

"Constable!" cried a familiar voice. "I say, man. Stop! There must be some mistake."

Hawkins released the pressure at Malcolm's collar but held on.

"No mistake, sir," Hawkins said. "I've gotta run the lad into the station. Now if you'll excuse us."

The policeman yanked Malcolm away and began hauling him toward the warehouse.

"I say, I will take responsibility for the boy. I know him. He's one of my students," Old Jones said, his tone urgent. "He's only just left my classroom. I can vouch for the fact that he's had no time for mischief."

That wasn't exactly true. Time had elapsed. Jones must have just exited the Widow Kramer's home.

Hawkins hesitated. He changed his grip from Malcolm's collar to his neck, still holding him from behind. His hot fingers pressed Malcolm's neck muscles tightly. Then, the pressure lightened and fat fingertips slid from the base of Malcolm's neck up to below his ears. Malcolm shuddered.

Hawkins pushed Malcolm toward the teacher. "Take him. Keep him out of trouble or I'll run him in."

"I will escort the young man home, constable." Jones stood tall. The sight filled Malcolm with shivers of gratitude.

Hawkins turned away.

Malcolm and Jones walked in silence toward the tube station.

Station lights failed to neutralize the grime. Malcolm slid surreptitious glances up and down the Underground's platform. His hip still stung. Would Hawkins seek him out again?

He would.

Rumbling advanced. The train swooshed in. And like ants swarming undaunted around an object, other passengers boarded. At the last minute, so did Malcolm.

Grateful to find a lone seat, he slid in and tried to force his lungs to breathe smoothly. His hands trembled like those of an old man with palsy. He clasped them together on his lap and then closed his eyes.

The idea of having to stay on his guard, watching for Hawkins at every turn, exhausted him. What could he do if nabbed again? Even if he was caught in a crowd, who would believe him, a youth, against the word of a policeman?

A small lurch, followed by rhythmic jostling, evoked both relief and panic. He tried to fight down his nerves. He was heading home, where he'd be safe. But something in the hurtling sensation disturbed him.

Helplessness.

He was not in control of the train. Vibrations and speed were as unwelcome as the touch of Constable Hawkins. A phantom-like feel of those fingertips on his neck made his flesh crawl. He half turned to make sure the policeman wasn't seated behind. An old man with bushy brows and a bulbous nose looked straight ahead, ignoring Malcolm.

The absence of Hawkins in the compartment failed to bring relief. He would be lurking about for endless days. Off duty, the policeman could be anywhere. He could ferret out all of Malcolm's haunts.

For the rest of the way, Malcolm stared at the floor.

Along Newington Green, moving outside the pools of light, he spotted the figure, lurking in the dark between Mrs. Doran's steps and the neighbour's.

The shape moved.

Across the street, Malcolm stood stock still.

But the form was small, a boy's.

It was Jun.

"Haroo, Malcolm. What took yer so long?"

Malcolm paused. Was Jun talking about crossing the street like a frightened girl or coming from school after dark?

"Sorry, Jun. How long have you been waiting? What's up?"

"I dropped off another order of eggrolls upstairs and thought I'd wait for yer."

Malcolm entered the ring of streetlight and sat on the front steps. He motioned for Jun to sit.

"What happened, Malcolm?"

The lad's insight shouldn't have surprised him. With effort, Malcolm fought down a cresting need to weep. Elbows on knees, his head in his hands, he sat. There were no words.

Jun waited.

He wanted to tell Jun that he'd had it. No more adventures. He was done solving crimes. Limehouse would have to take care of itself. He wished he could sink into oblivion, but he'd never confess to that.

Moments dawdled. Malcolm noticed the fog, low-slithering mists becoming denser, rising. City sounds muffled to a hum.

"It's either walls or windmills, my friend," Jun said, his tone serious.

He'd never known Jun to wax esoteric but was in no mood for enigmas. He ignored him. The fog's chill snaked around his ankles.

"Yer don't know the proverb, then?" Jun pressed.

"What are you on about?"

"Somethin' happened to yer. I can tell. I've seen that look lot s o' times in the opium den. That's where I learned the words."

"What words?"

"'When the wind blows hard...some build walls...some build windmills.'"

Jun looked at him expectantly.

Walls...windmills.

Malcolm shook his head and stood. "I know you mean well, Jun. Thank you. But I can't take that in tonight."

"Um..."

In the dim light, Malcolm considered Jun. It was the first time the lad had ever looked uncertain.

"Take care, mate," Malcolm said, mounting the steps. He entered the warm vestibule and closed the door without looking back.

Chapter Sixty-Six

Flecks of snow annoyed Malcolm, adding to his mounting angst. Despite his cap, tiny snowflakes moved in not only to tickle his nose but also finding his eyelashes and brow despite the hat's brim.

It had been a miserable commute and walk to the Metropolitan Police station in Limehouse. The blue lamp outside the place glowed against the grey morning light.

Silently, he both thanked and cursed Jun for the proverbial riddle.

Malcolm looked through the vapour before his face and focused past the blue lamp to the brick building beyond. He couldn't relinquish belief in the basic good of humankind. Nor could he overcome the dread he felt. He leaned against the building behind him. The air smelled of damp coal soot.

When he left the Newington Green flat, Auntie was still in her room, probably asleep. Adelaide frowned as he headed for the door. On some topics, she was a bit thick, but the lass had common sense; she was savvy enough to say nothing when sensing that he was up to something.

Adelaide might envy his freedom but she likely had no idea of its cost. It had cost Malcolm dearly. Joe's murder. Finding Batya Shuller with her head bashed in. Observing the intrigue that had led to Crocker's death. And learning of the trouble in store for the Chinese.

He doubted Smith's integrity now. After the newspaperman had chosen to elude him in Limehouse, Malcolm realized that he could not be trusted. The man's promise to alert the police meant nothing. Lying to him and Sid was probably an easy thing to do. Smith's story will be all the more sensational.

Limehouse might be a sordid place to London's civilized lot, but the borough was dear to Malcolm. It had been dear to Joe. The Asiatic culture around Pennyfields seemed more foreign than anything else he had come across, but the Chinese community was filled with family love like any other. Aside from the opium dens, the inhabitants appeared to be law-abiding, gentle and hardworking.

He again considered the blue light and then the station. Inside, he could conceivably run into Hawkins.

Malcolm's mouth and throat became dry as sawdust. There were only three days left before Chinese New Year.

He pushed himself from the building and set out across the street.

Chapter Sixty-Seven

A dragon arrayed in bright green, orange and red pranced side to side down Pennyfields. Its many feet were clad in Oriental shoes. Malcolm's view was partially blocked by the two constables crouching in the alley.

"Get along, lads. This ain't no time for yers to be here." The policeman ordered.

Another bobby turned to Malcolm and Sid. Even in the dim light, Malcolm detected a sense of empathy, as if adolescent interests were still fresh in the man's mind. The policeman gave them a friendly nod. A proper acknowledgement since it supported his fellow officer while affording them respect. Malcolm smiled, nudged Sid and retreated down the alley.

As Malcolm understood it, from having lingered unnoticed before exiting the police station, most of the alleys near Pennyfields and the Limehouse Causeway were to have two or more constables in hiding, ready for anything.

Before backing out onto King Street, he peered back along the alley and could barely make out the two silhouettes of the two they'd left.

From behind, a low voice said, "Move along, you two." It was Constable Hawkins. How had he come up on them unnoticed? "I suggest you get as far from here as you can."

Malcolm faced him. In the glow from a street lamp, recognition filled Hawkins' features and his expression said *I'll deal with you later.* "Off with you."

"Yes, sir," Malcolm said, his voice tight. He turned and ran, as did Sid.

At the corner, Malcolm looked back. Hawkins had disappeared.

A long stretch of tenement housing muffled the festive sounds on Pennyfields. Malcolm and Sid continued parallel to it, heading east.

The excitement at hand helped Malcolm to cast off that menacing image of Hawkins for the time being.

"Where can we watch if we can't be in the alleys?" Sid asked.

Malcolm waved his reply and then jogged north. After crossing East India Dock Road, he slowed down and began looking for some other vantage point, one on ground level so they could be poised for action.

"Mr. Smith said—before he cut out from us—that they were to start somewhere close to the Limehouse Cut, remember?"

Near Canton Street, Malcolm found an old brick building well-situated with a recessed front doorway. He pulled Sid along and the two shifted into the entry's shadows, hidden but able to scope out the area. Then a buzz of sound came from deep within the building. Numerous voices were advancing, approaching their very doorway. A chill shot through him.

"Come on, Sid."

He darted across the street to an alley. A form on the ground just within it came into view, a sleeping drunk. They would have to share space, but only for a few minutes. Malcolm hesitated.

Sid stood just behind him on the street.

Ignoring the drunk, Malcolm looked over his shoulder and considered the structure where the voices were coming from. "Oh, this must be the front of the Whittacker building. Cor! And if I'm right—"

"You most certainly are," said the prostrate body. Malcolm peered at the man.

"Mr. Smith. It's you."

"Be quiet."

Malcolm approached and crouched next to him. "Why did you run from me in Pennyfields?"

"Because you would have blown my cover. Two members of Crocker's gang were nearby."

"Oh, sorry. Uh, great disguise, this." He gestured at Smith's costume. "I thought you were a drunk."

"I had a bit of Dutch courage before coming here but I am decidedly sober. Wouldn't miss this for the world."

Sid entered the alley and also crouched.

Malcolm said to Smith, "What's going on across the street? It's *them*, isn't it?"

"*Them, yes.* And we can't have you giving me away this time either. Stay in the shadows."

Although Malcolm had guessed the situation before asking Smith, the moment's arrival ignited the air with energy, tingling the downy hairs on his arms.

"I've been here before." Malcolm couldn't add that it had been that night with Katja. "At the back entry, though. I didn't realize we were right here."

"Well you are. Now hug the walls, boys. They should be coming out any moment.

"Why didn't you tell the police that this was their base of operations, if you knew?" Malcolm demanded.

"That lot will be heading toward Pennyfields soon enough. I'm here to witness the event from the beginning. And by trailing them, I'll catch the action, all of it."

"You never reported any of this to the police? You'd said you would."

"It slipped my mind, I'm afraid." The coolness of Smith's intonation angered Malcolm."

Smith added, "Doesn't matter. I understand that the police are stationed near the festivities. I can't imagine who had informed them. Was it you?"

A noise came from across the street.

Smith hissed, "Now, be quiet and stay out of sight."

A drone of conversation came across from the building. Then, a single voice took control.

That voice.

Who was it?

After long moments, the double doors creaked open and a horde of men emerged, rounding the corner from Canton Street and facing East India Dock Road.

The leader, cloaked in shadow, crossed to the front of the forming phalanx, which seemed as if it were heading right for their alley. Fear flashed through Malcolm. Just then, a scrabbling sound rose from the coal chute next to him. The pattering feet of a rat ran across his legs and then Sid's. Malcolm felt Sid flinch, but the only sound his friend produced was an intake of breath. The rat scampered down the alley away from the forming army.

The leader faced their hideout. Had he heard? Did he suspect their presence? Malcolm could not tell if the man could see anything. But after two steps the face came into view—it was Mr. Lever, the bookseller.

An argument arose in the ranks. Lever turned back. The contending voices fell silent.

Lever commanded, "Now."

Countless dark forms marched past, wearing black, carrying truncheons. On some of the men, Malcolm saw the occasional bulging pouch secured at their hips by a belt. He knew they must contain cricket ball grenades. The marching men crossed East India Dock Road. The purposeful cadence filled the streets with evil.

"I'm off," Smith said. "If you tag along, you come at your own risk." He jumped up, walked to the centre of the street and followed the throng. Malcolm peered around the building. The mob's focus was Pennyfields. If anyone happened to look back, Smith, dressed in black, would look like one of their own, either trailing with purpose or straggling out of cowardice.

Malcolm and Sid leapt up and followed at a distance.

The suppressed energy of the gang juxtaposed against the distant twang and beat of the Chinese parade oppressed Malcolm's senses. The cold air smelled as it never had before. Did impending doom have a smell?

He and Sid crossed East India Dock Road and a roar of pandemonium erupted from Pennyfields. Up ahead, Smith took off, all elbows and heels.

"We're missing it!" Sid cried.

They ran along the pavement in the dark. An explosion erupted, then another.

"Cut through here," Malcolm commanded. He darted down the alley they'd been in before, now void of police. Out on Pennyfields, it looked like Dante's Inferno with its battling silhouettes against the flames.

Sid pulled him back. "Uh, we don't have anything to protect ourselves with."

Malcolm nearly toppled over as he stopped. He looked around the alley, now lit by the flames beyond it. Not a stick to be found. "Hey, there are dustbins here. Grab a lid and let's go."

Armed with bin lids like shields, they dove into the battle, passing through a wave of sound and insanity. Indistinguishable black-clad men and policemen wrestled for control; fury filled the entire stretch of Pennyfields.

Malcolm looked up and down the street, hoping to catch sight of either Mr. Smith or Mr. Lever, but the glare made that impossible.

"This way," he cried. Sid nodded and obeyed.

Malcolm headed for Hong's where he thought the centralized location would offer a better chance. He couldn't tell which group held the upper hand. He charged into the teeming mass and felt the hot breath of cursing men as they grappled. A loud crack off to his left startled him. He realized the sound was that of a truncheon meeting someone's skull. He hoped Sid was keeping close behind.

A sudden pain shuddered along his right shoulder as the tip of another truncheon grazed him. He raised the dustbin lid and held it over head and darted through the mayhem. An explosion rocked the street beneath his feet.

Hong's burst into flames.

Hand to hand combat not only continued but got louder. It closed in around him.

Clangs from advancing fire trucks rang out above the din but the intensity of battle blocked further approach. All of Limehouse would burn if they didn't get the hoses going.

Malcolm stood on his toes and searched for the nearest fire wagon. If he and Sid could mount one, they'd be safer. Just then, Sid was nowhere in sight.

Everywhere, men fought. Malcolm crouched then leapt upward but all he could see were grappling arms and legs.

What if Sid got trampled to death? Where was he? Panic surged.

A wall of flames shot from Hong's; and again glare and shadow blinded him. The fighting converged tighter and the smell of damp wool and blood filled Malcolm's nostrils. Near him, a man cried out and backed up; the man's boot heel nearly crushed Malcolm's left foot. He freed himself and stepped around. Then another man's elbow struck the side of his head. The sharp pain rattled him, but Malcolm kept on. Another hit to the head brought inner lightning flashes and his knees buckled. His shield hit the pavement and slid away. Spotting a clearing, he took a deep breath and scrambled forward.

The vice-like pain remained clamped to his head. With the roar of violence and acrid smoke, he thought death was upon him. Another clearing opened before him and he caught sight of two small figures huddled together.

Sid and Jun looked like younger boys as they clung to each other. Malcolm ran up and threw his arms around them both.

Clanging and commands rose louder. Malcolm turned and leaned against the building and watched the fire trucks make their way through. As intense as the scene was, breathless fatigue dragged him into a stupor.

Jun pointed in horror. "Look! The bullies are beating the firemen. This whole place is gonna burn."

Unbidden, a surreal calm settled on Malcolm. His feet, rooted on the pavement, became as those set in the mud of Belgium's trenches. He recalled those stories spoken into brandy snifters and envisioned his father at the Front—he was his father, commanding his men, witnessing their deaths, the flares, explosions and flying bits of earth. Malcolm stood tall.

"Stay here," he commanded the boys. He walked toward the nearest fire truck where troublemakers were climbing aboard, attacking the firemen. He made his way closer through a tunnel of men until he came up to the figure he'd seen outside Whittacker's, the groups' leader. Mr. Lever's gaze locked on Malcolm's, and the man read Malcolm's contempt. The bookseller raised his truncheon and swung it down. Malcolm flinched and heard a deafening crack next to his ear. He opened his eyes. Wendell was at his side. He had blocked the blow with his own truncheon. Before Lever could react, two constables grabbed him.

"I must get to that fire wagon," Wendell cried.

Malcolm followed in his wake.

He picked his way around debris and was shocked at almost stepping on a body sprawled in the gutter. The man held his bleeding head and moaned. Malcolm wanted to help, but he was losing sight of Wendell. At the fire truck, he could send someone back to help.

Three shots fired in the air.

A roar erupted from another mob pouring in from the far end and different alleys; their cries eclipsed the cacophony and the newcomers spread out on Pennyfields, filling the space between Malcolm and Wendell. Were they trying to rescue Lever? Malcolm lost sight of the policemen who had taken charge of the bookseller. A sharp jab against Malcolm's shoulder came from an elbow as two men grappled for control of a truncheon. Malcolm ducked around them, leapt away from another entanglement, and then came out into a small clearing. Next to burning heaps of rubble, two officers were getting an injured bobby off to the side.

Malcolm almost tripped over something and righted himself. He looked down and saw that the impediment was actually a fallen policeman. In the flickering light, he noticed two things: the wooden handle of a knife, like a kitchen knife, stood with its blade buried in the back of the man, the face of the man was turned toward him—it was Constable Hawkins. Glassy eyes stared blankly. A chill shot through Malcolm, as alarming as a blade slicing through him would be. *We will manage this in our own way.*

Could it possibly be? Was this new wave of men be commandeered by Bart? Was Hawkins' end the work of Katja?

Malcolm looked around. None of the combatants looked familiar.

Another body lay off in the gutter. It too had a knife in the back. Malcolm wove his way through the crowd and then sank to his knees next to it. The back of the figure could be anyone. The knife handle was similar, domestic, or from a restaurant's kitchen. Without hesitation, Malcolm reached down, gripped the man's shoulder and lifted. He turned the body on its side, just enough to glimpse the face.

It was Lever.

Malcolm got to his feet. He had to find Wendell. He stepped over Lever, walked on, his feet unsteady.

A deafening noise signalled the collapse of Hong's building. Burning shards and glowing ashes shot out against fleeing men. He vaguely noticed that there were fewer skirmishes. He limped around some more rubble. The clanging of the firemen's bell drew him on. He could see it.

Standing atop the fire truck, with luminous hair billowing in the wind and golden light, Jane Beardsmore commanded the hose, keeping it trained on the worst of the inferno.

The fire continued to roar. But the mayhem began dying away; the advantage of Lever's militia was collapsing like Hong's Tea House. Men carried off bleeding bodies. Policemen carted off gang members. Was Katja among them? Bart? He realized that he didn't care whether they were or not.

He stood on Pennyfields, transfixed at the sight of this Joan-of-Arc eccentric, his Aunt Jane. He then noticed a man scrambling up next to her. She relinquished control of the hose and embraced him. Malcolm peered at this familiar commanding figure. It wasn't Wendell. It was Jane's brother, the captain!

The captain spotted Malcolm's approach and scrambled down to him. Malcolm buried his face in his father's chest. The scent of wool and comfort blocked that of incendiary chaos. A sensation of weightlessness surprised him. It felt as if he were escaping a heavy suit of armour. The burden of loneliness lifted off his back and shoulders, allowing a flood of sobs.

Chapter Sixty-Eight

The occupants of Wendell's car smelled of smoke. Sid and Jun had been dropped off at their homes. Malcolm and Aunt Jane occupied the back seat.

For blocks on end, through London's late night streets they rode in silence, as if each had to assimilate all that had just transpired. Obelisks of light would come and go as they passed street lamps. Aunt Jane's cheeks were smudged, her hair a mess. But her head rested back, eyes closed, her smile beatific and steady.

At last, when she spoke, the suddenness of sound felt natural.

"I don't know what we would have done had the police not been there on the ready. How on earth did they know?"

Malcolm looked at his father's profile in the front passenger seat. He craved to earn esteem. Instead he asked his aunt and Wendell, "Why hadn't you informed them, if you knew about it?"

"We didn't know," Wendell said. A wisp of light passed over each of them. Darkness again filled the space.

Jane said, "At first we thought all those dreadful plans had fallen apart with the death of Julius Crocker. By the time we got wind of there being a new leader and an added impetus, we had been found out. They had spies, you know."

Malcolm did know. Parts of his body still ached from having been assaulted by such ones on his way to Katja's weeks ago.

"Their meeting place had been changed," she said, "and we couldn't find out a thing."

Wendell added, "Jane and I went to attend the Chinese New Year festivities for the event itself. We felt trouble was a possibility and were prepared to notify the police if we noticed anything suspicious. Chaos erupted soon after we got there."

Jane defended their decision. "We hadn't a bit of evidence before that. Why would they have listened to us? There is quite enough trouble demanding their attention in the East End at night. And we expected the local bobbies to be on hand."

"How did you come to be there, Father?"

"I'd sent a message to your aunt that I was coming, as a surprise for you. I've been making great strides and came for a visit."

Aunt Jane said, "I'd completely forgotten which day I was in, that is, once Wendell and I decided to check out the doings in Limehouse. I'm sorry, Robert. So glad you found us."

"Adelaide informed me of your whereabouts."

"Ah, I hadn't told her, but she listens, that girl."

"Thank goodness the police were there," Wendell said for emphasis.

"Indeed." Aunt Jane brushed down the front of her jacket and skirt.

"For the life of me," Wendell said, "I looked and never saw more than the odd injury among the Chinese. The hoodlums and some policemen got the worst of it."

Malcolm couldn't hold back the pressure. "I told the police."

"What?"

"How did you know, son?"

"A newspaper man told me of it. I hope he's all right. Sid and I lost sight of him in the ruckus."

"Well," the captain said, "if the man got out unscathed, he has quite a story to tell."

Wendell looked over his shoulder. "Did it seem to you like a new wave of people arrived?"

"Yes," the captain answered before Jane or Malcolm could. "Well organized, I'd say."

"I wonder if they were a rival gang." Jane said. Her tone left the notion dangling.

Malcolm held his tongue. Bart had been with Jack attending Crocker's meetings. He would have been part of the reorganized group after Aunt Jane had been found out. And he and Katja had their own agenda.

Malcolm wanted those details.

Chapter Sixty-Nine

Heady aromas from Auntie's kitchen lifted Malcolm's already high spirits and reminded him of those transcendent states that Wendell talked about. Malcolm didn't understand Nirvana but he did understand the pleasures of mince pie and plum pudding, delectables pungent with fruit and spices. And he found comfort in the knowledge that Adelaide had not been the maker of anything on the menu. The occasion was better than a holiday.

But there was the main course and more dinner conversation to enjoy before sweets would be served.

Bryn and Adelaide clanked about platters and tureens beyond the kitchen door, preparing to serve the meal. Malcolm sensed a possible competition between them in the handling of their responsibilities.

Anticipation ran keen, causing an occasional flutter of excitement in Malcolm's stomach.

Seated, at the head of the table, the captain looked at Malcolm and said, "I am hopeful for the first time since, you know." The reference to having entered the asylum was clear. "Well, hopeful that in time, I may feel right about returning to our home...together."

Malcolm wanted to look away. He'd hope that they would return home without much delay. But then the healthy gleam in his father's eyes and the notion of promise buoyed him up.

His father took a quick sip of tea and added, "Our new man, the good Doctor Walker, is a marvel. I'm doing better than ever, as are some of my fellows, but I feel it's prudent to make sure."

"I'm glad to hear that," Aunt Jane said.

Malcolm offered his father a smile. He wanted to ask how long it would take but knew better.

Wendell and Mrs. Doran began chitchatting to keep the mood festive. Herman Gold offered Malcolm a reassuring wink in support of the captain's good news.

Aunt Jane leaned back in her chair, pulled a slow drag on her cigarette and released her best smoke ring yet.

Bryn was first to bustle into the dining room, holding a large platter laden with a roast pheasant. Adelaide followed with a tureen.

While Bryn took charge of slicing and serving, Mrs. Doran gaily hummed a happy tune. She lifted her glass of wine and swayed it back and forth in time with the song's rhythm.

After the two servers had returned to the kitchen, Aunt Jane plunked an elbow on the table and said, "Malcolm, I'm sorry for brushing off your question before dinner. You deserve to know why my earring was found at Mr. Hasani's home."

Mrs. Doran's pencilled brows arched.

"At first, I wanted to verify for myself that this mentor of yours was ethical, to make sure that you were safe in his company."

"You went down to his ferry berth? You went to the docks?"

"I've been to worse."

Malcolm thought about this and said, "Joe would have known it was your earring when he found it. Why didn't he return it?"

"He didn't know where I lived. I called on him only twice, which was enough. I am a pretty good judge of character. He was a good man and he cared about you. I evidently lost the earring on the second visit."

"Or maybe it was from the first visit, and he was so taken with you, Auntie, that he kept it as a souvenir."

She waved the idea away.

Malcolm enjoyed dinner and was feeling stuffed. When the sweets arrived, he became hungry again. But before partaking, Malcolm looked again at his aunt. "Um, do you happen to know a Madame Thibodeau?"

"Poor woman. Life has not been easy for her."

"You *do* know her, then. You paid her to spy? To spy on me?"

"She needs a helping hand now and then and she's told me how exciting it had been to take on the role. Of course, being an older woman, she had trouble keeping up with you."

"But she stands out in a crowd," Malcolm said.

"That's her way. To divert suspicion by means of conspicuousness. You wouldn't believe what she's gotten away with."

Aunt Jane finished her cigarette, cleansed her palate with some wine, and finally began to slice a bite of pheasant. She stopped and added, "You'd also be well and truly surprised if you knew the highly placed gentleman who has hired the woman for courier assignments."

"You must have sent her to Jade's. How did you know that Sid and I go there?"

"Your father. We are both of us concerned about you. He's content giving you more freedom than my nerves could allow, but even with his, uh, distractions, he kept an eye out for you and knew about Jade's and your waterman."

"That's right, son."

Malcolm considered this for a while. Before he could concentrate on his pie and pudding, he asked, "Now that we've done what we could for Limehouse, life is going to get pretty boring."

The captain produced a look of surprise.

"I could take up knitting." Aunt Jane winked.

After studying Malcolm's expression and savouring her first bite, she then added, "You have but to look around. Causes abound. You'll find—I dare say you must have already—that happiness is connected with having engagement and purpose."

Wendell stirred in his seat. This had indeed been discussed before, but Malcolm appreciated it more than ever.

Jane continued, "Fascist groups, for example, have been springing up here and there about London." She waved her hand dismissively, as if Fascists were like so many types of ailments. "Someone needs to keep an eye out on behalf of his Majesty. I'm afraid there will always be something to keep this aging woman's hand in the game."

"You're not old."

"I didn't say *old*. But everybody ages."

"Do you work for His Majesty's government?"

"If I did, I wouldn't tell you…but, no. I'm simply nosey and help out when and where I can."

"I bet they know you, though."

"Doesn't matter. Now enjoy your pudding."

Chapter Seventy

"You'd think that nothing out of the ordinary had happened," Sid said in between bites of his scone.

"Because we're at Jades?" Malcolm considered the place. Other than the absence of Madame Thibodeau in the corner, their refuge remained the same: comfortable, congenial. The aromas just as delightful. The coffeehouse's pulse had the familiar rhythm of staid conversations and Billy's routine services at the counter.

Malcolm nodded in agreement with Sid and looked down at the newspaper that lay between them.

"Mr. Thaddeus Smith got his story, sure enough," Sid said. "Right on the front page."

"I like his spirit of adventure and way with words...but I wonder at his lack of humanity. He could have done something to prevent the whole thing."

"Like what?"

"If I'd been able to get in to those meetings, to be accepted and learn the details, I'd have tried to get policemen to, uh, come with me, you know, disguised like a regular. Infiltrate and conquer."

"Malcolm, you could barely approach a policeman to ask the time of day."

"You're right, but if I were older, like Smith, I might have. In any case, I did go. I made myself walk in there and report it—and it was okay. Once I started talking, first to the desk sergeant, then to the other policeman—I think he was an inspector or something—it proved to be okay. Didn't feel threatening at all."

"And now Hawkins is gone."

"Yes."

Jun entered, ambled up to their booth and slid in next to Sid, looking as relaxed as if he'd grown up in the confines of Jade's.

Malcolm smiled, recalling the nervous self-consciousness when Jun had first ventured in. "All's well?"

"Sure." Jun pulled some pennies out of his pocket and slapped them on the table, ready for Billy. His attention fixed on the counter, a silent call for service.

After Jun savoured his first sips of coffee, he looked ready to be civil.

They easily fell into hashing out all that had transpired at the ruckus in Limehouse.

"Those knives could've come from anywhere or anybody."

"Do you think the police will test them for fingerprints?" Sid asked.

"Sure. But it was a cool night. Many were wearing gloves. The killer would have been wearing them for that reason alone, not only to avoid leaving prints."

Jun cleared his throat and said, "They could have come from any of the restaurants in Limehouse."

Malcolm then thought of Donny Foon's. There would be plenty of knives in that kitchen. Had Hawkins abused Jun? Had Malcolm's young friend sought revenge? He studied Jun's face, and the boy met his gaze. Jun did not look away, nor were his eyes defiant. Clearly content with the surroundings, Jun looked like an innocent, younger than when he wore the mask of the streetwise. Was this an act, a poker face? Jun sipped, leaned back and then tilted his head, realizing Malcolm's attention.

"What?"

"Nothing." Malcolm smiled. Just glad that you're here.

Chapter Seventy-One

"I've got to find out how Katja and Bart discovered Joe's killers." Malcolm tossed a stone in the canal. Sid walked next to him.

Jun had gone to work at the restaurant. Not a breeze stirred under the grey sky. Sooty snow clung to surfaces shadowed within nooks and crannies.

"Um," Sid ventured, "I guess you don't want to just ask them?"

Shame rose up Malcolm's neck. With added clarity he realized the hurt and embarrassment at having been duped, used and abandoned.

"No."

"So how do we go about this?"

"By going back to the beginning. I've been a fool. I bet they followed some obvious lines of investigation that I completely overlooked."

"You're no fool, Malcolm."

"Well, we need to go back to the beginning."

The familiar smell at the docklands of Limehouse tugged at Malcolm's heart. Odours of dead fish and general muck rising from the brackish water would repel most folks, but it choked him with bittersweet memories.

His gaze lingered on the empty boat slip from where Joe had worked—from there he had taken his last customer out onto the Thames. How much pain does the mind register when the throat is slit? Had Joe lay dying with dimming thoughts of his loved ones? Of Malcolm?

The murderers, and likely there had been two as Smith had supposed, must have beckoned Joe out of his boat when they had reached their destination. No doubt the darkest, loneliest of docks. Had it been Hawkins and Lever together? Why?

Joe's body was later found in his boat drifting near Gravesend. With the tide's constant movement, how could one ever guess where to find the actual crime scene?

Sid kept to Malcolm's side. The sound of their steps along the pier was drowned out by the din of activity. Down at the front of Eggert &

Sons' warehouse, the crew of Chinese workers was loading merchandise onto a ship. Malcolm sensed from the tension manifest in Sid's body that he too was likely recalling the last time they were here, when they had learned of Joe's murder.

Malcolm scanned the area. Just off from the warehouse, Maisie stood with her tray of matchbooks. A couple of men walked past her. One offered her a friendly wave.

Just then, a sailor rounded the corner from the next building and approached the girl. The man dropped some coins on the tray. She handed over a box of matches. He tipped his hat, looked as if he wished to linger and chat. But Maisie pocketed the money, nodded to him, possibly ending the conversation in a way that indicated she was not there to meet men. The sailor left.

Malcolm realized that the sailor had expected to find Maisie there. She was a regular.

"Blast!" he cried.

"What?"

"I'm an idiot."

"You're not."

"Come with me."

"Hullo, Maisie."

"Oh," she gasped, "I'm afraid I should know you—you were Joe's friend—but I don't know your name, sir."

"No *sir* needed. I reckon we are of a similar age."

"Well, I recall you being with Joe quite a bit. I sure do miss him. Always had a friendly wave for me, he did."

Maisie's missing tooth detracted from her appearance but not from her speech. And he could tell she'd been educated from an early age, despite her casual phrasing.

After proper introductions had been made all round, Malcolm said, "Could you tell me whether Joe's niece, Katja or her, uh, boyfriend have been by?"

She nodded.

"Did they ask you about anything strange happening round here, that is, anything unusual?"

"Yes, the two of them came by my other post, though. Found me outside the Pig's Head Pub. Not long ago."

Malcolm said, "I would like to put this matter to rest; Joe was dear to me. If I could understand why someone would have killed him, it might help. It wasn't for the money in his pockets."

She nodded again.

"What did you tell them?"

Sid stood so still beside him that Malcolm imagined he might be holding his breath. Sid was trying not to detract from his inquiry.

"I told them about Esther Lever's father and Constable Hawkins and how they had Joe take them somewhere up river."

His mouth went dry as he had to decide how to approach his next questions.

"How do you know Esther?"

"She married Huang Jie." Sadness clouded Maisie's features or maybe a touch of envy. She frowned. "Her family cut her off for that. Couldn't stand the idea. But she was happy. They lived in a rooming house near here. I'd see them together sometimes. I knew Huang from the Pig's Head. He worked in their kitchen. He was a gentle man."

"Was?"

"He was killed weeks ago in the alley behind the pub. Police had said it'd been done during a robbery. We all knew that was a lie, or that rozzers are stupid. It's more like they don't care, of course. Who would bother to rob the kitchen help?"

Malcolm hated his next question. "How was he killed?"

"His head had been bashed in," she replied, "repeatedly." Her tone was as frank as the statement.

Waves slapped slowly against the pilings below while a lone gull cried out from the now empty gangplank. The Chinese workers hovered with restrained anticipation around one of Eggert's managers; the manager was flanked by two burly assistants. Wages were being doled out.

"How did you come to know Esther's father?"

"He'd come by; he came right up to me and asked me where the two lived."

Malcolm looked a question and waited.

"It was Constable Hawkins who had pointed Mr. Lever in my direction, I expect. The PC evidently assumed I knew of the couple and he had likely said as much to the man."

Maisie took to straightening the matchboxes on her tray. "Hawkins himself said afterward that I must notice a fair bit of life in my *occupation.* He had a way of making it sound bad. And he had those dreadful leering eyes.

In a flash, Malcolm feared for Maisie's welfare. If Hawkins thought she knew about his mistreatment of boys—

But Hawkins was dead.

Maisie said, "Mr. Lever was in a right rage. I gathered he'd come round looking for Huang after word reached him about Esther's death—she'd died during childbirth."

"Oh dear," Sid said.

"I believe the baby lived." The young woman's eyes returned to her tray and began studying each matchbox, as if they were babies lined up and in need of help. "I don't know what happened to it after Huang was killed. Probably the gran took him, the Chinese gran, that is."

The three of them stood in silence for long moments.

"Okay," Malcolm continued, "you said that, on another occasion, Esther's father and the constable were in Joe's boat?"

"Yes, Joe ferried them up river."

"Do you believe they killed Joe?"

"I think that's possible, though I don't know why."

"And Katja and her friend, after learning of this, seemed to believe that those two had done the deed?"

"From their reactions, I'd say they seemed sure of it, particularly the girl." Maisie shook her head. Malcolm couldn't decide whether her gesture questioned Katja's jumping to conclusions or came from another wave of sadness over Joe's death—or perhaps she was dejected at the low state of humankind in general—all of it: murder, corruption, prejudice and abuse.

"From just that much, they seemed so sure," she added. "The two of them are either loose cannons or had other details that fit their conclusion. They didn't share anything with me, though."

"Did you report your suspicions to the police?"

Her brows shot up as if to say, *are you serious?* Another shake of the head. "I didn't even have to consider it. PC Hawkins sought me out two days later. I mean after I'd seen him get in Joe's boat with Mr. Lever. Word was already out round here about Joe's murder. Hawkins came and told me that the River Police would likely be coming round and would be questioning folks about Joe. He then said they might even have good reason to suspect me. I didn't like the way he talked about it, as if he would be the one pointing my way. You know what I mean?"

"Yes."

"Police look after their own, they do. Who knows what the lecher would've said about me and Joe?"

The gap from her missing tooth looked more prominent somehow. Malcolm shifted his gaze up to her eyes.

"So, I avoided this post for a while and kept myself next to the pub."

"Which, I imagine, is exactly what Hawkins wanted you to do." Malcolm made sure his tone carried sympathy and not disdain. "And now you're back here."

"Everybody's heard that Hawkins is gone. None of us are too sorry to hear it."

Sid spoke up from behind Malcolm's shoulder. "He's gone all right."

"I only just returned." Maisie then grimaced and added, "May the bloomin' rozzer rot in his maggot-filled grave."

Chapter Seventy-Two

Snow crunched beneath Malcolm's shoes along Cable Street. He had passed by Merriweather in the early hours, well before the janitor would unlock its doors and before most of the city got moving. He was grateful for the prevailing hush induced by Nature's white blankets. Grimy trails stretched over the cobbles, but much of Whitechapel looked better in its winter garb.

He'd be late for school, he reckoned, and some discipline would get meted out, but he continued west. Muted grey, brown-grey and white blurred before him.

Had Joe known any details, held any evidence, of Hawkins' sins? Had that been the policeman's motive?

The police'll be of little use. You know how I feel 'bout them, and 'bout one in particular."

What about Lever?

Malcolm thought back to the late Julius Crocker, to the code, and to communism. He shook his head at the different elements that had stewed together and then festered, that had infected men's minds and then fomented the trouble for Limehouse.

Malcolm's deductions settled into belief. He'd seen no political motive in Lever. Bigotry and personal vendetta drove the bookseller to Crocker's side and made him a willing pawn. How they'd met, Malcolm would likely never learn. Crocker had wanted Joe killed. The waterman knew too much. He'd transported the weapons and had evidently learned of the group's intentions.

The river drew near and Malcolm felt some relief at seeing the majestic heights of Tower Bridge spire above other buildings. He'd be there soon enough. The rhythm of crunching snow matched his heartbeat, his emotion.

How long would it take for Katja's large, flashing eyes to leave him alone? He walked on. A gull cried overhead.

Malcolm had to suppose that Limehouse would have fared worse had he not reported the matter. Why did he feel like a failure, then?

The violent mob action haunted him every night since, daring him to sleep despite its vivid images of flames, destruction and death.

A beckoning panorama opened before him. Though the river pulsed with life—ships and small boats gliding along, workers off in the distance moving like ants—all of it sounded and felt subdued. Was he detached? Or was the sensation due to the buffering snowfall? In a flash, his spirits lifted. He floated high above the scene...looking into his mum's face, held fast in her grip at home, pearls around her neck, her teeth white like pearls.

Then wafts from the river drifted up his nose into his mind, a blend of rank and fresh smells, as familiar as anything. It gently lowered him to earth. He walked out on the bridge.

Death had visited many in his world, worst of all, his mum and Joe.

He strode on, having the immediate vicinity to himself. Loneliness was an odd thing; it felt both bad and good.

About midway, he turned, leaned heavily against the balustrade and looked east, toward the Isle of Dogs and Limehouse...and toward where Joe had conducted business.

Keep up with your studies, lad. Old Joe can tell you're gonna make a difference in this world.

Would he make a difference? Did he really matter? He accepted that he mattered to Sid and Jun. The three had bonded like brothers through the adventure. Malcolm could not imagine what the future would bring for each of them, though. Joe had believed in him. What had he seen?

Downriver, a ship's bleating call gave warning while a flock of gulls shadowed behind, moving in formation like a kite's tail in the wind.

Malcolm had to admit that he mattered to Aunt Jane, maybe even to Mrs. Doran's entire household. There wasn't one schoolmate who had a family like his. That pleased him.

The captain might even love him—does love him.

He bent over the wall. Below, the brownish water churned. He studied it for some time. Actually, it seemed to be revelling in seasonal cheer as mosaics of ice undulated along its surface. It was art. London was living art.

Bells chimed the hour. Malcolm realized with a start that he had better get to school. He didn't want to be late for geography class with Mr. Jones.

Just then, a flapping whoosh shot from below the bridge and brushed past so closely that Malcolm felt the disturbed air against his face. The bird continued upward. Out over the vista, it spread its wings and began to soar, catching a current and riding it out to sea.

###

CPSIA information can be obtained
at www.ICGtesting.com
Printed in the USA
FSOW02n0821061117
40818FS